Head
Over
Tails

Love Boldly!
Brianna Tibbetts

Uncommon Universes Press LLC
1052 Cherry St.
Danville, PA 17821
www.uncommonuniverses.com

Editing: Lauren Hildebrand
Proofreading: Hannah Wilson
Formatting: Sarah Delena White

Cover Design: Cover Culture

ISBN: 978-1-948896-37-5

To my grandmother,
for never giving up on a happy ending.

Chapter One

❧

Day 1

Jacob rearranged the old beach chair four times before he was happy with it. He didn't plan to sit on the yellow and white striped fabric. Its rickety wooden frame made him nervous. Still, if he did decide to sit down, the chair needed to be facing the perfect spot on the horizon.

His morning ritual, once finished, allowed him to turn his eyes to the ocean. No motion marred the translucent, glassy surface.

Already above the water line, the sun left behind a spectacular wake. The cascade of pinks and yellows urged Jacob to reach for the camera bag around his shoulders. He fished out the lens he wanted, attached it with a swift motion, and lifted the camera to capture the canvas before him.

The lens dipped as he adjusted his grip, catching the full glare of the sun. Jacob flinched and lowered the camera, rubbing at his eye to dispel the spots swimming in his vision.

"Stupid," he muttered, rolling his eyes. He was nineteen, not two. "Don't stare into the sun" was a pretty basic childhood lesson.

Jacob looked back up. In that brief moment of distraction, the sky had exploded into oranges and rose golds. He stared, stunned, then remembered the camera in his hands. He came down to the beach every day specifically to photograph his patch of Hawaiian paradise, but he often forgot the camera in favor of his own eyes.

He snapped a few shots before the sunrise could begin to fade, then lowered the camera toward the water itself. The ocean mirrored the sky, with soft waves creating patterns in the reflected colors. Jacob knelt down, using the lower angle to capture a few photographs with the roll of the ocean in the foreground. For as beautiful as the sunrises and sunsets in Hawaii were, the constant majesty of the ocean was what had drawn him to this beach in the first place.

The soft roll of the water was his daily background noise. Nothing drew the tension from his shoulders quite like the peace of his chosen paradise. The waves were small, but still managed to creep up the black, sandy shores and leave behind darkened patches in their wake. A few large rocks on the beach broke through the surface of the water here and there, like stepping stones for a giant.

This portion of beach lay at the base of Jacob's property, and rocky outcroppings protected it from large waves, most wildlife, and any human visitors. He could count on one hand the amount of times he'd seen another person anywhere near his beach. As far as he was concerned, it was *his* ocean.

Jacob tucked the camera back into its case but didn't bother to zip it up. Kicking off his flip-flops, he walked into the path of the tiny waves. With each step, his toes squished deeper in the ebony sand. He'd grown so used to his little pitch-black oasis that the far more common white sand beaches now seemed unusual.

When he was down here, he didn't have to worry about anything. All his concerns about his mental faculties faded into the distance. He spent plenty of time focusing on his father's health and what ramifications it had for his own life. While on the beach though, he did his best to set his fears aside. Nothing should disturb the peace of this small sanctuary.

A splashing noise caused Jacob's head to snap up. He narrowed his eyes at the disturbed ocean surface, daring the ripples to explain themselves. Nothing happened.

After a beat, Jacob relaxed and let out a soft laugh. "The mind's the first thing to go." Shaking his head, he started to turn back toward his yellow chair.

A woman's head popped out of the water.

Jacob blinked at the head once, twice, and then a third time. It was a nice head, all things being equal. The part of his brain that appreciated the art of symmetry was fascinated by her bone structure. Her nose was petite and pointed, her lips small and pink, and her eyes were a crystal blue that mirrored the ocean itself. Long, bright, unnatural silver-blonde hair framed her face, cascading into the ocean to swirl just under the surface. Her appearance was almost enough to distract from the excessive number of pearls draped around her neck. Another pearl dangled in front of her forehead, held in place by a thin gold chain.

Jacob's mouth hung open. He blinked again. The woman moved a little closer, offering a smile. Their eyes locked, intensifying the moment and doing nothing to alleviate his bewilderment.

She lifted one hand from the water, droplets flying as she gave him a little wave. "Hello!"

Jacob rocked back on his heels, his grip on the camera tightening. He closed his mouth, squeezing his eyes shut for a few seconds before reopening them. The call across the water made it undeniable. A real woman floated there, in the ocean, watching Jacob. A beautiful, pearl-laden, impossibly blonde woman. He gave her another once-over. She didn't have goggles or any kind of breathing apparatus.

"You're not real," Jacob called back, which wasn't what he'd meant to say at all. "I mean, where did you come from?"

Is this what it felt like to lose his mind? Surely he would have noticed someone swimming toward his beach. Jacob examined the woman again, his photographer's eye unable to dismiss how perfect she looked in the water. She seemed real enough. Then again, maybe he wasn't the best person to judge that.

Her head tilted to the right. The pearl dangling over her forehead rolled across the furrowed skin. She matched his volume. "I swam here."

"Sure." That would make sense. Except Jacob *would* have seen her approaching. There was only one way to access this part of the beach. She would've had to swim in underwater. Except she didn't have snorkeling gear, let alone scuba equipment. Which brought him back to his original assumption: she wasn't real. His heart seized at the implications.

The woman seemed to sense Jacob's doubt. She moved closer. Taking advantage of one of the rocks near the shore, she gripped it, pulled herself up onto her stomach, and settled atop the rock with her chin nestled on her folded hands.

She grinned. "You're here a lot." It was an announcement, like he might be unaware.

"I live here." Jacob returned to a normal speaking volume. He examined her again, now that she was closer, reassuring himself she wasn't just a talking head. She wore some kind of corseted bodice the color of the sky, with more pearls holding it closed. She could put any of the pearl-peddling tourist traps on the island out of business.

"Is that your house?" The woman indicated the octagonal structure at the high point of the hill behind the beach.

Jacob stared at her graceful and delicate hand. It reminded him of dancers on a poster for the ballet. Having never actually gone to a show like that, it was hard to imagine people so lithe in the real world. He cleared his throat and replied, "Yes. Yes, that's my home." He forced his wits back where they belonged. "I'm sorry, who are you?"

"Sevencea."

She said her name like it answered any possible follow-up questions, like that one word solved every mystery about her. Maybe it did, but Jacob was not the type of man who understood what strange, impossible women in the middle of his ocean meant by the way they introduced themselves.

"I'm Jacob." It was all he could think to say in response. "Pearson," he added as an afterthought. It was probably unnecessary.

Sevencea raised an eyebrow. "Does your surname serve a purpose?"

Definitely unnecessary.

"I've never thought about it. I guess it helps distinguish me from everyone else called Jacob, but Pearson isn't a rare surname, so…" He shrugged and stopped himself. Fear of boring this ethereal being derailed his train of thought.

"I've never needed one." Sevencea blinked, then gave a slight shrug of her shoulders. "It's nice to meet you, Jacob Pearson. What do you do all day, out here on the beach?"

At this point Jacob decided to use the chair. Abandoning his previous notions of an excellent horizon view, he stepped back, grasped the chair, and dragged it forward. All of this was just strange enough to leave him feeling a little shaky. He also wanted the best view of Sevencea. She seemed real enough so far, which meant indulging in this conversation couldn't hurt anything.

He sat down with half an expectation that his rear end would land in the sand, but the frame held. Good. He'd never really used the chair. He allowed himself a small moment of relief, then refocused on his visitor.

"I just take photographs." He held up his camera bag as evidence. Photography was his first love. Life may have prevented him from pursuing a career, but he would never give up his camera.

"What does that mean?" Sevencea's eyes widened with a curious gleam, focusing on the bag around Jacob's shoulders.

Jacob hesitated. Did she need him to explain the concept of photography? Wouldn't most people already know? Better to redirect to avoid creating awkwardness.

"What about you?" Jacob asked. "What do you do? Other than watch me?"

Sevencea looked offended. Her nostrils flared and her brow furrowed slightly. "I do not watch you," she protested, "I've just seen you when I swim past." She gestured toward the opening between the outcroppings. "I was curious because you're always on the beach."

That was true; Jacob regularly spent entire days on this stretch of black sand. Still, he was certain he would have noticed if she'd really been swimming past his beach.

"You didn't answer my question," he reminded her.

She relaxed. Her hair shifted around her in the water where it draped off the rock. "I explore. There's not much else for me to do. I have an appreciation for what's around me, but no way to use that to make a living." She smiled, but there was a tightness in her expression; the admission must have cost her.

"I understand." Of everything she'd said so far, Jacob found this the most relatable. At least the camera in his hands was proof that he hadn't given up on his dreams, right? So what if his plans for his own photography business sat in an untouched folder on his laptop? Being there for his father was worth it. Being cautious about his own health was worth it.

Jacob had an urge to hug Sevencea, but wading out to her rock felt presumptuous. His expression slid into a frown as his mind drifted back to her earlier assertion. "Listen, I don't mean to be rude, but I don't understand how you could've been swimming around here multiple times without me noticing. And why are you still in the water?" He made a move to stand. "You can have my chair."

"Oh!" Sevencea's expression lightened, and she shot him a playful smile. "Sorry, I didn't realize you didn't know already. I'm a mermaid."

Jacob blinked.

Sevencea still lay there, smiling.

He closed his eyes, counted to ten, and then opened them again.

The sky was radiant with new morning. The ocean was peaceful and rhythmic. The sand evoked midnight. And the bewildering woman with champagne hair was still in the water smiling at him.

"I don't believe you." Jacob selected this response because it was true, and not as rude as his first impulse. Tension gripped his chest—a physical manifestation of his brain shouting at him that mermaids did not exist. At all. He didn't have the luxury of being unsure about things like that.

A spark of mischief glinted in Sevencea's eye. "What would convince you?"

"I…" Jacob opened his mouth, then closed it again. "I don't know," he admitted. He'd never had to think about it before.

Sevencea examined him with a slight furrow in her brow. The glint of mischief in her eyes grew more pronounced. "Will you faint if I do anything shocking?"

"I've never fainted before." While that was true, Jacob had to admit he felt a little off kilter at the moment. Worst case scenario, at least he'd already taken the precaution of sitting in his beach chair.

Without further warning, Sevencea slid backward off the rock, ducking below the water. Her hair streamed out behind her as she glided away from the beach. Something else seemed to move underwater behind her, colors he wasn't expecting. Before he could figure out what he was seeing, sunbeams splintered off the ocean's surface and obscured his view. He squinted, trying to track where the alleged mermaid had gone. The water was caressing the shore as it had done all morning, like it wanted to reassure him. Jacob inhaled deeply, grounding himself in the salt-rich scent of the air.

Jacob studied the water further out from shore, shielding his eyes with one hand. Had he really been talking to a woman? Perhaps he'd imagined the whole thing.

Near the entry to the inlet, the water rippled, drawing Jacob's eye as Sevencea launched herself into the air. Her head emerged first, pearlescent hair unfurling with a cascade of water droplets. Her body followed, light dancing off the tiny pearls holding her bodice together. Then there was her tail—a kaleidoscope of several shades of pink, from the palest rose to the brightest fuchsia. Even a few brilliant teals and purples caught the sunlight as the tail twisted through the sky.

Jacob stared at the tail. He knew mermaids had tails. But—he hadn't expected there to *be* a real tail. It was so long! How tall was Sevencea? Jacob was over six feet tall. If mermaids could stand on their tails, she could definitely look him in the eyes. Was that even a thing mermaids could do? He doubted it, but it wasn't like he had prior experience to base that assumption on.

It was hard to tell where Sevencea's torso met her tail. Her bodice blended into the trove of colored scales. She reentered the water, head first. The end of the tail, an almost translucent, pale-pink fin, disappeared below the water with a splash. Was fin even the right word? That was another question Jacob didn't have an answer to.

Too stunned to react, Jacob watched the water until Sevencea's head reemerged, moving back toward her previous perch. She pulled herself back onto the rock, adjusted her pearls, and refolded her hands, settling her chin on them once more.

"So," she said with a broad smile, showing off slightly pointed teeth, "do you believe me now?"

"Yes," Jacob conceded with a wry smile. "But my prevailing theory is that I'm just imagining you." The tension in his chest hadn't faded, but he would worry about that when the hallucination was over. He spared a moment to be grateful that he'd planned ahead for his sanity's departure.

"Is that so?" The corners of her lips twitched upward. "Are all humans so disbelieving? I've heard about them, but I haven't actually met one before. I could be imagining you."

"There's more precedent for me to imagine impossible things than you," Jacob pointed out. "Unless you've also got a family history of madness, but I doubt that's common."

"Not that I know of," Sevencea agreed. "Still, you don't seem out of your mind to me. I think we can at least agree that you and I are both real."

Jacob decided not to debate that for now. If he was actually losing his mind, he already had a contingency plan. Plus, his father was always telling him to be more optimistic. "So, I'm the first human you've ever spoken to?" He allowed curiosity to take the reins from his fears.

"Quite an honor, isn't it?" Sevencea winked. "My clan lives far from shore, and most of us don't like traveling too far anymore. We used to have a treaty with the islands, but that was a long time ago. Besides, the islands are always overflowing with visitors these days. It's hard to tell who can be trusted." She shrugged, the movement almost too casual on her.

Jacob huffed a laugh. He was hearing a mermaid give him a variation of the same locals-versus-tourists argument he'd been hearing since he moved to Hawaii a year ago. "How did you know I wasn't just visiting?"

"You're here every day," Sevencea reminded him.

"That's fair," Jacob agreed.

"I was just curious to talk to someone different," Sevencea concluded. "You're not merfolk."

Jacob actually glanced down before nodding. "True."

"And you never have anyone with you," Sevencea continued. "I thought you might like the company."

"I don't think I can argue with that." Jacob smiled. When was the last time he'd been social? He hadn't set out to isolate himself. Not intentionally, at least. He wasn't convinced that his sanity was still intact, but maybe, for now, it didn't matter. His current problem was how he was supposed to be interesting to a mermaid. He'd only seen the Disney movie once, and that had been at least ten years ago.

"So, are you friends with fish and stuff?" Jacob winced. He had the sneaking suspicion he'd just asked a ridiculous question.

Sevencea snorted—a remarkable, unattractive sound that somehow made her more real and appealing at the same time. "Fish aren't like merfolk," she explained, laughter in her voice. "They understand us, if we need them to, but it's not like…" she trailed off, waving her hand as she searched for a comparison. She snapped her fingers. "Humans have dogs, right?"

"How do you know about dogs?" Jacob's mouth fell open as his imagination went into overdrive. Maybe there was an as-yet-unknown breed of dogs with gills?

"I've seen them," she explained. "And my clan has interacted with humans before. In any case, creatures of the sea, most of them at least, are sort of to us what dogs are to you." Guessing Jacob's next question, she added, "And no, I don't have a pet fish that follows me about."

"I don't have a pet either," Jacob announced. He cringed at the awkward declaration, though he felt relieved he'd kept the dogs-with-gills theory to himself.

Sevencea laughed. "I told you, this will be good for both of us. We clearly don't socialize enough."

"So you just want to talk?" Jacob raised an eyebrow, leaned forward in his chair, and balanced his elbows on his knees.

"Isn't that how all relationships begin? Human or merfolk, true connection begins with conversation." Sevencea's smile was warm and genuine.

The simplicity of the sentiment sealed the deal. It didn't matter if Sevencea was real or not. Jacob was lonely, and she was offering a connection. He'd had no idea how desperate he was for friendship until she'd offered it, but he was eager to accept.

"So, you don't have a pet and you like to swim," he summed up, allowing his sense of humor to crawl out of its hole and take a peek around. "What else do you do?"

"I make maps sometimes." She gave him an encouraging grin. "I like to map unfamiliar areas for my clan, but it's just a hobby. I don't have an official job. What about you?" She glanced at the camera bag.

"I don't really have a job either," Jacob admitted. "I've always wanted to be a professional photographer, but I've had other stuff on my plate. Besides, I own the house outright, and my bills get paid." Not due to any of his own money, but he couldn't help that. He did work, sort of, but going into the nuances of freelance photography felt like too much for right now. At least Sevencea didn't look confused by his explanation.

"You feel purposeless," Sevencea surmised. "What good is an endless supply of time if you've no adventures to spend it on?" She trailed her fingers across the surface of the water in front of her, watching the ripples. "I know that feeling well."

Jacob nodded. She'd captured the sensation he'd battled since first moving to the island. "Any time I feel restless, I combat it by doing things I like, and trying to make those activities mean something. It sounds like you do too, with the exploring and the maps."

Sevencea inclined her head to the right and considered his assertion. "I hadn't thought about it like that, but you're right. My father has an endless supply of, well, everything, so there's no need for me to do anything in order to be comfortable. It's a rather stifling form of security."

"I understand." Jacob scoffed and shook his head.

Sevencea gave him a questioning look.

"My mother," Jacob clarified.

Sevencea nodded once, but didn't pursue the subject. "We seem to have strayed into deep waters," she observed with a soft giggle. "I didn't mean for our conversation to drift that way so soon."

Jacob glanced down at the sand, digging in with his toes, then met her eyes again with a shrug. "I don't mind. There's still a part of me that doesn't believe you exist, so it seems safe to talk about anything we want."

Sevencea laughed out loud, her head falling back and her hair glinting in the sunlight. As she recovered, the pearl on her forehead rolled back and forth and settled into place. "I don't know why you think you're crazy," she said, "but you seem just right to me."

Jacob felt his cheeks warm and grinned. She only meant his sanity, but it still might've been the best compliment he'd ever received.

Chapter Two

Sevencea did not swim home so much as glide. A smile danced across her lips, and she twirled with a laugh as she made her way toward her clan.

"That went much better than expected." There was no one around to hear the pronouncement, but it was worth saying anyway.

It had been years since anyone in her clan had bothered to go near the islands, let alone get close to a human. The fact that she'd spoken to one? Well, Sevencea could only imagine how her father would react. Not that she'd have to imagine long. She planned on telling him at dinner. Secrets bred enemies, and Sevencea had no intention of making enemies of her family.

Meeting Jacob had been a thrill in so many ways. It was new, risky, and even fun. Once she'd convinced him she was real, he'd turned into a sweet, funny, personable man. Although, she wasn't sure she'd *really* convinced him. It sort of felt like he was humoring her. That was the main reason Sevencea intended to return to the beach tomorrow. Jacob seemed lonely. She knew what that was like.

"Welcome back, dear!" An older mermaid looked up from the oyster shell bowl she was constructing, offering a bright smile.

Sevencea started, and just managed to wave a greeting in response. She hadn't realized she was so close to home already! Her clan wasn't large, but they kept busy, moving around often. It was easy to think there were far more of them in a given area.

Swimming over the next ridge brought her home into view. The spacious caves her people lived in were surrounded by rocky mounds and vibrant coral. The area teemed with sea life, most of it completely ignoring the merfolk floating amongst them. Sevencea relaxed automatically. She'd done something new today, but nothing had really changed. Home was still home.

"There you are! My girl, you've been away all day. Adventuring again?" The broad-shouldered merman surged forward, stopping just in front of her with his arms wide open in invitation.

And her father was still her father.

Sevencea closed the gap between them and gave her father a hug. Brineus kept their whole clan safe, and there was no one she trusted more. Sevencea was half his size, in height and width. A snail shell, carved so it could emit a loud whistling noise, hung from a cord around his neck, just visible below his long, braided beard. The soft look in his eyes warmed her, though behind that gentle expression was a merman who could be fearsome when he needed to be. Sevencea didn't feel that she resembled her father much, though his beard was the same shade as her own hair. Still, they were family.

"Adventuring is a word for it." She glanced up at him, trying and failing to suppress a grin.

Her father raised one eyebrow, then shook his head and snorted. "I suppose I'll get a full update at dinner. You have perfect timing, as always." He released a belly laugh. "My minnow can be expected to show up for meals!"

Sevencea rolled her eyes, but didn't argue. Father and daughter swam together toward the communal dinner table, set up in the center of their home. It had once been a row of rocks, but someone's magic had been used to connect the rocks and create a smooth surface on top. It was visible from the mouth of every cave they inhabited, so all the merfolk would know they were always welcome to gather. The whole community contributed to the daily feast, so there was always something for everyone. A wide variety of plants could be relied upon to sustain the clan. Not everyone ate together—they came and went as they pleased—but it was still a good way to stay connected to the others. Sunlight still streamed down from the surface, though the light would dim by the time they finished eating.

Waving to the merfolk around her, Sevencea flashed a shy smile at a few of her siblings. They smiled back, but made no move to approach her.

Brineus made a tutting noise. "I wish you all could spend more time together." His expression hinted that he might be planning to do something about that.

"They all have work to do," Sevencea reminded him. She was the youngest by many years, so her bond had always been with her parents, not her grown siblings.

"Still." He sighed, watching his older children swim across the space, away from the dinner table and back toward their own homes and families.

"Shall we eat?" Sevencea gestured to the table, where no one was waiting. On cue, her stomach rumbled, reminding her she'd not eaten since first thing that morning.

Brineus released the tension in his expression with a laugh. "That seems to be a yes! After you."

They swam forward and filled empty shells with their choice of plants. At the end of the table, Sevencea faced her father and raised an eyebrow. "Where do you want to eat?"

"Do you mind a bit of a swim?" Brineus's smile was conspiratorial and contagious.

Sevencea couldn't stop her responding grin. The two moved away from the clan's space and swam back the way Sevencea had come, toward the island. Did he already know where she'd been today? Sevencea was about to ask when her father turned around a reef and began moving off toward the left. Now she knew exactly where they were going.

Years ago, before her mother had died, her parents would sometimes take her above the surface to watch the sunset. There was a place where a particular rock formation jutted just above the surface. Her parents would swim up there with her and set her atop the rocks to gaze at the sky. It was a special treat—rare, but the foundation of many sweet memories.

"What's the occasion?" Sevencea asked as the rock formation came into view. She was mature now, no longer prohibited from poking her head above the surface whenever she liked. Since she'd spent most of the day above water, the uniqueness of this place was only preserved in her memories.

Brineus made his way toward the surface, motioning for her to follow. "I've been so busy lately, I haven't had a chance to feel the air on my face. Besides, it isn't as though we stopped doing fun things just because your mother is no longer with us."

Sevencea's smiled softly and a little wistfully. "That's true," she allowed. "We just haven't been here, specifically, in a long time."

"Maybe I just want to see if my grown minnow can still fit on top of the rocks." Her father shot her a mischievous wink, then put on a burst of speed toward the surface. His hand covered the shell he carried to protect his meal from being swept away.

Rolling her eyes, Sevencea covered her own shell, flicked her tail, and took off after her father. "That's not fair!" she called after him. Her father's tail, glistening with navy blue and teal scales, held far more power than her own. In a race, he would always win.

Brineus faced her, floating just below the surface. "Oh come now," he teased, "you've always been a quick one."

Sevencea reached him and stuck her tongue out. "Your tail is still twice the size of mine." With a laugh, she dodged the swipe of her father's tail. "Nice try. Come on, are we going to eat or not?" She pushed forward and breached the surface with a deep breath, savoring the exotic transition from water to air. The rock outcrop was beside her, a little smaller than she remembered it. Then again, she was bigger now.

Popping up beside her, Brineus inhaled slowly, tilting his head back and closing his eyes. "I always forget how nice this is," he murmured.

"I like exploring above water." Sevencea nibbled at her lip, wondering how best to explain she'd been above water most of today. She set her shell down on the rocks, picking at her food.

"I know you do." Brineus held up his shell and tipped his food into his open mouth. With a few chews and a swallow, he made a satisfied noise and waved his empty shell at Sevencea.

Rolling her eyes, Sevencea continued eating her own plants at a normal pace. "I was up here most of today," she blurted. Best to get it over with.

"All right." Brineus moved closer. He set an elbow on the rock outcrop and focused on her, his expression neutral. "Doing what?"

The water lapped softly against the rocks. Sevencea considered the best way to answer. "On the big island, there's a beautiful little beach with black sand. I've been by there often recently. There's always a man on the shore, alone."

Brineus raised an eyebrow, but did not otherwise react. It was hard to tell what an eyebrow meant. At least he wasn't angry. She wouldn't have to guess if he was. Her father was uncompromising about the safety of his children.

"So, today, I introduced myself." There. She'd said it. No more secrets. It was at once a release of the tension in her chest and a blossoming of fluttering jellyfish tentacles in her stomach.

"To a human?" Brineus asked.

Sevencea nodded. She didn't quite trust her voice.

"Hmm." Brineus cocked his head ever so slightly and examined her, his eyes unreadable. "How did that go?"

The jellyfish sensation began to settle. "He seemed to think he was imagining me." She giggled, the conversation replaying in her mind. "But I think I brought him around in the end."

Brineus chuckled, a deep, oddly soothing sound. "Many young men might think they were imagining you, my girl."

Sevencea flushed and shook her head. "I suspect it was my appearing from the water with a tail that startled him, Father."

"Ah, well, I'm sure the fact that you're a lovely young mermaid didn't have a thing to do with it." He winked, a teasing lilt to his lips.

Her flush did not dissipate. "Well, whatever it was, he was nice. I'll probably go back tomorrow."

"So you like him too." Her father was nothing if not forthright.

Sevencea sputtered for a moment, but couldn't bring herself to disagree. "He was so sweet," she finally said, unable to keep her lips from forming a small smile.

Brineus smiled back at her, his expression sympathetic. "Your mother loved her work with humans."

Sevencea nodded; this was not new information. "Right, but she stopped."

"Indeed. The relationship between man and merfolk grew apart before you were born, but your mother's ambassadorial work was important to her. She believed it was important to maintain those relationships, and was disappointed when the humans didn't share her passion." Brineus sighed, a wistful glint in his eyes. "Selfishly, I don't mind that we had her home for her final years."

Sevencea rested her hand on her father's arm and squeezed gently. "I don't think it's selfish at all. We were just as important to her."

"True." Brineus patted her hand and offered her a grateful smile. "My point is, I think she would be proud of you. I know you're just making a single connection, but it was those types of bonds she valued. You never know what it could lead to. Perhaps we've been isolated long enough."

"Why didn't the humans want to keep meeting with her?" Sevencea glanced down, trailing her fingers through the water. "I asked Mother, once, but she just said it was a season of change. I always assumed it made her sad, so I never asked again." She looked back up, meeting her father's eyes. "If I'm going to spend time with them though, I'd like to learn whatever I can."

Brineus nodded. His brow furrowed slightly as he laid a comforting hand on her arm. "I understand. I'm sorry her illness took her away, that she can't be here to experience your foray into the human world with you. I can only tell you what I know." His lips twitched toward a wry smile. "Which, of course, is hardly a fraction of what your mother knew!"

Sevencea laughed, reaching up to squeeze her father's hand. "I'm still grateful for anything you can tell me, Father. It's a way we can remember her together."

Brineus relaxed a little, a more natural smile in place now, and flipped his hand to return her squeeze. "You're right. We don't do that as often as we should." He pulled his hand back, stroking his beard as he gazed over the surface of the water. "So, you asked why the humans stopped meeting with us?"

Sevencea nodded and shifted into a more comfortable position. She focused her full attention on her father.

"Well, as I recall, it really was a season of change. Cultures often evolve over time. New people come into an area, new ideas are adopted, conflict may break out. Some cultures may be pushed out or fade away entirely. Obviously that happens in merfolk communities as well, but the humans outnumber us, so they do it on a larger scale. These islands, they've changed over the years."

Brineus paused, his gaze focused not on Sevencea or the water, but on some point in the past. "It used to be that merfolk and humans could have a mutually beneficial relationship. Particularly in seafaring, humans often looked to us for wisdom and help. But, as time has gone on, the humans have invented new ways of making seafaring safer. They don't need us in the same way; their own wisdom has evolved." He shrugged, his focus coming back to Sevencea. "Relationships take work, my minnow. And when one party believes they've advanced beyond needing the other, that relationship may quickly sour."

Sevencea's eyebrows drew together. The pearl bounced on her forehead. "That must have been hard for Mother. Did humans say that to her? That they no longer needed her? Or wanted her?"

Brineus shook his head before she'd even finished speaking. "No, no, it was nothing so cruel. It was merely a gradual distance. As their need lessened, so did their efforts toward maintaining our relationship. Eventually, your mother stopped going to the islands. If she had continued to put her all into her work and receive nothing in return, it would have been devastating. So, she returned home, to invest in her life below the waves. In me, in your siblings, and ultimately in you." His fond smile lingered as he watched Sevencea take in his words.

"It's hard to imagine," Sevencea murmured. She thought of Jacob's reaction to seeing her tail. It was difficult to picture a world where the sight wouldn't be a shock. "The world is so large; is it like this everywhere?"

Brineus shook his head again, this time with laughter, and gestured broadly around them. "As you said, my minnow—the world is large. There are many clans of merfolk in many bodies of water. Some still communicate with the humans nearby, I am certain. Things may change, but they do not change everywhere at the same pace. It has been many, many years since I have traveled very far from our lands, but I saw much of the world in my youth, and merfolk can be as varied as the humans, I assure you. Maybe one day you'll see it for yourself. I know you like to explore, and you're running out of room here at home. Perhaps your future is with human interactions, like your mother. Or to travel the world, like me. Who knows, maybe you will do both." He fixed her with a broad grin, reached for her hands, and clasped them in his own. "Whatever you do, Sevencea, I would like to see you safe and thriving."

A matching grin spread across Sevencea's face. "So it's all right with you? If I spend time around the humans?"

Brineus rolled his eyes with a chuckle. "I may still call you my minnow, dear, but you've seen eighteen migrations now. You're grown, Sevencea. I can offer you wisdom and guidance, but your choices are your own." He squeezed her hands, then released her.

Sevencea threw herself forward and hugged her father, knocking them both backward into the sea. As the bubbles cleared, their laughter filled the surrounding ocean.

Chapter Three

After hours of conversation, Sevencea had bid Jacob farewell and ducked underwater, leaving behind only ripples. Jacob watched the ocean until it grew still, ignoring the tension in his chest. Then he packed up his beach chair and walked home. Nothing about the well-worn path up the hill was different. But everything seemed brighter. All the flowers growing in the grassy patches along the path shone with new life.

He closed his eyes and took a breath, trying to recalibrate his senses. When he opened his eyes again, everything still had a hopeful glow. He suspected he knew why—the flutter in his heart was not subtle. Jacob glanced over his shoulder, expecting some evidence on the beach of the encounter. The black sand was empty though, and he was far enough away that even the marks from his chair were no longer visible. The flutters began to sink, becoming a growing weight in his stomach.

Setting his chair against a tree and fishing his key out of his back pocket, Jacob unlocked a glass door—the only entrance to his home. Most of his house had glass walls, although his bedroom was constructed with plaster. The living room, kitchen, and entryway were all one large space, designed to expose as much of the ocean view as possible.

In the spacious windows, Jacob's reflection followed him as he crossed to the kitchen. He didn't look any different. He scowled, examining the healthy glow of his sun-warmed skin. It was just a façade. Being in great shape on the outside meant nothing if his mind wasn't healthy too. There was no reassurance to be found in his reflection, no peace to soothe the mounting fear that had grown with each step away from his beach. A spike in his forehead warned of an impending headache. He closed his eyes and took a deep breath.

When he opened his eyes again, a blinking light on the counter caught his attention. Mobile service was spotty by the ocean, so he gave the landline number to anyone whose calls he didn't want to miss. Jacob hung the camera bag on a peg by the door, strode across the room, and pressed the message button.

"First message," the system intoned. Jacob squinted at it. He rarely had more than one.

"Hello, dear—" Jacob hit the skip button before he could learn why his mother was calling. They hadn't really spoken, other than by email, since his high school graduation. That conversation had been, for lack of a better word, disastrous.

"There's not an official diagnosis … the doctor expressed concern it could be hereditary … no way to be sure when or if it will develop…" Snatches of that conversation, in his mother's precise, unconcerned tone, often intruded on Jacob's thoughts. It was hard to remember a time before that conversation. That fight, really.

The ache in his forehead pulsed, reminding Jacob that he was scowling. He had to make an effort to relax.

"Second message," the system informed him.

"Hey, Jake!" His father's excessive enthusiasm was unmistakable. Jacob relaxed, reflexively smiling at the machine. There was no better distraction than a message from his father. "Sorry I missed you. I'm having a really great day, all things considered, so I wanted to try and catch you while I'm not, well, you know. They're giving me some great stuff, I gotta tell ya. Doc's going to forward you the paperwork, since I told him you'd want it. You know how he gets though. You might need to email the poor guy. Anyway, call me back when you get this!" The machine beeped, and Jacob hit the save button before the machine could give him his options.

He always saved his father's messages, just in case.

Glancing at his watch, Jacob nodded. It was just before five. He still had time to try and catch his father before the facility's schedule prevented him from answering.

Choosing to multitask, Jacob grabbed the handset and hit redial. He pinned the phone to his shoulder with his ear, opened the fridge, and retrieved a Tupperware bowl full of soup. He managed to open the microwave with his elbow, slid the bowl inside, and set the cook time.

"Mana'o Treatment Center," a generic, pleasant voice announced through the phone.

"Room forty-three, please." Jacob hit the start button on the microwave and relaxed against the counter, adjusting the phone so he was actually holding it. He gazed through the microwave window, counting the rotations to ground himself. He could worry about his own mind later; this was the time to focus on his father.

"Oh, Mr. Pearson, of course. One moment." A click sounded, followed by soft, traditional Hawaiian music.

Jacob wasn't surprised the front desk person had identified him, though he couldn't remember her name to save his life. He knew his father's doctor, a few of the staff specialists, and one of the nurses well enough. Everyone else in the facility was a blur. If he visited more often, maybe it would be different, but it was hard to bring himself to do so. That was the main reason he lived an hour and a half away from the facility. Close enough to stay connected; far enough to live in denial.

"Jake?" His father's eager voice answered the phone. Gerald Pearson was the only person who ever sounded that thrilled to talk to Jacob. It was the main reason Gerald was allowed to call him by a nickname. Everybody else called him Jacob.

"Hey, Dad. It was good to hear from you. It's awesome you're feeling better today."

"Oh, not just today! It's been this whole week so far. I don't want to jinx anything, but they might have found me a drug that actually works this time. I haven't had a memory lapse in almost four whole days!" No small amount of pride accompanied the announcement.

Jacob straightened, his eyebrows drawing together. "Seriously? No memory lapses at all?" The weight in his stomach lessened ever so slightly. Hope was a drug with interesting side effects.

"I remember everything," Gerald declared.

"You certainly remember your tendency toward the dramatic," Jacob pointed out. He popped the microwave open with his elbow just before it beeped.

Gerald let out a belly laugh, the warm sound traveling straight from Jacob's ear to his heart. He couldn't help his responding smile. He really needed to visit his father again as soon as possible.

Maneuvering the phone back to the space between his ear and shoulder, Jacob carefully extricated his soup and set it down on the counter so he could hunt for a clean spoon. The tension in his chest eased as Jacob relaxed into the familiar back and forth with his father.

"Let's test this newfound memory integrity," Jacob challenged. He picked up a spoon from beside the sink, examining it. Good enough. He stirred the soup, adjusting the phone to a more comfortable position.

"Hit me!" If *fearless* had a face in the dictionary, it was Gerald Pearson.

"What's my favorite color?" The pale pink that dominated Sevencea's tail swam to the front of Jacob's mind. He chased it away, only to have it followed by metallic teals, purples, and soft blues woven into the pink. An ache pulsed in his jaw—he was clenching his teeth. He tilted the phone away from his mouth and took a deep, centering breath. It was selfish to focus on his own situation right now.

"Blue," Gerald stated, his confidence undeniable.

Jacob grinned, a relaxing wave dissipating the unsettled whirlpool in his gut. "Well, there you go. Looks like you're cured." Blue had been the right answer for the first nineteen years of his life. Jacob didn't intend to debate his father's memory with a newly acquired fondness for the color palate of a mermaid tail. Blinking away the intrusive thought, he eyed his steaming soup. He might have heated it too long.

Gerald snorted. "Well, not yet, but you just wait. It's a process. I'm not completely symptom free, but, I mean, you can hear it, right? I think I sound pretty healthy."

It was true. Jacob could recall multiple times when Gerald's particular cognitive impairment had rendered him almost incapable of communication. The days when he sounded like his old self were often pockmarked by lapses in memory, among other issues.

Jacob resolved to email Dr. Wilcox as soon as he got off the phone. No one, aside from Gerald's doctors, knew more about Jacob's father's treatments than Jacob. He researched them all thoroughly, to understand exactly what could happen. Gerald had no official diagnosis, so treatments were often haphazard. That was also why no doctor had been able to declare with certainty that Jacob wasn't at risk of developing the same condition.

"You do sound great, Dad," Jacob acknowledged. "You said not symptom free though, so I'm guessing you're still hallucinating." It was more a statement than an actual guess.

Hallucinations were the biggest issue with Gerald's illness, often the most debilitating one. That symptom had resulted in the round of diagnostic testing which landed Gerald in a treatment facility on the island of Hawaii.

"Not big things," Gerald assured his son. "I thought there was a swarm of bees in here earlier, but I knew it wasn't real as soon as I saw it."

Jacob breathed a sigh of relief. He tilted the phone away so he could slurp some soup without treating his father to the auditory experience. The prospect of his father developing an awareness that his hallucinations weren't real while they were still happening was promising. Gerald had often experienced hallucinations he believed in fully, which terrified everyone who cared about him. Jacob couldn't think of anything more frightening than thinking something was real, only to find out his mind had betrayed him. Sevencea smiled from the periphery of his thoughts. He redirected his focus.

"I'm going to have Dr. Wilcox send me the info on this new treatment, okay? It sounds like great news, but you know me." Jacob took another sip of soup and silently repeated the prayer he'd been saying since his father's diagnosis—a prayer of gratitude for everything he had, and a petition for everything his father didn't.

"I figured." Gerald huffed a laugh. "Enough about me, Jake. Give me news about you! Still in the fancy beach house, right?"

Jacob snorted again. "Yeah, well, it's got a great view. I'm still doing photography, of course." He had a handful of freelance clients who bought his photos, but it wasn't quite the thriving business he'd hoped to open one day.

"Hardly new information," Gerald grumbled. "I know you moved here because of me, but it's not like you're stuck in here with me. Your lack of a life is kind of sad, kiddo." The elder Pearson's sense of humor came through in the jibe, but so did a hint of sincerity.

Jacob hesitated, unsure how to reply. He'd had a lot of friends at boarding school by the time he graduated. At this point though, his social life had gone into a metaphorical box, just like his diploma had gone in a physical one.

What if his father needed him without warning? What if he finally developed symptoms of his own? It was hard to justify going out and making friends when he knew he was a ticking time bomb. So he stayed home, keeping himself available in case of an emergency at Mana'o. The beach was as far as he went most days, unless he needed groceries or was visiting his father. He'd intentionally kept some distance between himself and the treatment center though. If he'd chosen to live close by, the shadow of his father's illness and his own potential future would have loomed even larger. At least here, overlooking his beach, he could pretend that there was still a future where his mind was his own and his father was healthy.

"You talked to your mom lately?" Gerald prompted.

"We email." Jacob injected as much finality into the response as possible. He knew his father wanted to see him reconcile with his mother. More importantly, Gerald knew that Jacob didn't like talking about it.

Gerald sighed heavily into the phone, but thankfully didn't push the issue.

Stirring his soup, Jacob gazed absently through the glass wall, cleared his throat, and said the first thing that popped into his head to change the subject. "I met someone." He winced. Why even admit that? Wasn't the tail proof enough that his brain had made up the whole thing? Worrying his father was just cruel.

Gerald was quiet for a minute. "Really?" he breathed, palpable hope in his voice. "Who? How? Details, Jake, details!"

Jacob's grimace morphed into a small, sad smile. Maybe, if only for this conversation, it didn't matter. Allowing his father to believe he was happy was worth it. Setting aside his soup, he walked to where he'd hung his camera bag, digging the device out and turning it on so he could scroll through the SD card's memory.

"She's a little enigmatic," Jacob offered, dimly aware that he hadn't answered his father's actual question. He continued scrolling through the photographs. Surely he'd taken one of Sevencea? That would be all the proof he needed! "We met on my beach," he added as an afterthought.

"Isn't your beach private property?" Gerald asked warily. "I thought that was the whole point of living out there."

"Yeah, well, she doesn't strike me as a 'bound by traditional rules' sort of person." Jacob scowled at his camera. No photographs of Sevencea. That settled that. "Then again, there's the ever-increasing likelihood that I imagined her, so…" He kept his tone as light as he could manage, but he couldn't fight off the pulse of disappointment which worsened his budding headache.

"You. Do. Not. Have. My. Disease." Gerald said, each full stop growing more emphatic. "How many tests did you make your mother pay for after my diagnosis? Twenty? Thirty? You're completely free of any of the markers I showed, kiddo. You're fine."

"For now," Jacob retorted. He laid his camera on the counter and picked up his soup. He gave it a stir out of habit. "And you don't have a diagnosis, Dad. You have a degenerative brain condition no one can effectively treat or conclusively say isn't hereditary. If the doctors can't say I'm in the clear, you definitely can't. Plus, you weren't symptomatic until you were a lot older than I am. I've got plenty of time to lose my marbles."

Gerald snorted, but there was no humor in the noise. "I may not have been full on hallucinating and forgetting my own name, but there were signs. I didn't just wake up with a disease like this, Jake. It got worse over a long period of time before we figured it out. But I've never hallucinated meeting someone new. I've hallucinated people I already know, and sometimes I talk to them for a while before I figure out it's a hallucination or a doctor gets to me, but it's never anyone new."

He paused. Jacob was quiet too, surprised to hear his father breathing hard. This wasn't the first time they'd had this conversation, but something about Gerald's intensity felt new. A small, wistful smile crossed Jacob's face. Maybe his father just didn't want him to lose hope.

Slowing his speech and lowering his volume, Gerald continued, "Trust me, Jake, if you met someone, they're real. You are not crazy."

"Everyone's a little crazy." Jacob sighed and sipped at his soup, relaxing against the counter. Fighting with his father sucked, no matter the topic. His father's urgings on this issue were usually somewhat reassuring, but it was hard to be reassured when you'd spent most of the day with a symptom.

Gerald made an irritated noise in the back of his throat. "You might look like your old man, kiddo, but we're far from the same person."

Jacob hummed in response, glancing at his reflection in the closest pane of glass. When puberty hit, Jacob had become used to people telling him on a near-daily basis that he looked like Gerald. After a growth spurt, Jacob ended up brushing the edge of six feet and two inches, so he was basically the same height as his father. Their rich, dark brown hair was a shared feature too, although Gerald wore his in a business professional cut, and Jacob only cut his when shoving it out of his eyes got annoying. They also shared brown eyes, but Jacob was pretty sure his were darker. They both had square jaws, Jacob's clean-shaven, whereas his father only picked up a razor when forced. Their biggest difference was that Gerald had the build of an office worker, while Jacob's high school hobby of running track had kept him lean.

"Anyway," Gerald dragged the word out, "you going to see this girl again?" Hope had reentered his voice, but with an edge. There would be no further argument about his son's mental state.

Jacob hummed again, switching the phone to his other ear. "No idea. I don't know much about her, so she'd have to come back to me." A forceful part of his brain interjected that even if the beautiful mermaid was real, a romantic future with a fictional species couldn't happen. To his annoyance, the rest of Jacob's brain had no comeback for that.

"She'll be back." Gerald certainty was absolute. "You're a catch, Jake. It's just a fact."

"You're kind of obligated to believe that, being my dad and all,"

Jacob teased, slurping his soup. He didn't bother to shift the phone away this time.

"I take it back," Gerald deadpanned, "you're clearly an animal with no social graces. Were you raised in some kind of barn?"

Jacob paused, a grin spreading across his face and shoving his concerns to the back of his mind. "When I was ten..."

It took Gerald a moment to catch up to where his son was leading, then he began sputtering. "A barn converted into a quaint bed and breakfast does not count!"

Slurping his soup again, Jacob tried not to choke on his own laughter. "Still a barn!"

"I don't know where you got all this snark," Gerald huffed. Jacob could practically see his father's good-natured grin and accompanying eye roll. "Anyway, there's an orderly here giving me the side-eye, so I think I'm about to be chased outta here for dinner. You come visit me soon, okay?"

"Sure, Dad." That was a request Jacob would never decline. "I'll be out your direction before you know it."

"You'd better!" Gerald said something unclear away from the receiver, likely to the orderly, then addressed his son with, "I'll talk to you soon, Jake. Love you."

"You too. Bye, Dad."

Jacob hung up the phone and swallowed down what remained of his soup. He had a list of things he needed to accomplish now, including emailing his father's doctor, but his mind kept running back to the beach. The headache had mostly faded, but the lingering prickles of pain behind his forehead were hard to ignore.

"It wasn't real." Jacob made the pronouncement to the empty room. Nothing happened. The tension inside him did not fade, nor did the niggling of doubt in the back of his mind. What difference did it make that there was no photographic evidence? If he really had met a mermaid, it made sense that he'd be too distracted to think of taking a photo. Jacob glanced back out the window at the ocean. No one was out there, blonde and impossible or otherwise. He shook his head, put his dishes in the sink, and headed to the little room he called an office to get some work done.

Maybe he'd find a mermaid waiting for him in the morning.

Chapter Four

Day 2

Sevencea pulled herself up on the rock perch she'd used yesterday, adjusting until she was comfortable. Jacob was already on the beach, fiddling with whatever it was he had slung around his torso. He wore less clothing today, but more color. She squinted at the fabric on his bottom half. It was garish, and floral in a way that made her want to blink rapidly, even from this distance. A piece of fabric that she couldn't identify was slung around his neck. His bare skin caught the light in random spots, where he was streaked with a white substance.

"Jacob!" she called with as much cheer as she could muster. He wasn't smiling yet, but she could fix that.

The young man twisted toward the sound of her voice. As soon as he laid eyes on her, his whole body relaxed. A genuine smile bloomed on his face, and he held his hand up in a half-waving motion. "Hey!" His smile grew even broader.

Sevencea studied him. The moment Jacob had seen her, it was like a thousand stones had lifted from his mind. She knew he'd struggled with the idea she was real, but was that really the cause for such relief? It seemed too deep a question for so early in the morning. The sun still hadn't fully risen, the orange sunrise painting the sky behind her.

"How was the rest of your night?" Jacob rubbed at his shoulder where some of the white stuff still glinted in the light.

"Mediocre." Sevencea shrugged, suppressing a smile. She twisted the pearls at her neck around her fingers. "I just wandered aimlessly, thinking about you."

Jacob's jaw didn't drop, but it was a near thing. The sunrise began to fade into softer colors as he stared at her. She could almost see the list of possible responses flying through his mind.

"I'm kidding." Sevencea grinned at him and winked. "I went home and had dinner with my father. I did think about you, I just haven't built a shrine."

Some merfolk used human things from the ocean floor to decorate their caves, but Sevencea always found that creepy. Making use of discarded items, sure. Pilfering shipwrecks, no. That was inappropriate.

Jacob barked a laugh, and his whole expression lightened. "You had me going for a second." He shifted in the sand, shivering a little. Sevencea focused on the air briefly, but couldn't tell if a human would feel chilled. Maybe he did—there was no direct sunlight yet.

Sevencea gave Jacob a pointed once-over. "You look … different today." She paused, unsure if that was rude. Were humans easy to insult? Merfolk could be awfully touchy.

"Swim trunks." Jacob gestured to his patterned garment. "It's for wearing into the water. I know these are ugly, but I didn't own a pair when I moved here, and it was peak tourist season. You get used to it. It's the main reason I haven't replaced them."

He paused, nibbling on his lip. "I was thinking that, if you wanted, I could come in the water and show you how the camera works. You seemed interested yesterday." He winced, though what his mind was objecting to was anyone's guess.

"Of course!" Sevencea was most interested in getting that uncomfortable look off Jacob's face, but the whole camera thing was interesting too. What had he called it yesterday? Photography? A thought occurred to her, and she raised an eyebrow. "So, even though you weren't certain I was real, you still made plans for us today?"

Jacob blinked at her, and it almost looked like his cheeks were pinking up. "I guess so," The words sounded like they surprised him.

"I'll accept whatever belief you can offer." Hoping her smile conveyed reassurance, Sevencea gestured for him to come closer. "It might be a little cold for you right now," she mused, reaching down to twirl her fingers in the water, "but I think I can fix that."

Jacob's eyes narrowed, but he didn't question her. He moved into the calm water lapping at the beach and waded toward the rock Sevencea had claimed as her perch. The water slowly swallowed him, settling around his belly button as he reached her. His eyes stayed trained on her the whole time, like he wasn't aware there was a world around him anymore.

The singular focus was almost enough to make Sevencea blush now. He was staring at her, but not in a rude way. More like she was the sunrise, the thing he couldn't take his eyes off of. As soon as she had the thought, Jacob thrust his eyes down at the ocean. Maybe he thought he'd been staring too long. As soon as his gaze was gone, she missed it.

"The water's warm!" Jacob blurted. He thrust his hands under the surface and turned them a few times, staring at his palms like that would tell him something.

Sevencea smirked a little, but shifted the expression into a softer smile before Jacob looked back up. "Merfolk can affect the water around them," she explained. She pushed herself off of the rock, floating in the water at a level even with Jacob. Speaking from above him felt weird. Her tail moved a little beneath the water, something she wouldn't have even registered, but it was clearly distracting Jacob. She ignored his divided attention. "Temperature is an easy fix, but I have to be careful not to hurt any fish that might happen by."

"Wouldn't want to harm your friends." Jacob grinned. His body relaxed again, at least a little.

Sevencea rolled her eyes, then almost did it again when Jacob's eyes went to the pearl at her forehead. She didn't even notice it moving anymore. It was hard to think of all the things that would be fascinating to a human. So much of her day was mundane, but nearly every facet of it would probably overwhelm Jacob. His gaze shifted back to the water, and his eyes grew even larger. She glanced down to identify what had caught his attention this time. Her hair, silvery-blonde in the sunlight, looked luminescent under the water. Just another thing that distinguished her from a human. Maybe the things that made her so other to Jacob were the reason he doubted she was real?

"Tell me about your camera." Sevencea's words made Jacob jump, his eyes going wide as he looked up at her again, though he recovered swiftly. She really couldn't blame him for staring. If she'd never seen a human before, she'd probably do the same thing.

"Well, only the bag is waterproof." Jacob tapped the bag he'd slung across his torso. He opened it and retrieved the device he'd been holding yesterday. "In other words, the camera can't go in the ocean, or it won't work anymore."

Sevencea nodded and inched closer, shifting her head to take in the camera from different angles. "How does it work?"

"I'll show you." Jacob began fiddling with the device, twisting the tubular portion and holding it to his face. He adjusted his stance, then the camera. "Think of the funniest thing you've ever seen."

Sevencea's eyebrows drew together and she pursed her lips. The funniest? An image of her father accidentally tying his hair in knots when one of his own whirlpools had gotten away from him flashed into her mind. She grinned. It might not be the funniest thing she'd ever seen, but it was up there. Her father hadn't been amused, of course, but as a child, she'd found it hilarious. A sort of soft clicking noise distracted her, and she snapped back to the present, leaning forward toward Jacob. "What did you do?"

"Hang on." Jacob fiddled with something on the device, then flipped the camera over to face her.

A window on the device showed the image that had been captured. It was her! Sevencea had never seen her own face in such crisp detail. Reflections were one thing, but this was a masterpiece.

"This is incredible magic," she breathed, unable to tear her eyes away. This was a unique kind of vanity, to be unable to look away from oneself. She looked ethereal; no wonder Jacob had trouble believing she was real.

"It's not magic." Jacob's tone was hesitant. He shifted in place again, hunching his shoulders a little.

Sevencea tore her eyes away from the camera to pin Jacob with a pointed stare. "I didn't mean the device was magic." She didn't want to sound scolding, so she added a small smile. "I mean you,

Jacob. You're the one with the magic. You have a gift in how you perceive the world, and it allows you to create beautiful images. What is that, if not magic?" How could such talent be considered anything other than magical? She couldn't fathom it.

Jacob was staring at her again, his mouth actually hanging open this time. It was difficult to guess what was going on behind his guarded eyes. He didn't seem upset. Rattled was a better word.

"I've surprised you." Sevencea brushed a few hairs away from her face, then laid her hand on Jacob's shoulder. It was the first time they'd touched, and she tried not to let that distract her. Jacob seemed aware of it too. He straightened when they made contact. "Surely you've been told you have a gift before now?"

Jacob nodded. "In school, I had teachers tell me I should take photography seriously as a career."

"Is that what you were educated in? This magic?" Sevencea made a point of maintaining eye contact. Jacob had a tendency to retreat within himself; she wasn't going to let him get away with it.

"Sort of." Jacob gnawed at his lip, looking torn.

Sevencea tilted her head and examined his expression for clues. "What's wrong?"

"Nothing, I just don't want to…" Jacob trailed off, waving his hands in a way that made it look like his words had run away from him.

He hadn't explained, but Sevencea suspected she'd figured it out. "You're afraid of confusing me?" They'd been getting on all right so far, but they weren't the same. There were bound to be things they didn't understand about each other. Jacob nodded, and Sevencea relaxed. "You don't need to change how you speak or what you say, Jacob. I catch on quick. I'll ask if something doesn't make sense to me."

Surprise flitted across Jacob's face before he settled into a small, grateful smile. "You're a quick study when it comes to me, that's for sure."

Sevencea laughed and gestured toward him. "You say everything you're thinking without words."

"Fair enough." Jacob snorted and ran a hand down his face. "All right, I'll try and explain. For humans, normally from ages fourteen to eighteen, you attend what's called 'high school.' There's a bunch of different versions, depending on what country you live in, how much money you have, and who knows what else."

Merfolk had education too, though less formal than whatever it was Jacob was describing. Sevencea nodded, offering Jacob what she hoped was an encouraging smile. It was a natural instinct to smile at him. For a man who stood so surely, he seemed ready to crumble in on himself with little prompting. His tone bore no signs of hesitation, that was all gathered behind his eyes. If Sevencea could discover the way to chase his worries out of him entirely, she'd be sure to do so.

"My parents have their own business, so they do pretty well," Jacob continued. For some reason a furrow creased his brow, but he seemed aware of it, because it smoothed out almost as soon as it appeared. "I mostly learned at home or with tutors—like teachers you hire into the home—until I was fourteen. We moved a lot, all over the world, so it was practical. When I was about to start my first year of high school, my parents sent me to boarding school. It's a type of high school where you live full-time, go to school, everything. I saw my parents during breaks in the year, but that's about it."

"That must have been difficult." Sevencea tried to imagine being apart from her father. He was gone sometimes for work, but never for longer than a day or two. She didn't have to imagine being apart from her mother. She cursed death for many things, but that most of all.

"It was," Jacob admitted. The wrinkle in his brow broadcast a story behind those simple words. "Anyway, you take lots of classes while you're at school, and sometimes you can take classes about things you're interested in that wouldn't otherwise be part of the curriculum—er, normal class load, I guess." He held up his camera. "I was most interested in photography, so I took a bunch of classes about cameras and working with them."

Sevencea tilted her head, considering that. She mostly understood what he meant, but some of the complexities escaped her. Jacob's passion though, that she could follow with ease. Passion she understood. "What about this form of magic spoke to you?"

Whatever burden sat around Jacob's shoulders slid off. The smile that appeared on his face was so natural she wondered how he didn't always wear it.

"It came so easily! The first time I held a real camera, not some cheap one I'd bought for fun, I just loved its weight in my hands. It was the most natural thing in the word to look at everyday scenes for what should be captured, and then people were telling me I was good at it! I was a pretty ordinary kid. I didn't skip grades, and I didn't excel at anything in particular, so I had no idea what I was going to do with my life. No clue at all. Then teachers, people I respected, told me I was great with a camera. Finding out I was good at something was like a drug."

Jacob paused, as though he'd forced himself to halt. Maybe other people had told him to stop gushing before, but Sevencea had no intention of joining that list.

"That's what magic is like." She let the words out in a soft, teasing tone. When Jacob flushed, she laughed and spoke normally again. "So, is that what you do with your days? Take photographs?"

Jacob nodded, then paused and tilted his head from side to side instead. "Sort of. I'm a freelance photographer."

Sevencea didn't disguise her blank stare. She had promised to let him know if she didn't understand something.

Jacob noticed quickly. He waved his hand in the air, like he hoped to snatch the right words. "Basically instead of working a normal amount of hours for the average adult, I work when I feel like it and when the project interests me. I need to be available if my father needs me, and my parents are wealthy enough that I don't actually *have* to work. I choose to work so I can pretend I'm self-sufficient. I've tried throwing my mother's money back at her, and it doesn't work."

Comprehension dawned, and Sevencea let out a noise of acknowledgment. He'd mentioned his mother yesterday, and she'd been able to tell that was a much more complicated story than he was ready to dive into. She could identify. For as much as she loved to speak about her own mother, it still felt like tearing off her scales with lobster claws to speak of her death and subsequent absence. Some things were complicated.

"Being available for your father is noble," she finally said, offering a smile she hoped was reassuring. Some things required a bond to discuss. The pulsing in her chest told her that they were well on their way, but a mere day of companionship was not enough to weave together those kind of connections.

Jacob nodded. "I want to run my own photography business, full time. That was the plan, but my father got sick. It's really complicated, but he lives here now, so I moved here to be close to him. I've put my whole," he paused, waving in the air for words again, "life, I guess, on hold."

Sevencea raised an eyebrow. "You can't have your own dreams and be there for your father at the same time?" She knew what it was like to have a sick parent, but it was her mother's example, even after she was gone, that drove Sevencea to want to live a full life. Even if she didn't know what that looked like for herself yet.

Jacob scowled, although there was no anger in his eyes. "You sound like my dad."

A surprised laugh escaped Sevencea. She felt her cheeks warm as Jacob peered at her quizzically. "Your father must be a smart man then." She winked and started giggling again.

Jacob's face lightened, and his lips twitched toward a smile. "We have an expression, here on land. Great minds think alike."

"I like that. Great minds think alike." Sevencea tested the words on her tongue and nodded once. "I would like to meet your father." Jacob's expression shuttered. Sevencea held her breath. Had she said something wrong?

Jacob caught her eye and shook his head. "Sorry, I don't mean to look like that. I'd love for you to meet him too. Dad's great. Funny, smart, supportive. It's just … remember when I said he was sick?" He waited until she nodded. "It's basically his brain that's sick. Sometimes he's okay, and sometimes he sees things that aren't there and can't remember anything from the last decade. It varies so much every day, and we don't know if he'll get worse, or if there's a chance he'll get better. Either way, he doesn't leave the treatment facility where he lives." Jacob's tone was matter-of-fact, but in a soul-crushing kind of way.

"I'm so sorry, Jacob." Sevencea reached for his face and pulled his forehead to hers. "I know what it is to watch a parent suffer." She'd meant the touch to be comforting, but where her fingertips met the hair at the back of Jacob's neck something sparked. She inhaled; he smelled earthy, a rich, grounding scent. The world around her faded, his closeness drawing her in and blocking out everything else. She closed her eyes just briefly, then let him go, drifting back to a less intimate distance.

Jacob's eyes glistened, though his face stayed dry. "Thank you."

Loss and suffering, especially when it was family, was such a personal subject. Sevencea hesitated to say anything more, but Jacob was still here, with her. He wasn't hunched in on himself, nor turning away. If he was sharing himself, she wasn't going to reject that opportunity. "If you don't mind, why is his future so uncertain? At least with my mother, we knew the end was coming. It was hard, but certain, and certainty helped, in the end."

"I'm sorry about your mom." Jacob reached for her this time, resting a hand on her arm and giving it a gentle squeeze. "I don't mind explaining. My father's illness is similar to a lot of things doctors know a lot about, but also different from all of them. He has something new, or at least something rare. It means they can't predict for sure what will happen to him. They can guess, but there's no certainty. And you're right, certainty would help."

"That's true." Sevencea offered him a small, teasing smile.

Jacob tilted his head. "What is?"

"I'm always right. That's lesson number one." Sevencea winked at him. Jacob laughed, and a wave of relief filled her chest. If they couldn't punctuate the sadness of life with laughter and love, then they weren't living well. It seemed like Jacob needed someone to help him with that.

Jacob gave a dramatic roll of his eyes, but the new lightness to him was the important thing.

They shared a moment of peaceful quiet. There was no need to fill the silence, just a shared enjoyment of being present together. The sunrise had faded, and the sky was now a bright blue. The ocean was calm, sending small waves past them and toward the shore. The slightest breeze caressed them, causing a shiver to race down Sevencea's spine.

"What's your father like?"

Sevencea started a little, her eyes widening. She pursed her lips. "He's quite a presence," she finally said. "His magic allows him to create whirlpools."

Jacob opened his mouth, did a double take, closed his mouth, and stared at her. "Do you have magic?" The words stuttered out, like they were tripping over his tongue on their way out.

Sevencea laughed and nodded. "Yes, all merfolk do. We're all very different, though sometimes magic passes through family members. For example, one of my brothers can also make whirlpools, though not as large as Father's."

The undefinable bewilderment on Jacob's face was endearing. "What does he use the whirlpools for?" His hands tightened on his camera, like he was imagining a whirlpool sucking it away.

"My father is in charge of our clan's security," Sevencea explained. "He uses whirlpools, small ones, to break up fights or to herd sea creatures away from or toward places. That's about it. He's not one for destroying things."

Jacob's expression shifted to understanding. "So he's like law enforcement? That sounds like a big responsibility."

"Yes, law enforcement! Exactly." Sevencea beamed at Jacob. "My clan doesn't get up to too much trouble, but he still takes it seriously. He works hard to make sure we're all safe."

"I respect that—a lot. I'm glad it's not too dangerous."

"Me too."

Jacob tapped his fingers on his camera. Sevencea hadn't had time to learn his habits, but she'd wager a sand dollar that the tapping was one of them. He drummed out an unconscious rhythm across one of his prized possessions.

She gestured, drawing his attention back to the camera. "Will you share your magic with me? I'm interested in how it all works."

Jacob's eyes lit up. "Sure!" He grasped the fabric around his neck and pulled it off, handing it to her. "Here, wipe your hands on that first. Like I said before, the camera can't get wet."

Nodding her understanding, Sevencea took the fabric with a soft grip. It was textured, and seemed to draw the water from her skin with little effort. As she handed it back, she flexed her fingers, studying her palms. "I don't think my hands have ever been dry before."

Jacob paused, then shrugged. "Honestly, I'm not sure why that surprised me." He shook his head and extended the camera. "Hold it carefully. I'm going to put the strap around your neck, just in case." He grimaced, his grip tightening on the camera for a split second. "Please don't drop it."

Sevencea met his eyes and nodded. He didn't let go until she had a solid grip on the camera. Jacob's hands went to the strap, lifting it and placing it around her neck. His fingertips brushed her hair, sending a shudder through her body. Her hair was damp, starting to dry in the sun, and everything about the brief touch was *new*.

Recovering with a deep breath, Sevencea raised the camera with care. She rotated it slowly, evaluating it from different angles. "How does it work?"

Jacob shifted so he was beside her. "This switch turns it on." He pointed out each essential function as he spoke.

Sevencea asked clarifying questions when she needed to, but her shoulders relaxed as it became clear she understood the majority of what he was telling her. She held the camera up, keeping her grip gentle. "What do I take a photograph of?"

A broad smile took over Jacob's face. "Sorry, can't help you there." He shrugged. "It's completely up to you. You're the only one who can decide what you think is worth capturing. Everyone has their own thoughts on what should be photographed. It's totally subjective, like most art."

"You're not helpful," Sevencea chided, setting her lips in a petulant twist.

Jacob's smile morphed into something softer. "Doesn't mean it isn't true." His posture relaxed, and he floated back a little. "Go on, just try it out. It's your first time. You don't have to be a master of technique on your first try."

Sevencea narrowed her eyes, turning in place as she scoped out the landscape. The ocean, the black sand, the rock formations, and the sun itself all sparkled under her examination, but she didn't raise the camera. After another moment of quiet consideration, Sevencea brought the camera to her eye. She aimed at the water breaking softly on the shore, just over Jacob's shoulder. It took a little finagling to get the camera to do what she wanted, but she was confident when she pressed the button. What had he called that part? Something to do with the shutter.

When she looked back to Jacob, there was a spark behind his eyes. Some portion of him clearly felt joy in teaching. Sevencea met his gaze with a smile. She didn't share his passion there, but the camera she understood. It was intoxicating to preserve the world's wonder.

"Can I see?" Jacob's posture was upright once more. He looked like he was having to hold himself back from just taking the camera to see her handiwork.

Sevencea laughed. "It's your camera," she reminded him. She held it out for Jacob to take. He accepted it with care, taking back the strap and wrapping it around his hand. His own grip on the device was much more certain. It was like an extension of him, which made it all the more thrilling that he'd let her handle it.

Jacob slid his thumb over the switch he'd told her accessed photos already taken. His mouth dropped open, and Sevencea fought back a laugh. He was seeing his own face, in focus, just to the side of the blurred beach behind him. Until she'd actually altered the camera's focus, she hadn't known it would work. With practice, it was something she could see herself getting really creative with. For now, shocking Jacob into awed silence was well worth it.

Jacob continued to stare at the camera screen, making little noises under his breath, but not actually saying anything. Sevencea huffed and demanded, "Well?" There was only so much one could glean from a facial expression!

Jacob's eyes snapped back up to meet hers, and an easy smile slid into place. "Whatever magic I've got, looks like you have it too." He passed the camera back to her. "I'm impressed. And flattered, honestly."

Sevencea's cheeks warmed. Part of her wanted to tell him what her actual magic was, but she also didn't want to overwhelm him. She played off her blush with a soft giggle and tightened her grip on the camera. There were plenty of things that could go wrong, but her dropping his camera into the ocean wouldn't be one of them. "I think you should credit my results to another magic I've decided you have." Jacob's brow furrowed, and he raised an eyebrow. "Teaching," she clarified. "It's a rare gift to be able to instruct someone in a skill you effortlessly possess."

Jacob blushed. "I don't know about effortlessly," he muttered, but he was still smiling. "Thank you, really. Most of the best influences in my life have been teachers, so that's a real compliment. I have to say though, teaching someone who has natural talent is just as magical, in its own way." He gnawed at his lip, then released it and scratched at his neck.

Sevencea beamed at him. "I think that proves we make a wonderful team." Her own excitement reflected back to her from Jacob's eyes, plus a genuine twinkle that made her heart stutter.

Chapter Five

※

Day 3

Jacob's cell phone buzzed—his first hint that something was wrong. Nobody called him at that number. He opened his eyes, bleary with sleep. The old-school alarm clock on his nightstand confirmed his fears. There was no good reason for his phone to ring at four in the morning.

Grasping blindly in the dark for his phone, Jacob grabbed it and flipped it over. His blood ran cold. "Mana'o" glowed on the screen.

No good phone calls came before the sun was up. And certainly not from his father's treatment center.

Jacob accepted the call and brought the phone to his ear, then reached with his other hand for the bed frame. He tightened his grip, using the solidity of the furniture to keep him grounded. "Hello?"

"Jacob, it's Dr. Wilcox."

He tried to open his lips to respond, but his face was a wall of tension, immovable and trembling all at once.

"Jacob, take a deep breath for me. Please." Dr. Wilcox had known both Pearson men pretty much since they arrived in Hawaii, and was one of the few people who understood exactly what kinds of things would be flooding Jacob's mind at receiving a call this time of day.

Jacob grabbed hold of the command and used it as a weapon against the fear gripping him. "What's going on?" he managed. "Is Dad okay?"

Dr. Wilcox hesitated. "He's having a pretty bad episode, Jacob, I won't lie. But he should be okay."

Jacob closed his eyes, then reopened them right away. "What can I do?"

"Normally we wouldn't bother you, since you're not exactly next door—"

"I don't care," Jacob interrupted. "If you need me, I'm there. You know that. I can speed if I have to."

Dr. Wilcox muttered something under his breath Jacob couldn't make out. "Well, don't get arrested. I'll explain more when you get here. Remember, Jacob, he's going to be fine. This is just kind of a rough one, and I'd rather have you here."

"Okay. Okay. I'm coming. See you soon." Jacob hung up before Dr. Wilcox could try and reassure him again. Focusing on his breathing, Jacob shifted so his legs hung over the bed. Having his feet touch the floor helped. It was too early to be awake, but he wasn't dreaming. He'd received a real phone call about a real problem. His father needed him.

Jacob got to his feet and went through the motions of getting dressed and brushing his teeth as quickly as he dared. He didn't bother turning on any lights, using his cell phone to make sure he didn't trip on anything. He'd have to trust that he'd put his pants on the right way. He ran his fingers through his hair instead of brushing it. It would have to be good enough.

The moments between finding his keys and finding himself driving toward Mana'o were a blur. Jacob rubbed his eyes, doing his best to focus on the road. He wouldn't be any help to anyone if he drove off the side of the highway. Even as he had the thought, his foot sank down on the gas.

"He's going to be fine," Jacob repeated, trying to fight back the chill in his blood and bones. He let up on the gas just enough to ensure he wouldn't roll the car around a turn. Trying to keep his focus outward, Jacob sent up a prayer of heartfelt gratitude that his phone had woken him. If he'd slept through a moment when his father needed him, he wouldn't be able to forgive himself.

Jacob made the final turn and saw the generic architecture and white walls that made up his father's treatment facility. A single tear escaped down his cheek, encapsulating his sheer relief at having arrived. Jacob parked, wiped his face, turned off the engine, and jumped out of the car. He slammed the door behind him. Street lights lit the parking lot, though the barest hint of impending sunrise showed on the horizon.

Dr. Wilcox must have been waiting in the lobby, because he came outside as soon as Jacob parked. His sharp countenance was pinched as usual. "Come on, Jacob. I'll take you to him."

Jacob followed, thankful he didn't need to speak right away. He focused on his breathing as they walked. When they got inside he needed to direct all his attention on his father.

"As I'm sure he told you," Dr. Wilcox began, "the new medication we were trying significantly improved your father's memory retention this week. He was recalling new information fine, and had full access to his long and short-term memory. He was still having mild hallucinations, but you know we've had trouble treating that symptom. Without a true diagnosis, it's hard to treat him accurately, which is frustrating for us all."

"Right," Jacob murmured, nodding. He grasped each piece of information, absorbing it and using it to focus his energy and shove his panic away.

"Anyway, Gerald had an episode in the middle of the night that woke him up. An orderly found him and couldn't calm him, which is why they called me. When I got here, he just seemed to be seeing something. We're not sure what, but he was talking to whatever it was. It was fairly mild, so we thought it would pass. But he became more and more upset. Eventually he was yelling, and he still hasn't calmed down." Dr. Wilcox talked with his hands as they walked. The part of his hair that was slicked back with gel bounced slightly upward from the nape of his neck.

"Why call me?" Now that he knew the problem, Jacob felt resolve replacing his panic. The chill started to leave him. The tension didn't, but he ignored it.

Dr. Wilcox hesitated. "A few reasons. One being, even with the length of your drive, I suspected he wouldn't pull out of the episode before you could get here to help. Of course, as family, you have a bigger chance of helping him through it. But it's also because he keeps yelling at someone he's calling Merry."

Jacob stopped dead in the hallway. "He's seeing Mom?!"

Dr. Wilcox's lips twisted, and he nodded. "Unfortunately. As far as we know, that's never happened before. I wasn't positive he was talking to his wife, but—"

Jacob interrupted him again. "That's because he doesn't call her Merry anymore. Not since she decided to leave him here."

Dr. Wilcox inclined his head and began walking again, motioning Jacob to follow him. "Well, since you're family, you seem best equipped to deal with what appears to be a very family-oriented situation. I'm glad I could reach you."

"Me too."

Yelling drifted down the hall. Jacob quickened his pace. He pulled ahead of Dr. Wilcox and turned into the correct hallway. Reaching the door, he pushed it open, bracing himself.

Gerald faced the opposite wall, his trembling fists at his sides. "What did I do, Merry? What was it about me that made abandoning me easier?" The words were loud and aggressive, but sounded like sobs.

Jacob felt a lump in his throat, formed of emotions he usually ignored. He moved further into the room, closing the distance, and caught a glimpse of Gerald's face. His father was dry-eyed, but clearly choked up.

"Dad?"

Gerald whirled, his eyes darting between Jacob and the wall. "Jake! Tell your mother, would you? Tell her that I don't need to go to some, some, some kind of crazy house!" He gritted his teeth and glared at the wall. His head cocked slightly, like he was listening to his hallucination. He scoffed and turned back to Jacob, his expression expectant.

This was the reason Jacob hadn't spoken to his mother since he'd moved to Hawaii. His parents might still be married, but clearly his mother didn't care about either of them. His heart seized at memories of similar words coming from his own mouth.

"Jake?" Gerald's expression faltered. For the first time his eyes trembled, as though preparing for moisture.

"Dad, you did not deserve this," Jacob said firmly, grabbing his father's hands. "Mom was wrong, okay? We should have stayed together. She doesn't need to run the company all by herself. You're right. You don't need to be anywhere but with family. I'm so sorry she did this."

Gerald scoffed, glaring back at the wall. "You hear that, dear? My Merry, who I swore to love in sickness and in health. Well? I kept up my end, didn't I? I still love you. Why don't you love me?"

His father may not have been crying, but Jacob was. Small tears raced their way down his cheeks, no matter how desperately he blinked them away.

"She does love you, Dad," he choked out. "This was how she thought she could love you best, by sending you to a place that could help." He didn't believe the words, but that didn't matter. His father believed them when he was his normal self, when his mind wasn't fighting him. Jacob may not have forgiven his mother, but Gerald had never once hinted that he resented her.

Gerald drifted away from Jacob toward an armchair and slowly fell back into it. He glanced again at the wall. "Well, Merry? Is that true? Is this what's best for me? For us?" He looked back at Jacob, his eyes narrowing slightly. "Jake. Jake. Son. Jake. You're here?"

"Yeah, Dad, I'm here. How are you feeling?" Jacob gave his father a once-over, holding his breath. He squeezed his eyes shut for a brief moment, ensuring no more tears were coming. His heart ached, a consequence of thinking about his mother at all, but as always his father made for a good distraction.

Gerald glanced back at the wall with a furrowed brow, then looked to Jacob and tilted his head. "Jake? Did I know you were coming?"

"I was in the area." Jacob kept his tone level with a great deal of effort. "Are you okay?"

Understanding flooded Gerald's expression. "I was seeing

something."

Dr. Wilcox entered the room, the motion tentative. "Yes. You had a long, extended episode. You were seeing your wife."

Gerald paled and shifted in his chair, like he could escape the conversation if he just fidgeted enough. "I was seeing Meredith?"

"Yeah." Jacob folded his arms, the tension easing now that he could see his father was really here. The adrenaline that had filled him moments ago was fading, and he felt like his strings had been cut.

"Huh." Gerald mimicked his son, folding his arms and slouching a little in the chair. "Never done that before."

"Indeed." Dr. Wilcox glanced between father and son, his gaze pausing on Jacob. He inclined his head toward the hall. "Jacob, do you mind?"

Jacob blinked at the doctor for a second before understanding. Perhaps he was more tired than he'd realized. Turning to his father, he rested his hand on Gerald's knee. "I'm going to let them take care of you now, okay?"

"Jake, I'm sorry. I don't remember—I'm guessing it wasn't pretty." Gerald winced, flicked his eyes up to meet Jacob's, and cast them down again.

Jacob leaned forward to hug his father, ignoring Gerald's hesitation before reciprocating. "I don't care, Dad. That's why I'm here. I'll always come when you need me. I'll try to visit soon, when you're feeling better, okay?"

Gerald smiled. "Yes, please. Thank you, Jake. For everything."

More than ever, Jacob felt like he was being thanked for not being his mother and not following her example. He forced the resentment out of his mind, offered his father a smile, and stepped toward the door. "Try to get some rest, okay? Behave for Dr. Wilcox."

"You know me." Gerald winked. The first real sign that he would be okay.

Jacob relaxed a little, nodded, and stepped outside the door. He followed Dr. Wilcox a few steps down the hall. Coming to a stop, he scratched at the stubble he hadn't had a chance to shave and yawned. "What's up?" Jacob asked. "What do you need?"

Dr. Wilcox offered him a sympathetic smile. "It's not what I need, Jacob. You look dead on your feet, and I'm uncomfortable letting you drive back home right now. Please, take one of the spare rooms and get a few hours' sleep, all right?"

"Oh." That wasn't what he'd expected to hear. Jacob briefly debated protesting, but one long, slow blink was almost enough to allow his knees to buckle. "You might be right."

"You're emotionally exhausted on top of regular exhaustion," Dr. Wilcox pointed out, his tone wry. "I'll accept the blame for calling you in, although I'm grateful it worked. Please, get some rest. A few hours should help, I'm sure."

Jacob nodded, recognizing the weariness in his bones. It was not worth arguing. Plus, his insurance would thank him for sparing it the certain car accident if he tried to drive.

Jacob sighed heavily. "Which room is free?"

Chapter Six

The beach was empty when Sevencea arrived. That was new. Two days in a row, Jacob had beaten her to the shore. If nothing else, the sunrise was stunning. The lack of a young man holding his camera to capture it seemed a shame.

Pulling herself onto her rock, Sevencea studied the hill behind the beach. The structure on top was Jacob's home, but with how reflective it was, it was difficult to tell if anyone was inside.

"Hello!" Sevencea called out. She scanned the beach, as if Jacob might be hiding somewhere, waiting to surprise her. Where was he?

They'd made no official plans to meet. She shouldn't be frustrated by his absence. No promises had been broken. Still, hadn't it been clear to him too? He was always on the beach, and she'd all but told him she'd meet him here each morning.

"I'm overreacting," she decided. Slumping down on the rock, Sevencea let her hair hang into the water and closed her eyes, content to wait. Jacob wasn't absent, he was just late. She was sure of it.

Once the sun reached its midday height, Sevencea was forced to admit that Jacob wasn't coming. She slid off the rock and into the water, then swam away from the beach. A surge of irritation powered her movements. What could have been more important than meeting her? Was he hurt? Was his father hurt? His mother? A friend? Had he gotten sick in the night and been unable to get out of bed?

Usually, time on that beach passed in seconds. Today, Sevencea had memorized each grain of sand as the agonizing moments dragged on. If something really was wrong, there was no way for her to know it. Her heart picked up its pace at the mere thought that Jacob might be harmed, and she felt a little dizzy.

Sevencea froze, her tail seizing in mid-motion. Her momentum carried her forward, but she wasn't paying attention. This distractedness, this ache, this concern … what was it? Her face felt warm. She lifted her hands to her cheeks to make sure she wasn't coming down with an ailment. She felt normal. Except… maybe nothing was normal. It had only been two days! How could such a short time have such a great impact?

Pushing forward with her tail again, Sevencea began muttering to herself under her breath. It was too early to speculate about her feelings, much less the condition of her heart. Surely it was too early to wonder about Jacob, especially if he couldn't be bothered to come to the beach today. Unless he really was hurt.

"Stop it!" Sevencea ordered, flicking herself in the temple. "None of this is helpful."

Until tomorrow, she couldn't know what was going on with Jacob. Assuming he came tomorrow.

For tonight, she could at least make sense of some of this. She needed to speak with her father.

It was evening before Sevencea worked up the nerve to ask her father. He was floating in the mouth of the cave they shared, watching their clan wind down for the day. She swam up behind him and asked, "How do you know when you're in love?"

Brineus whirled to face her, his eyebrows shooting up. "I'm sorry?"

Sevencea ducked her head and retreated, picking a comb up from her things and running it through her hair. She scowled and picked at a tangle. "You heard me, Father."

"I did, I'm just confused." He cleared his throat, drifting closer to her and crossing his arms. "Is this about the human?"

The dark ocean water would make it hard for her father to see her blush, but Sevencea could feel the heat in her cheeks. "I didn't say I was in love. I just asked how I can know, when it happens."

"Uh-huh." Brineus uncrossed his arms and reached up to stroke his braided beard. "Love is a complicated thing, my girl. I'm not sure words do it justice."

Sevencea finished combing her hair and swept its length back over her shoulder. "Well, given it's your job to dispense justice around here, I hope you're up to the task."

Her father snorted. "Corralling our clan is not the same as explaining the thing that brings us all together, but I'll do my best." He flicked his tail, driving himself toward a rocky surface. He rested against the water-worn stone. "Let me think on it a moment."

Sevencea hummed in response and closed her eyes, letting the ocean's natural current rock her gently. Their clan lived in a network of cave-like rock formations. Fish often came in and out of the caves at will, and the ones that glowed naturally helped keep the caves from getting too dark. The soft light wasn't much, but there was something comforting about the light from a living creature. Most of the caves also had a few spots where luminescent plants grew, waving gently in the water. Merfolk had good vision no matter how much sunlight was available, but Sevencea liked the dark. Home, in the dark and the quiet, with only a soft glow for light, felt peaceful. She opened her eyes again and could just make out her father, watching her.

"I'd like to preface this by pointing out, once more, that you met this human *this week*." Brineus's tone wasn't harsh, but it was firm.

Sevencea smiled. "I know, Father. Trust me. I may be your youngest, but—"

"Exactly." Brineus nodded once, wagging his finger at her. "Eighteen migrations is enough to be considered mature by the clan, but you will always be my youngest child. I don't want to see you hurt, especially not if it can be prevented. That's my responsibility, no matter how old you are."

"What if I promise to consult you before making any major life decisions?" Sevencea ducked her head a little to hide her grin. She didn't begrudge her father his protective streak. It was his nature, and she loved him for it. Besides, he wasn't one to override her decisions, so long as she made them wisely.

Brineus sighed, a long and drawn out noise. "My girl, I don't want you to feel as though you need my permission to grow up. I just want to make sure you're safe while you go about it."

Sevencea pushed herself off of the rock she'd been resting on and swam to her father, pulling him into a half-hug. "That's not what I'm saying. I value your guidance, Father. I always will. I'm going to grow up, and I'll probably fall in love. If not this time, then another. I'm not going to do anything to significantly alter my life without seeking the advice of the man I trust most."

It was true. With her mother gone and her siblings so much older, there was no one in the world she trusted more.

"All right." Brineus returned the hug, squeezing her tightly before letting go. "So. Love, then."

"Love," Sevencea agreed. She settled herself across from her father so she could see the glow dancing across his face as the water moved.

"There are a few things that really define love, for me. You understand, it looks and feels a little different to everyone, but its core is the same. Oh, of course, not all love is the same. The love I feel for you, for example, is different than what I felt for your mother, or what I feel for our clan. But it's all unconditional." Brineus paused, his fingers going to his beard. He stared into space.

Sevencea watched him, at ease with the quiet. She knew this expression. This was how her father looked when he thought about her mother—a beautiful, smart, and wonderful mermaid who had been taken far too soon. His eyes didn't glisten and his face didn't crumple. Instead, he always smiled, a soft, gentle thing. His brow would smooth, and his frame would relax, like he was hearing a beloved melody.

"This is what I know of love," Sevencea said, keeping her tone soft. There was something sacred about the ocean at night, something quiet she wouldn't disturb.

Brineus's eyes drifted to hers, and his eyebrows drew together. "What's that, my minnow?"

Sevencea gestured to his face. "The way you are about Mother. I know what it looks like, when someone truly loves. I've seen it firsthand. I just don't know how to tell it for myself."

"I'm pleased you're able to see your parents as an example of real love, my dear." Brineus didn't quite sound choked up, but it was close. "There are emotions, of course, that are signs of love, but love has more to do with what you're willing to do."

"What I'm willing to do?" Sevencea repeated. She mentally swam through the ramifications of that.

Her father leaned forward. "Let me put it this way. When I met your mother, right away my heart sped up. She was beautiful, and making eye contact with me! It was more than I could have hoped for, young and awkward as I was."

Sevencea arched an eyebrow and deliberately drew her eyes across her father's broad physique. He was a commanding presence. There was no point in her life where she would have referred to him as awkward.

Laughing, Brineus shook his head. "Trust me, my minnow, I have grown in many ways since my youth. Regardless, as I began to court your mother, I noticed changes. The speed of my heart slowed, not because she was less beautiful, but because it was growing in sync with hers. Being apart caused a stumble in my heart, an inconsistency in rhythm, because a piece was gone. We were becoming two parts of a whole, and I could feel that physically as well as emotionally. Then I met her family for the first time."

Sevencea leaned in, eyes wide. She'd never known her grandparents. Merfolk often lived for generations, but they were susceptible to illnesses, injuries, and other normal means by which one might die young.

"Your grandfather pulled me aside with such a stern expression that I was certain I would be forbidden to court your mother any longer." Brineus chuckled. "It wasn't that. He asked me, in his grave, gravely voice, what I would be willing to do for your mother. I was so shocked he wasn't demanding I leave that I blurted out, 'Anything!' That was the first time I saw him smile. He told me that any other answer would not have been enough. Until that moment, I hadn't realized it, but I would have laid down my life to protect your mother."

Sevencea hummed under her breath, nodding. "Love is a willingness to sacrifice."

Brineus waved his hand back and forth. "Almost. It can't just be willingness. There's no hesitation, just certainty. There would be no other option. For many, it never comes to that. Sacrifice is a smaller, more intimate thing between the two of you. But that knowledge that you would give all of yourself, no hesitation, for the other person, that's how I define love. It's a decision, not a feeling."

"Thank you, Father." Sevencea swam back to his side and pressed a soft kiss to his cheek.

He clasped one of her small hands in his own. "Anytime, my minnow."

Sevencea left him and drifted toward the place where she typically took her rest. Her mind raced. It was true, she'd not had nearly enough time to define what she felt for Jacob. Love was a multi-faceted thing that took effort. It didn't spring up unannounced after a few conversations. Especially given they'd skipped today. The emotions which could build that foundation though—there could be something there. Sevencea considered it all, her thoughts circling around the way her heart had stuttered earlier. No, this feeling wasn't everything, not yet, but it was the start of something.

Assuming Jacob was on the beach in the morning.

Chapter Seven

Jacob stood in the parking lot of an electronics superstore, only marginally more alert than he had that morning. He'd woken in the middle of the afternoon to discover the staff at Mana'o had let him sleep most of the day. He must have needed it, but the extra rest left him feeling fuzzy and off-kilter.

Now he stood beside his car, unable to bring himself to walk toward the building. What was he doing here? He'd had an idea when he woke up. Realizing the time had brought Sevencea bursting back to the front of his mind. He still needed to keep the idea of her at a distance, but he'd possibly left a beautiful woman—or, mermaid—alone all day with no explanation.

The sweet, musty smell of the pavement bit at his nostrils. He glanced down. The cracked asphalt gleamed black and wet. Had it rained while he'd been asleep? Jacob closed his eyes, pinched the bridge of his nose, and took a deep breath. The rich, fresh scent of a new rainfall was oddly relaxing. He opened his eyes again, feeling more centered. He glanced up, and his gaze settled on the store.

Right. He had a plan.

His father's voice echoed in his head, pulling his mind away from the task at hand. Jacob hadn't had time to process the incident since it happened. Now, he felt his father's pain as deeply as he had in the moment. Nothing was so destructive to the heart as the pain of someone you love.

Jacob sighed and dragged his hand down his face. How often were his father's episodes that bad? This was the first time Dr. Wilcox had summoned him before the sun was up, so surely the episodes weren't frequent. Despite his proximity, Jacob hadn't witnessed many true episodes of his father's illness. His parents had both signed documents that allowed him to make medical decisions for his father, especially given how often his mother was away. He should be grateful for that. He was, but his gratitude was overshadowed by that unnamed force that clenched his teeth and twisted his gut.

His mother should be here. If she was, maybe his father's episodes would lessen. Maybe things would be different somehow.

Choices had already been made, and lines had already been drawn. Jacob squeezed his eyes shut again, blocking out everything that threatened to overwhelm him.

His father's illness.

His mother's choices.

His words, hurled in anger.

Jacob exhaled slowly, forcing each aspect of his pain to the back of his mind. It all would be dealt with, but not today. Not in this moment. All he could do right now was move forward.

Which meant walking into the store.

Jacob scanned the parking lot for something else, anything else, to focus on. His eyes fell on a family walking past. The mother, father, and two boys all wore matching Hawaiian shirts. Goggles rested on their foreheads. They laughed loudly, the sound a solid anchor to the present. Jacob was almost grateful enough for that to overlook the garish evidence of tourism they sported. He still rolled his eyes, but even that felt normal. Solid. He relaxed a little, and began actually moving toward the store.

He glanced at himself as he moved, noticing for the first time what clothing had made its way onto his body in his dash to leave the house. He'd grabbed a t-shirt for a local marathon, which was a relief. He'd rather people assume he was local, even if he'd only been here for a year.

The closer Jacob got to the store, the more he relaxed. All of his worries couldn't be dealt with in that moment, but it seemed he'd successfully made his brain recognize that. He wasn't always so lucky. It was time to focus on the plan that had brought him here.

If, as he hoped, Sevencea was very real, then he didn't want her to think he'd left her alone willingly. They may not have had an official date, but their beach mornings had at least become a standing date, right? Hopefully she thought of them that way too. Family came first—a sentiment he suspected she'd agree with—but he could still apologize. And that would go over better with a gift.

Tuning out the ambient noise of straggling shoppers, Jacob moved on autopilot toward the camera aisle.

"Can I help you?" The practiced sales voice belonged to a teenager with a perpetual smile and an obnoxious neon uniform shirt.

Jacob twitched, biting back a surprised expletive. "Oh! Hi, uh, sure. I'm looking for underwater cameras. Something that can last for really long periods underwater. Like seriously prolonged exposure." He could probably find one himself, but the sooner he found what he wanted, the sooner he could go home and shut down for the night.

"Ah, so not just waterproof then?" The kid studied the aisle with a look of practiced consideration.

Wait, why was he thinking of someone no younger than sixteen as a kid? Was he an old man at nineteen? So much for his roarin' twenties.

Jacob gave a slow blink and forced a polite smile. "Right, I'm not looking to be protected if it gets wet. I need it to be capable of being underwater for hours at a time."

"All right, well, let's take a look at these models here." The kid guided Jacob further down the aisle. He swept his arm toward a range of models designed for scuba diving and similar activities. "Looking for something reasonably priced for your vacation, huh, sir?"

Jacob chomped down on the inside of his lip to avoid scowling. "I live here. I'm looking for something long-term and high-quality."

Why was it so hard to be nice to people when he was tired and upset? This was why he lived in the middle of nowhere. The ocean didn't require him to have a good attitude and a positive outlook on life.

The kid appeared off-kilter for a second, but he bounced back right away. "Oh, yeah, of course! Here, take a look. This guy is waterproof up to like fifty feet. There's a bunch of other stats here." He thrust the box into Jacob's hands, pointing out the statistics on the side.

Jacob could evaluate a camera with a glance. There was nothing like using a camera with your own hands to teach you about the device, but he knew enough about photography to make pretty accurate snap judgments. "Only fifty feet?" he prompted, raising an eyebrow. He'd been hoping for something with a little more depth flexibility.

"Well, yeah, but you can get a housing for it," the kid suggested, holding up a second box.

"Which would increase the depth to...?" Jacob's eyes were starting to droop with exhaustion.

"Oh, about two hundred fifty additional feet." The kid rushed the words out, an apology for not mentioning that in the first place.

Jacob nodded and accepted the second box. "All right, that should be fine. Thank you for your help, uh..." He squinted at the kid's chest for the first time, identifying the name tag. "Brad."

"My pleasure!" To Brad's credit, his chirpy reply didn't carry a hint of insincerity.

Jacob walked toward the check out, feeling chagrined. He was a grumpy old man. His dad was the most young-at-heart person he'd ever known, so Jacob couldn't blame it on genetics. When Gerald felt well, he was just as positive and welcoming as he'd been for Jacob's entire childhood. Somehow that must have skipped Jacob. Or maybe he could blame it on the scene he'd witnessed at Mana'o earlier.

Jacob focused on being polite to the cashier, and made it back to his car without actually noticing he'd been walking. Man, he needed to go to bed. He still had another hour and a half on the road before he could sleep. The whole point of this excursion was to find a gift for Sevencea. At least he'd been successful in that.

Now he just had to hope Sevencea would still come to the beach after he'd abandoned her with no explanation today. Assuming she was real. If she was real, then he couldn't wait to see the look on her face when he gave her a camera of her own. If not, well, he was a photographer. It was hardly a wasted purchase.

Chapter Eight

❀

Day 4

Sevencea rose early. Her father had already left. She was used to him being gone when she awoke. Their clan didn't cause much trouble, but her father believed his vigilance would keep it that way. Hardly anyone else bothered to rise as early; the water was still as Sevencea left their dwelling. A few of the younger merfolk were already mingling around the communal table as she made her way to it. Sevencea selected a few plants she could easily eat on the go, then waved to the young ones as she swam away. The soft echo of their conversation, peppered with giggles, brought a smile to her face. It wouldn't take her long to get to Jacob's beach, but his absence yesterday still caused her heart to twist. She flicked her tail to drive herself forward, toward the island.

"Sister, wait for me!"

Sevencea jolted to a stop and twisted around, her eyebrows raised. Surely she'd heard wrong. Her siblings rarely sought her out. But no, her ears had not deceived her. One of her many brothers propelled his way toward her, his reddish tail swirling the water.

"Athys?" she questioned, tilting her head. "What is it? Is something wrong?"

The older merman slowed and drifted close to her. An easy smile crossed his face. He winked at her. "What, something has to be wrong for me to want to see my littlest sister?"

Sevencea rolled her eyes and folded her arms across her chest. "It's not like there's much precedent for anything else."

Athys pretended to scoff. "You wound me."

She narrowed her eyes at him. "I don't mean to be rude, but it's true. Don't you have work to do? I'm sure our clan is full of customers for your potions and whatnot." She'd never had need of her brother's magic before, but plenty of other people did. As long as Athys had a specific goal in mind, he could combine ingredients to achieve all manner of results. She'd seen his skills improve singing voices, heal long-set injuries, grow muscles, and more than one member of her clan had purchased a potion from Athys to change the colors of their tails.

Her brother grinned. "I am quite successful these days, but I didn't find you to talk about myself."

Sevencea arched an eyebrow and moved her tail in a slow drag, using the motion to back away from her brother. "Then do you need something? I have somewhere to be."

He pointed at her and nodded. The water ruffled his auburn hair. "That's what I came to talk to you about. I ran into Father this morning, as he was beginning his route. He mentioned you're seeing a human."

Sevencea scowled, although it wasn't as though the information had been secret. "I'm not *seeing* a human," she huffed, "I've just been ... well, seeing one."

Her brother snorted. "Well, now that that's cleared up..."

"You know what I mean, Athys!" Sevencea paused and inhaled deeply. She didn't like seeming irrational. The best way to prevent that was to keep her brother from riling her up in the first place. She closed her eyes for a brief moment, then reopened them and leveled a glare at her brother. "I'm not courting a human, which I'm sure is what you were trying to infer. We've only just met. We've been visiting."

Athys shot her a wry smile. "I know how it must be, little sister. Being the only child left, with the rest of us grown. None of us intended to let you be an only child, it just sort of happened. I guess I want to make sure you don't do anything reckless because you're... I don't know, lonely." He ran his teeth over his lip, then licked his lips and relaxed. "We do care, you know. About you."

Something bitter was tightening her eyes. Sevencea blinked a few times before replying. "I know you do, Athys. All of you. You all have families, responsibilities. I don't resent you, I promise." That much, at least, was true. It wasn't her siblings' faults that she'd been born well after they'd reached maturity and moved on. She knew they cared, in their own ways. Those relationships may have been built out of infrequent talks and distant smiles, but they were still relationships. They still mattered.

His lips twitched. "That's good. I was worried you were planning something nefarious, what with your running off alone all the time."

Sevencea rolled her eyes again. "If I was mad at you, Athys, I'd make sure you saw me coming." She allowed a grin to punctuate the statement, just in case he actually got worried.

Athys chuckled. "I appreciate the warning. So, you're seeing a human."

Sevencea threw her head back with a groan. Her hair floated

around her, catching the sunlight from above. If she didn't hurry, she'd be late to meet Jacob. If he was there.

"I'm not doing anything reckless, Athys, I promise. We're just getting to know each other. I already promised Father I wouldn't make any major life decisions without checking with him first."

"Well, if you need anything, I want you to know you can come to me, okay? I mean it, Sevencea. I'm your brother. One of many, but still. I reserve the right to be a little overprotective. If it makes you feel better, I'd be the same way if you were hanging around a merman I didn't know." Athys grinned and glanced around like he expected to be swarmed by imaginary suitors.

Sevencea laughed, relaxing a little. "I need to go, really, but thank you. If I need anything, I'll be sure to reach out."

Athys spread his arms. "I'm here for anything, Sevencea. Romantic advice, gift ideas, body disposal, whatever."

She glared at him again, but without venom. "I'm leaving, Athys."

Laughing, he waved her off. "Go on, have fun. I just would have felt guilty if this human captured you with a net and I hadn't given you an overprotective brother speech."

Sevencea didn't dignify that with a response. She turned and swam off, hiding the smile on her face.

Chapter Nine

Before today, Jacob had never realized how difficult it was to wrap a gift for someone who lived in the ocean. Wrapping paper wasn't waterproof. To be fair, the boxes holding the presents weren't either. Jacob finally opened both boxes and put all the pieces of the underwater camera together. Once assembled, he wrapped it with a shammy towel and used a twist tie around the ends. It wasn't elegant, but Sevencea wasn't elitist or—more notably—human, so what did it matter?

Jacob set up on the beach the same way he always did and waited at the edge of the lapping waves. His bare feet squished the sand between his toes, released it, and then squished it again. Would she come? Would she be upset about yesterday? So many unknowns, but instead of the familiar tension in his chest, his heart raced in a way that made him feel alive. He raised his camera, capturing a few images of the horizon. Glancing down at the display with a smile, he flipped through the photos, deleting one with a little too much glare from the sun. That was one of the advantages of living where he did—there was always a market for pretty ocean photos.

Finally, Sevencea's head popped up from beneath the waves.

Water cascaded down her pearlescent hair as she moved toward her usual rock.

"You're here!" Her face lit up with a combination of relief and genuine happiness probably similar to Jacob's own expression.

Jacob released his camera, letting it hang from his neck by the strap. He bent down to retrieve Sevencea's poorly-wrapped gift, then immediately moved toward the water. Hesitation brought him to a halt at the water's edge. He fumbled for the right words to say. He'd spent so much time on the gift, he hadn't worked out the apology.

"I'm sorry," he finally said. He ducked his head briefly, then forced himself to meet her eyes. "I didn't mean to not show up yesterday. I had to go into town really early in the morning—my dad wasn't doing well." He cut himself off before he could ramble. She didn't need the gory details.

Sevencea's expression softened, and she almost looked relieved. "I'm glad you're all right. I was worried. Is your father well now?"

Jacob hesitated. "He's ... the same as always, I guess you could say."

"Well, I'm sorry for that, but at least whatever ill required your attention yesterday hasn't prevailed?" She raised an eyebrow, her expression hopeful.

Jacob quirked a wry smile and nodded. "Last I heard, he's no worse. It was a temporary issue. Still, I felt bad leaving you, even though it was an emergency."

"I waited," Sevencea admitted. "Until about midday, just in case. That's why I was worried for you. If something had happened to you, would anyone know? You live alone, right?"

Jacob scratched the back of his neck and shifted a little, squishing the sand between his toes. "Yeah. But nothing happened to me. I'm fine, Sevencea. Really." He paused, then added, "You really waited? For me?"

"Of course." Sevencea said pointedly, like he shouldn't have had to ask. "Wouldn't you wait? For me?"

Jacob smiled, a warmth filling him and complementing the racing of his heart. "Yes. I would." In that moment, he'd never been so sure something was true.

Sevencea's gaze drifted to Jacob's hand and the package he held. Her eyes widened. "What's that?" She pushed herself up with her forearms to get a better look.

"I got you a present. It's sort of part of my apology for being gone yesterday." Jacob waded the rest of the way out to her and presented the shammy-wrapped bundle with only a slight shiver of trepidation. "The present is inside the yellow thing. The wrapping is just a towel … thing." Jacob cut himself off, cringing.

Sevencea smiled. She took the gift and touched his shoulder. "You didn't need to get me anything, but I'm grateful for your thoughtfulness, Jacob."

Jacob returned her smile easily, his cheeks warming. He made an awkward gesture to redirect her attention to the present. "Go on, open it."

Sevencea removed the bright towel with care and set it on the rock along with the twist tie. She turned the camera in her hands, evaluating it with a focused gaze and pursed lips. It didn't much resemble Jacob's Canon to begin with, and the housing made it look even less like a normal camera.

"Is it a camera?" Sevencea lifted her head and caught Jacob's eye. "Some of the buttons seem familiar, but it looks different."

Jacob couldn't help his proud grin. He nodded eagerly, shifting closer to her rock. "That's because it's not a normal camera." He waggled his eyebrows at her, and was rewarded with a soft giggle from the mermaid. "It can go underwater. It's not one of the industrial ones, mostly because I can't get something like that locally. But this'll work up to about three hundred feet below the surface. I got it so you can practice using my, uh, magic," Jacob fumbled the word, flushing a little, "in your own world. It's often easiest to photograph what you already know well."

The mermaid lifted the camera to her face. She glanced through the viewfinder and practiced holding the camera the way Jacob had shown her. "This is incredible, Jacob!" She lowered her present. Gratitude shone in her eyes. "I can't wait to show my family!"

"You're welcome. I hope you'll get a lot of use out of it." Their eyes met again, but Jacob dropped his gaze. "Do you have a large family?" he blurted.

Sevencea hesitated, considering. "Sort of." Her pink lips twisted into an uncertain expression.

"Okay." Jacob wasn't sure what else he could say. That didn't qualify as an answer, did it?

"Sorry, I don't mean to sound mysterious." Sevencea's hands went to the pearls around her neck. She twisted them around her fingers as she gnawed gently at her lower lip. "I have my father. I've told you about him already."

Jacob nodded. "Right. He does security."

"That's right!" Sevencea beamed. "My father has twelve children, including me."

Jacob's mouth dropped open in surprise, and it took him a second to remember to shut it. "Twelve?" he finally managed, struggling to mask the shock in his voice.

Sevencea raised an eyebrow. "Are large families uncommon among humans?"

"Well, no," Jacob admitted. "I mean, between one and five is more common. But some families have way more kids. You just surprised me, I guess. I'm an only child, so eleven siblings sounds like a lot."

Sevencea inclined her head, allowing that. "Well, I said 'sort of' because all of my siblings are much older than I am; they've long since reached maturity and moved on. I barely know them." Her tone was wistful, but she didn't appear troubled.

Given the mermaid's previous revelation that she'd lost a parent, Jacob hesitated for a moment before asking, "What about your mother? How long has it been since…?"

"Seven years or so." A small, sad smile played across Sevencea's face. "She was ill, so we were prepared in some ways. We weren't prepared in others. But how could we be?" She glanced down for a moment, then met Jacob's eyes. "I would love to still have my mother, but I'm forever grateful that I had a chance to say goodbye."

A lump lodged in Jacob's throat. Sevencea's words cut to the heart of one of his biggest fears. "Ever since Dad got sick, I've worried that one day I'll show up and he won't remember me. Or he'll be having a fit and think I'm some kind of monster. His brain's turning on him. He's always getting worse in different ways. Sometimes they find a treatment that helps for a while, but it always gets worse again. They aren't sure what he has, so treatment is a gamble every time." Jacob blinked rapidly, trying to avoid contributing to the saltwater he waded in.

Sevencea's right hand returned to Jacob's shoulder. Her left grasped the camera. "You came here to be near your father, didn't you? Even if the illness does take his mind one day, he must have known this whole time that you love him."

"You're right." Jacob stared at her, the words a surprise as they left his mouth. "He does know it, even if he won't always."

"I hope you never have to see him like that," Sevencea's voice was soft. "But if you do, I hope you'll let that knowledge give you peace." She paused, her words resting between them. Sevencea leaned forward, the pearl on her forehead rolling over the furrow between her eyebrows. "If you don't mind my curiosity, where is your mother in all of this?"

Jacob rolled his eyes. Fear's grasp on his heart released as irritation and frustration marched in. "My mom is…" he paused, unsure how much diplomacy to bother with. "My mom is insanely smart," he decided on. He took a deep breath. "She runs her own company, so she's on the road constantly. Dad was her business partner. When he got sick, Mom found a treatment facility where he could stay full time. She kept working, kept traveling, and hasn't been to see him even once." Resentment colored his last words, but he didn't care.

Sevencea's eyebrows pinched together, and she tilted her head. "She just left him?"

Jacob almost smiled at Sevencea's bewildered expression. "Mom thinks she's helping," he explained. "She's never been good at relating to people. Which means she does awful things for the right reasons. To her, the best thing for Dad is for him to have consistent treatment in one place without interruptions. She wants him to be safe and comfortable, which is good. The problem is that he's also lonely. I don't think that even registers for her."

Sevencea hummed as she looked down at the underwater camera, running her thumb across the top of the housing. "What about you? How did you end up here?"

Her focus distracted him, her wide, blue eyes an ocean of empathy. Jacob ran a hand through his hair and gathered his thoughts. "Well, growing up, I lived kind of all over the place. I traveled with my parents to wherever their work took them. When I turned fourteen, I was sent to a private academy on the mainland." Jacob hooked his thumb over his shoulder, although for all he knew he was pointing at Japan instead of the general direction of his school in Colorado. "That was another of my mom's ideas. She shows her love with money, but she's also a really good manipulator. I finished school, but I found out Dad was sick the day I graduated. He was supposed to come to the ceremony. Instead, I got Mom letting me know she'd checked him to a treatment facility in Hawaii."

"That must have been difficult." A comforting warmth shone in Sevencea's eyes, without a trace of pity. It bolstered Jacob's confidence.

"At first I was furious," Jacob admitted. "When I realized she meant to just leave him here, I was furious. And I yelled. A lot." He looked down, a deep breath escaping.

"Not my finest moment. Mom and I are very different, but she's still my mom. I know she means well. She didn't deserve that from me. Anyway, one of my loudest declarations was that I was going to move here and take care of Dad, since she refused to." Jacob winced, rubbing his temple with the back of his thumb. "Again, a horrible thing to say. She tried to talk me into 'living my life,' as she put it, but eventually gave in and bought me the house and land." Jacob gestured to the structure on the hill behind them. "She also got me a car and takes care of my bills."

"Why would she pay for all of that?" Sevencea's brow was furrowed again, jostling the dangling pearl.

Jacob smiled wryly. "It's her way of showing that she cares about me, and in a way, that she cares about Dad too. We sort of have a deal though. She thinks I'm putting my life on hold. I have to bring in some kind of income on my own to show I'm not sitting on the beach all day. I always wanted to be a professional photographer, so I keep a handful of freelance clients. Not many. I wanted my own business, but … I can't afford to be too busy, in case Dad needs me. Though if I stop working completely, Mom will take everything back and force me to return to the mainland. Or, she'll try anyway."

Sevencea's brow had yet to unfurrow. "I don't think I understand your mother."

Jacob shrugged. "I've known her for nineteen years, and I don't either." He laughed, relaxing a little. "Mom's a complicated person. If I just up and decided to leave Dad, she'd be upset with me. If I were to stay here and mooch off her forever without working, she'd be mad about that too. It's an odd agreement, but the balance works for some reason. It's probably the best our relationship's ever been. I mean, I haven't spoken to her in like a year, which is a good sign."

Sevencea's eyes went wide. "You haven't spoken to your mother in a year?"

"We've emailed," Jacob allowed. At Sevencea's blank look, he clarified, "We send each other letters using technology. We don't talk on the phone or in person though." He gnawed on the inside of his cheek. Just because he didn't pick up didn't mean his mother didn't call. Talking was harder than emailing though. If he thought about what he said before he said it, it was better for everyone. Phone or in-person conversation was a recipe for disaster.

"That's sad," Sevencea murmured.

"Probably." Jacob shrugged. He hadn't questioned his relationship with his mother in a long time.

Sevencea offered a small smile. "To be fair, I often go months without having a real conversation with my siblings. So I'm hardly one to talk."

"Maybe that's what makes love significant," Jacob offered. "Love's a choice, right? Even with family, you have to make that choice, sometimes every day. It doesn't matter if you talk to the people in your life every day, it just matters if you're still choosing to love them. I still love my mom, even when it feels like we're on different planets. Do you love your siblings?"

"Each and every one," Sevencea confirmed, her smile growing.

Jacob matched her smile. A wave of peace flowed over his heart. Explaining all of that had been more cathartic than he expected.

"Maybe," Sevencea said, the ocean sparkling in her eyes, "the choice to love is magic everyone has."

Jacob met her gaze and felt a sudden urge to exercise that magic right then. He swallowed it down. His head emphatically reminded his heart that beings potentially constructed by his imagination were off limits.

Chapter Ten

Day 5

Sevencea put on speed, racing toward the beach. After leaving Jacob the night before, she'd spent most of the evening and plenty of this morning playing with her present. Having something as magical as a camera that actually worked in her world? It was magnificent! She couldn't wait to show him what she'd captured, but she was running a little late. The problem with anything truly wonderful is that it could make you lose track of time.

As she neared the shallows, Sevencea popped her head out of the water. She spotted Jacob right away. He sat on the black sand, staring at the water by his toes, his posture tense. He seemed to be muttering to himself, but the breaking waves covered the words. Before she could call out, Jacob's gaze shifted, and he caught sight of her. His eyes went wide, and his body went slack with relief. Guilt pinched at Sevencea's gut. She knew what it was like to wait on this beach alone. She hadn't meant to do it to him.

She waved and called out, "Jacob! I have to show you what I've done!" She lowered her arm and lifted her other hand, where she clutched the camera he'd given her. The camera strap looped around her neck for extra security. Moving past the rock where she normally lounged, she swam as close to the beach as possible. She propped herself up on her elbows and wiggled closer until she was more or less level with Jacob.

Her hair pooled around her, looking whiter than normal against the black sand. The water still covered most of her tail, but the waves ebbed and flowed, revealing glistening scales in their wake.

Jacob moved to her side without hesitation, dropped to the sand, and crossed his legs. His own camera dangled around his neck, just like hers. Whatever his concerns had been a moment ago, his eyes were now bright and his smile easy.

A wave crashed on the shore, splashing Sevencea. She laughed and dragged her fingers through the water. "The ocean's a little excited today!"

Another wave engulfed Sevencea's normal rock, drenching it. Jacob's eyes widened. "It's probably a good thing we aren't out there."

"You keep coming to me, so I figured I'd come to you." Sevencea glanced at her normal perch with a wry smile. "Keeping your camera from getting wet is simply a welcome consequence. I fear you took more care choosing my camera than you did your own."

Jacob grinned. "Hang on, let's be fair here. Until a few days ago, my camera never needed to be this close to the ocean! Or any water, for that matter."

Sevencea snorted and flicked a droplet of water off her finger toward him, hitting his knee. "I suppose that's true. Speaking of cameras though, I have to show you all that I was able to capture!"

Sevencea adjusted her pose so she could easily angle her camera toward him and pulled the strap from around her neck. The strap brought with it most of her wet, white-blonde hair, dumping it around her neck. With a huff, she shoved the mass of hair back over her shoulder, letting it fall on her back. It was probably a tangled mess, but she'd deal with that later. The water usually sorted her locks out eventually.

"I can't wait to see your photos." Jacob inched closer, leaning in a little. "How did the camera work out for you? I didn't really get to test it before I gave it to you, so I hope you didn't have any issues."

Sevencea turned on the camera and navigated to her recent photographs. She shrugged. "I can only really compare it to your camera, and the two devices were created to serve very different worlds."

Jacob's cheeks took on a light flush. "Okay, that's fair. I only meant, was it easy to use? Any issues?"

"Yes, it was easy. No, there were no issues." Sevencea met Jacob's gaze and offered him a reassuring smile. "It was a wonderful gift, and the education on your own camera was certainly a help." She angled the camera so he could see her most recent photo on the display. Her breath caught in her throat, waiting for his verdict.

Jacob inspected the photo for a moment, then made a low whistling noise. "Is that a coral reef?"

Sevencea nodded, pressing the buttons to shift through a few coral photos she'd taken. "Coral is so naturally beautiful; it seemed like a good thing to practice on."

"I've never seen coral in person," Jacob admitted, his eyes fixed on the camera's display. "Not underwater, anyway. It's absolutely stunning." He tilted his head to look at her.

Warmth built in Sevencea's cheeks. Clearing her throat she gestured to the camera again. "I swam to the next island over this morning so I could capture its beauty in the morning light. Aren't the colors just so ... rich?"

Jacob stared at her, both eyebrows raised high and his eyes wide. "Wait, did you just say you swam to *Maui* this morning?" His mouth hung open for a second, then he blinked and closed it, though he still looked incredulous.

Sevencea shrugged. "I ... yes? I don't know what the humans call all the islands, so you'd know better than I would." She lowered her eyes, then darted them back up to see if Jacob's expression had shifted. He still looked awed. Was that a good thing?

Jacob rocked backward, his eyes still wide. He whistled under his breath. "How far can you swim before you'd have to stop? Like, before you'd be so exhausted you'd have to take a break."

Sevencea nodded. It would seem she'd done something unusual—if she were human. If swimming between islands was all it took to shock Jacob, she'd have to be careful not to give the man a heart attack.

She tilted her head in consideration. "I could probably make it all the way around this island five or six times before I'd want a break. I've never exactly tried, so I can't say for sure. I've never had a reason to swim to the point of exhaustion. I'm of average strength for merfolk, I think. Some are weaker, and plenty are stronger than I am. We're all different, much like humans."

"Average," Jacob scoffed. His gaze darted over her, then he met her eyes with a smile. "I can't imagine a world where someone like you is considered average."

Sevencea ducked her head, positive her cheeks were rosy. "Thank you." The awkwardly quiet words escaped her lips.

"You could explore the whole world, if you wanted." Awe still filled Jacob's voice, tinged with something that might have been envy.

Sevencea met his eyes again. A wry smile took over her expression. "I could, but long journeys are best with company. And none of my siblings or friends care much for exploring. That's always been my thing." A wave crested over her tail. She flicked her fin a little, sending water droplets flying through the air.

Jacob's eyes moved to her tail. A wistful expression crossed his face. He blinked and it was gone.

"Here," Sevencea lifted the camera a little to draw Jacob's attention back to the moment they were sharing. "These are the photographs I took last night."

Jacob accepted the camera and shifted his position so they could both see the display. He thumbed through her photographs. First were a handful of small sea creatures, though she'd struggled to get any ocean life to pose for her. Jacob made a few approving noises as he moved through what she'd captured. The sound wrapped around her like a warm current, and she couldn't help her smile. Jacob moved to the next photo. He audibly gasped, his eyes going wide.

A thrill surged through Sevencea's veins, and she sat up a little. "That's my favorite place." She glanced out toward the water, then back to the camera. "There's so much out there that's amazing and beautiful. But this place—it stuns me every time."

"It looks like a privateer ship." Jacob brought the camera closer to his face. "It's not really my area of expertise. It can't be that old, because I'm pretty sure a wooden boat like that would have disintegrated after all this time. Maybe it's a replica? I don't know. Where is this?" He lowered the camera and met her gaze. Excitement gleamed in his eyes.

Sevencea turned to the water, squinting at the horizon. "About…" she paused, tilting her head as she tried to orient herself above the water. "I'm not positive from here," she admitted, "but I think it's that way." She pointed to their right. "It wouldn't take me long to get there from here, but I'm afraid I don't actually know how far it is. In human terms, at least."

Jacob nodded. His eyebrows drew together and he looked deep in thought.

"I don't think humans know it's there," Sevencea clarified. Jacob looked surprised, and she giggled. She'd guessed his thoughts correctly. "I know humans sometimes go underwater with containers of air, but I've never seen them near the wreck. I'm there often, so I would have seen something by now. There are other wrecks in the area plenty of humans visit, but not this one."

"You've never seen anyone around it? Ever?" Jacob's tone betrayed his surprise. "Hawaii gets so many tourists, and a shipwreck is the perfect kind of thing to monetize. You'd think someone would have found it by now."

Sevencea wasn't entirely sure what that meant, but she could guess. She shrugged. "It rests in a bit of an ocean valley with a lot of large rocks. Maybe it's just hidden? If anyone does know it's there, they haven't left behind any trace of themselves."

Jacob's eyes returned to the photograph. He tilted the camera back and forth a little, like the motion would bring the shipwreck out of two dimensions. "Do you know her name?" He gestured toward the display.

"Keep going." Sevencea nodded to the camera and leaned in to peer over his shoulder. Her damp curls fell forward, brushing against his back and arm.

A slight shiver ran through Jacob, but he obediently thumbed through the next few photographs. As he went, he made a few noises of approval. Warmth bloomed throughout Sevencea's chest. She smiled at the back of Jacob's head. Finally, he paused on a close-up of faded paint on the ship's side. Once, the paint had shown the ship's name. Now the text was a guessing game.

"It's been like that as long as I've known about the wreck." Sevencea kept her voice soft, hyper-aware of how close she was to Jacob's ear. "I wish I knew what it looked like when it was new."

Jacob took a deep breath, then turned his head to meet her eyes. "There are plenty of paintings out there of old privateer ships. I'm sure I could find one for you, if you wanted. It wouldn't look exactly like this, but it would give you an idea of what she might have been like when she was new." He looked back at the camera, humming quietly to himself. "I can only tell what a few of these letters were." Frustration colored his tone.

Sevencea squeezed his shoulder. "I've always guessed it was called the Heating," she suggested, "and thank you for the offer. I'd love to know what it looked like in its glory."

A bright smile lit up Jacob's face. "Of course." He traced the letters that could be discerned on the ship's side—a capital H, and lowercase letters e, t, and n. He nodded thoughtfully to himself. Sevencea watched, her lips twitching toward a smile. Jacob wet his top lip, then held the camera up a little. "Whatever letter was there," he pointed to the lack of paint between the e and the t, "probably wasn't another vowel. It almost looks like an x, but there's not enough paint left to be sure."

"Hextant?" Sevencea volunteered, leaning in again so she could squint at the letters.

"Or Hexton?" Jacob wagged his head back and forth, like he was weighing both options. He shrugged and offered Sevencea a more relaxed smile. "She's been down there a while, so I doubt she'll mind much if we can't figure out her proper name."

Sevencea shifted back a little, tilting her head and raising an eyebrow. "Why is it that humans refer to ships as women?"

"Tradition, I think." Jacob shrugged. "I don't know how it started, but ships are always female. Some people use female pronouns for their cars too."

Most of the islands had roads that ran parallel to the shoreline in places, so Sevencea was familiar with cars. It was always a relief when Jacob mentioned something she already knew about. She grinned. "Perhaps ship builders knew that the good sense of a woman would see them safely through their travels."

Jacob threw his head back, and a hearty laugh escaped his lips. The light expression was startlingly different from his ordinary demeanor. "I'll give you that," he admitted, still chuckling, "although I think it used to be superstition that a woman on a boat was bad luck."

Sevencea scoffed, but was too distracted by Jacob's smile to form a retort. Watching him forget his burdens for that moment, she knew there was much she would do to make Jacob smile. And he didn't do it nearly enough, if such a small moment could have such a big impact. She reached for him again, resting her hand close to his free hand. Wet black sand sprinkled their fingers. "You've seen my favorite place. You should tell me about yours."

"That's fair." Jacob hesitated for a brief second, then stretched out his fingers and laid them across hers. He watched the water and the sand rippling between them, then looked up and met her gaze. "I really like Mauna Loa." Sevencea's brow furrowed, so he hurried to add, "It's a volcano here on this island. It's pretty impressive, and a gorgeous place to take photographs. I have to be careful when I go though. It's a big draw for tourists, so there are often too many people for me to really be able to appreciate it."

Sevencea's eyes were wide. "We have volcanoes underwater. But I imagine they're quite different on the surface." She looked up the hill, toward Jacob's house. From this angle she couldn't see anything that looked like a volcano, but she found herself wishing she could.

"Probably." Jacob shrugged. "I think places like that fascinate me because of how amazing they are. I mean, potentially terrifying and dangerous, sure, but also literally awesome. It always gives me some kind of comfort. Like, it can't be possible for something like Mauna Loa to exist, or even something beautiful like this," he gestured to the black sand and the water around them, "without there also being something greater at work."

"You mean the way the world sings, rejoicing in its design?" Sevencea leaned back, gazing up at the sky. Her hair, a tangle of soft curls, felt heavy against her back. It was still damp, but much drier than it ever became normally—a reminder of how unique this was. She smiled softly at Jacob. "I agree completely."

Jacob shifted to face her, keeping his grip on the camera. Their fingers still touched in the sand. "Do merfolk believe in God?"

Sevencea laughed. "Of course. Everything has a purposeful origin and future." When one saw merfolk magic up close, or experienced a storm for the first time, or saw any part of the beauty beneath the sea, it was impossible not to see the elegant design behind it all.

Something pure and hopeful danced across Jacob's expression. It stole Sevencea's breath away. Jacob pushed his fingers forward, fully interlacing his hand with hers. Sand glistened on their damp skin. He met her eyes. "Nothing happens by accident."

A spark raced through Sevencea from their clasped hands, running down her spine and through her tail. She flicked her fin, the splash spraying water droplets at them both. Jacob laughed, but didn't look away. A new wave crested, and Sevencea tightened her grip on him. "Everything has a design."

Chapter Eleven

❀

Day 6

Jacob had purchased snorkeling equipment upon moving to Hawaii. He'd never used it, but it seemed like something he ought to own. After a full year he still hadn't opened it. He was too embarrassed to take it back, and the box had been shoved into the depths of a closet. Gerald, who knew nearly everything about his son's life, found the whole thing hilarious.

Given that the ocean was his literal backyard, Jacob had to admit his lack of initiative in using the snorkeling gear was kind of sad. And a little funny.

"Well, Dad, look at me now," Jacob muttered. He rechecked the bag he'd dragged down to the beach. All the snorkeling stuff was there, finally out of the packaging.

There was no shortage of advertising about the beauty of the ocean in Hawaii, but Sevencea's photography had made Jacob long to experience the sea in a way no advertisement ever had. He'd found himself daydreaming about being a part of her world—then spent the rest of his evening trying to get the Disney melody out of his head.

"What's in the bag?" Sevencea called. Her head bobbed above the waves a way out from shore. With a swift push of her tail, she glided closer, reached her rock perch, and pulled herself up. The sunlight glinted off her hair and exploded in starbursts off her fin, which danced in and out of the water.

Jacob moved closer until he stood ankle-deep where crystal blue water met ebony sand. The ocean was calm today, sparing them the hassle of shouting over background noise. "It's…" He paused, giving his bag a quizzical look. How was he supposed to explain a snorkel to someone who could breathe underwater? He gnawed on the inside of his cheek. Memory struck him, making him feel silly. Sevencea had told him yesterday she knew about divers. She must already have some idea of how a snorkel worked.

"Yes?" Sevencea arched an eyebrow, a familiar expression.

Jacob opened the bag, retrieved the snorkel mask, and held it out. Without a face to give it shape, it looked like a lump of plastic.

Sevencea studied it for a second, then shot Jacob a look of mild exasperation. "Jacob, you're going to have to explain what I'm looking at."

Jacob snorted and obediently moved the mask to his face. He pulled it on and adjusted the straps. "This," he pointed to his face, "is for breathing underwater and protecting my eyes." He pulled two gigantic pieces of hardened rubber out of the bag and held them up. "These are called flippers. They help humans propel ourselves when we swim." He dropped them and slid his feet in, growing more and more self-conscious at how silly he must look.

"Oh! Like fins, just detachable." Sevencea looked far more fascinated than amused. "Is that normal? For humans to strive to be more than they are?"

"You have no idea." Jacob rolled his eyes. "Remind me to explain science fiction to you some time." He adjusted the dangling mouthpiece of the snorkel so it wouldn't bump his chin.

"Humans seem to be good at finding ways to counteract weaknesses," Sevencea mused. She dragged her eyes up and down Jacob's snorkeling-equipped form.

Jacob shrugged, jostling the snorkel again. "We try. There are a lot more practical ways for humans to go underwater than what I've got. But I didn't want to fork over the amount of money an industrial scuba suit would cost, so…" He considered explaining. Sevencea regarded him with an amused face rather than a confused one. His point must have been clear enough.

Sevencea's lips curled up on one side. She leaned in a little from her perch. "Is all of this so you can come explore my world?" Her voice was tender, but her eyes sparkled with mirth.

If anyone asked, the flush in Jacob's cheeks was sunburn. "Yeah." He cast his gaze down, fidgeting in his giant flippers. He forced himself to meet Sevencea's eyes again. Why should he be embarrassed? She wasn't making fun of him. Yet. He shooed the thought away and smiled at her.

"I mean no offense to all these human attempts to join the ocean. But I may have a better idea." The mermaid's tone was tentative. Jacob raised an eyebrow at her, and she beamed. "Do you trust me?"

"Yes." Jacob would question his lack of hesitation later. For now, he was confident enough in her existence to willingly follow her anywhere. If she did turn out to be his imagination … Well, he trusted himself.

Most of the time.

"Then take that stuff off and come out here."

Jacob removed the snorkel, accidentally smacking himself with it.

Sevencea giggled. "Careful!" she said. "And on second thought, keep the flippers. They're silly, but they'll help you keep up."

Ditching the snorkel and face mask with a laugh at his clumsiness, Jacob waddled out into the ocean. Why was it so much harder to walk through water in flippers? He stumbled a little and thrust his hands outward to regain his balance. The water lapped at his legs as he moved deeper. Sevencea's rock wasn't far enough from shore for him to just give up and swim to it, so he stuck to awkward waddling until he stood in the water beside her. He felt ridiculous, but she still wasn't laughing at him.

Sevencea slid off the rock, immersing herself in the water for a brief second before rising again beside Jacob. Her hair, always somehow more silvery when wet, covered her face like a curtain. She swept the wavy mass out of the way, then held her hands out toward Jacob's face. Water droplets raced away from her fingertips and down her arms.

"Still trust me?" The question was soft and quiet, settling in the air between them.

"Yes." Jacob breathed the answer. The air between them thickened. A torrent of possibilities flooded his mind. Was she going to kiss him? She was so close to him. They'd been close before, but this was different. He could practically feel the warmth of her hands, and she wasn't even touching him. Yet.

Sevencea's delicate hands rested gently on his cheeks. His eyes fluttered closed. Her hands were smooth, devoid of the prune-like texture his own skin gained from the water.

"Jacob."

His eyes reopened and fixed on her.

Sevencea kissed him.

Somehow, even with all the build-up he'd created in his own head, Jacob was still surprised. It was a sweet, tender thing, conveying in a moment what neither had managed to say with words. After a prolonged moment, Sevencea drew back and met his eyes with a confident smile. Her cheeks held a flushed tint.

Speechless and without air, Jacob forced himself to inhale.

There was still no air.

A full second of sheer panic dominated Jacob's mind. He was underwater.

"Wha…?" Jacob recoiled, whipping his head around as he tried to orient himself. Sevencea still held him. Had she dragged him under the surface during their kiss? Jacob paused. He'd just heard himself speak clearly underwater.

Most importantly, he could breathe.

Jacob blinked rapidly. Sevencea floated before him, her hair fanning out in a pearlescent halo. She studied him with a look of mild concern.

"Are you feeling okay?" The layers of pearls around her neck floated in the water. She looked far too ethereal for Jacob's floundering mind to register.

"I'm breathing."

Saying it made it easier to believe. He cycled through dozens of possible questions before settling on the most important. "How?"

"Everyone has their own sort of magic, Jacob." Her voice was muted slightly by the water, but still clear. "This is mine. You shared your magic with me; I'm simply returning the favor."

"You can magically make humans breathe underwater by kissing them?" Jacob's tone was more aggressive than he'd intended. His face grew warm as mention of the kiss slipped out.

Sevencea laughed, and the sound surrounded them in the water. "It only lasts until you lift your head above the water, so be careful. Come on, if we go deeper it'll be easier."

She reached out without waiting for a response, took his hand, and pulled him far enough out to sea that he could straighten without fear of breaching the surface. The black sand followed a gentle slope until it disappeared just past where they'd paused. The depths of the ocean spread out before them. Sunlight sparkled, refracting through the surface and dancing along the ocean floor. It was almost like staring at a painting. Was he truly underwater?

"It doesn't need to be a kiss."

Sevencea's admission pulled Jacob out of his observations.

"All I needed to do was touch you with intention. But I wanted to kiss you." She ducked her head slightly, one of the first times she'd seemed anything other than confident.

Jacob grinned and squeezed her hand. "Me too." When she met his eyes again, he reached out with his other hand, a slow motion through the water. Her eyes widened, and her lips twitched upward into a smile.

Jacob cradled her cheek, and Sevencea leaned into his hand, welcoming Jacob's kiss. His hand was large, but he held her gently. Their lips touched, the moment infused with passion and mutual desire. They parted, opening their eyes in unison. Gazes locked, mermaid and human began to giggle, a magical sound in an underwater paradise.

Chapter Twelve

Sevencea glanced over her shoulder, wincing when she realized how far ahead she was. Again. She didn't even need to think about using her powerful tail to cut through the water. Jacob struggled to mimic her though. He was moving, but it wasn't exactly graceful. His brown hair floated around him like an anemone, and his tongue stuck out when he was concentrating.

He looked up to see her staring. His lips twitched into a sheepish grin. "With how close I live to the water, you'd think I'd have more practice."

Sevencea released a light chuckle and twirled a little as she returned to his side. "I don't know, I think you're doing all right." She squinted at his legs, which were moving a little haphazardly. She reached for his knee and gave it a gentle squeeze. "Don't bend so much. You don't have to move your legs together like a tail, either. You're a human, it's okay to swim like one."

"I may be human, but I'm currently breathing underwater," Jacob pointed out. He gnawed on his lip, then twisted to face her. "Okay, I'll admit it. I'm a little freaked out."

Sevencea raised an eyebrow. "Maybe I can help. You mentioned breathing, but you seem to have gotten used to that."

He'd choked a couple times when they first began to swim, but he was breathing naturally now. This was Sevencea's first time bringing anyone under with her, so she'd sighed in relief when he'd started to relax.

Jacob nodded. "That part, shockingly, I'm not as weirded out by." He reached up to tuck his hair behind his ears, and the locks ran through his fingers and fanned out in the water. "How do I keep forgetting I'm underwater?" He shook his head.

Giggling, Sevencea reached forward and ruffled her fingers through his strands of floating hair. "This isn't your world. It's okay for it to feel strange."

"I can see," Jacob declared. He waved a hand at his face.

Sevencea squinted at him. "Why would that be odd?"

"Human eyes aren't designed for underwater use." Jacob said wryly. "You know all the stuff I had on at the beach? The piece that went over my eyes is to help me see while I'm underwater."

"Oh, I see what you mean. That's part of my magic," Sevencea explained. "You're probably a comfortable temperature too."

Jacob's eyebrows rose, and he nodded. "So not only can I breathe underwater, your magic makes me comfortable while I do it?"

Sevencea laughed and nodded. "Why would breathing under-water be of any use if you couldn't do it in comfort?"

Jacob relaxed a little and began experimenting with the motion of his flippers again. He propelled himself forward. "Can you imagine what it's like, at all? To do this for the first time?"

Matching his pace with ease, Sevencea shook her head. "No, I've never had that sort of first-time experience. I wouldn't even know what to compare it to. Can you describe it?" It hit her, as she asked, that this was the first time in many years that a human from the islands had come underwater with a mermaid. She was following in her mother's wake.

"Maybe. Let me think about it for a second." Jacob gnawed on his lip again. They swam on in companionable silence. He finally nodded. "Have you ever been above water on a really humid day?"

Sevencea shrugged, not recognizing the word. "I'm not sure." There was still so much she didn't know about the world above water.

Jacob nodded again. "Humidity is when the air is full of moisture. So your skin feels sort of damp even when you haven't been in water, your hair gets all frizzy and misbehaves—at least mine does—and it feels a little like breathing water." He paused, looking to her.

"I haven't experienced it, but I think I understand what you mean." Sevencea ran her eyes over Jacob, trying to imagine his beautiful hair in any sort of disarray. The way it floated above his head right now was definitely unusual, but still appealing.

A soft smile crossed her face as she watched him. She could have stumbled on any human, but she'd found Jacob. They'd found each other. Was there anyone better she could have brought underwater with her?

"This is like inhaling liquid air," Jacob continued. "It feels natural, which is freaking me out just a little, because it shouldn't feel natural. I'm guessing that's also your magic. It's beyond amazing—I don't even have words for what it is—but it's far outside anything I've experienced."

He ran a hand through his hair, pushing it all back along his scalp. It floated upward as soon as he dropped his hand. "Have you ever had a moment like that? Where something was so incredible you couldn't actually explain it?" He stared into the sea ahead of them.

The blood rushed to Sevencea's cheeks, and she ducked her head in case he looked back at her.

"I have," she murmured. Her face felt like it was on fire. That was definitely something she wasn't used to. How long was it supposed to last?

Jacob looked back at her right as she glanced up. He seemed to catch up with her thoughts in an instant, for his own face grew pink.

"Right. That too." He cleared his throat and gestured to her. "So, how exactly does this all work?"

Grateful for the conversational escape, Sevencea's lips twitched and she winked. "Magic."

"Ha ha." Jacob rolled his eyes and utterly failed to hide his smile. "You're hilarious. Seriously though, why do you even have magic that's designed around human contact? I didn't get the impression that merfolk interact with humans all that often."

"We don't," Sevencea admitted. "But we used to. My mother had the same magic I do. It was her responsibility to bridge the gap between our peoples. Over time, the humans stopped needing us, so she came back home to stay. She died before we could explore if there would ever be a purpose for my magic. There are other parts of the world where merfolk and humans still have contact. Or so I hear, anyway. Just not around this area."

Jacob hummed in acknowledgment. "That's fascinating. So, there are parts of the world where people wouldn't be at all surprised if a mermaid stopped by to say hi."

It wasn't really a question, but Sevencea nodded.

Jacob shook his head, looking a little dazed. "Wow. Well, if you've never met a human before, how did you even know what your magic was?"

"Mothers always know." Wistfulness tinged Sevencea's voice. She cleared her throat. "Before birth, mothers can sense what magic their child will have. It helps parents prepare, in case that child has a potentially destructive magic."

"Like your dad, with the…" Jacob mimed a whirlpool with his finger, causing a small stir in the water that dissipated almost immediately.

Sevencea nodded, a small burst of pleasure exploding in her chest. He'd been paying attention.

"Exactly. My mother knew what I could do, so she told me as much as she could when I was small. But then she was gone, and I never had the opportunity to use it for real." Her fingers twisted the strands of pearls at her neck. She loved remembering her mother, but hated the pain that always followed those memories.

"I'm sorry." Jacob reached for her hand, squeezing it lightly. "I'm sure it was hard, not having her there."

Sevencea squeezed back. "It was. But I am grateful that my father was there for me, and I for him." She cleared her throat, blinking once to make sure her emotions were in check. "Let's not dwell on the sadness of the past. We have a future to explore."

"I can get on board with that." Jacob relaxed, a teasing smile on his lips.

"Speaking of on board, let's go see the Hextant." Sevencea waggled her eyebrows and gave a strong push of her tail. She thrust herself forward, dragging Jacob behind her.

"Hexton," Jacob corrected, his grin turning ornery.

Sevencea shot him her most exasperated look, but she knew her eyes betrayed the warmth in her heart.

Chapter Thirteen

It's impossible to fully describe the sensation of swimming around a boulder and discovering a shipwreck, debauched by time and the sea. The wreck itself was muted, time having leached away the life from its hull. There were spots of color though, plants that had made their home between cracks in the wood. The entire vessel reeked of abandonment and hopelessness, much like a castle ruin. Only the inherent intrigue of something so old and untouched by other explorers gave it the spark of life Jacob felt in his chest.

"She's incredible," he whispered. It somehow seemed disrespectful to raise his voice. How was it so much quieter here than just a moment ago? He couldn't feel the current, or see its effects, like it didn't dare disturb the wreck. There didn't seem to be any fish either, no motion catching his eye as he took in the ship. It was a silent memorial to a different time, laying still before its two visitors.

Sevencea nodded. "I went inside once." She matched Jacob's volume.

Jacob raised an eyebrow. "Only once? There has to be enough to explore to occupy more than one visit."

She shook her head. "No, only the once. All the men are still in there."

"Oh."

Jacob evaluated the wreck again and shuddered. Men who had never returned home were entombed before him. The inherent mystery of a shipwreck held endless fascination, but he had no desire to ogle the bones of dead sailors. Now he knew why it felt disrespectful to raise his voice.

"I couldn't stay away from the ship entirely though," Sevencea admitted. "It … I mean *she*, calls out, whether I intend to listen or not."

Jacob understood completely, as if he'd visited the wreck in his dreams and somehow forgotten it. "It's odd," he mused, his voice still low. "In this moment, I want to know her story more than almost anything. But at the same time, I hope I never know."

"The urge to solve the mystery versus the thrill of a mystery that cannot be solved." Sevencea glanced at him with a wistful smile. "I know exactly what you mean."

They floated in place, and a chill settled in Jacob's bones. Was he imagining it? He rubbed his arms. He felt as comfortable in the water as he had before. It wasn't the water, then, but the eerie nature of the scene. Part of him wanted to move closer, but he didn't want to infringe on the unplanned graveyard.

"I wonder how long she's been here," he said. The way the ship lay nestled in the sand on its side, it almost seemed like she must have always been there. He had a hard time imagining the vessel above the waves.

Sevencea shrugged, her expression fond. "Time is hard to judge underwater."

Jacob had no trouble believing that was true. It couldn't have been long since he'd been pulled under by Sevencea's kiss, but it felt like days. He could barely remember what it was like to not have her in his life. That was all sorts of dangerous. He'd been a solitary creature most of his life. Wanting to share every moment with someone was a terrifying, earnest sensation that burned in his chest. At least the desire drowned out his anxieties. Unless this was the most vivid dream of his life, he couldn't say Sevencea wasn't real anymore.

"Let me show you something." Sevencea swam forward, her tail fluttering as she moved through the water.

His own flippers were less graceful, but he followed. She led him toward the bow of the wreck. At least, he was pretty sure it was called the bow. The ship wasn't in great shape. As they got closer, he could see where the sea had claimed the ship's wheel. Coral encrusted the wheel, the original structure almost invisible beneath the hard, thick coating. In a few places, the coral formed a mass jutting outward from the wheel. Jacob made mental notes of everything he laid his eyes on. The ship's structure, the plant life, all of it. He'd have to research when he got home to learn more about what he was seeing. All he knew for sure was that it was amazing.

"Whoa."

"Isn't it fascinating?" Sevencea swam up to the wheel and ran her hand just over it, not quite touching the twisted growth. "This is for steering, right?"

Jacob nodded, raising an eyebrow at her. "Yeah, how do you know that?"

"Merfolk do talk about humans," Sevencea laughed. "I knew what a ship was long before I found this place. I've never seen one like this above water, but I'm sure this type of ship is quite old."

"You're probably right," Jacob acknowledged, examining the

ship's wheel up close. It seemed fragile. He'd been right before: there was no way this was an original privateer ship. Up close, it was easy to see some of the metal structure of it. The ship's wheel appeared originally to have been both wood and metal once he got up close to it. Abruptly, he found himself with a desire to go to a university and study the history of shipping. His gaze drifted to Sevencea. She watched him with a soft smile. The feeling in his chest surged forth, and he ducked his head. He'd known guys in school who'd done weird things for girls. He'd never understood before.

Sevencea straightened, her tail swishing beneath her. "Let's go around, so you can see the whole thing." She held out her hand. Jacob took it.

Being underwater was a sort of out of body experience. As they swam around the shipwreck, Jacob wondered how his life had changed so utterly in such a short time. His fears, though ever-present, were being drowned out by Sevencea's hand in his. She was warm, somehow. Nothing underwater was as cold as it should be anyway, but being with her was a new kind of warmth. Her eyes kept flicking between the ship and his face, like she wanted to make sure he was enjoying himself. He smiled each time their eyes met. He honestly wasn't sure he'd ever enjoyed himself more.

They completed their circuit and paused near where they'd first approached the wreck, taking one last look at the drowned moment in time. Finally, Jacob tore his eyes away from the ship. He focused on the impossible creature beside him. "What other places do you love, besides the Hexton?"

"Hextant."

He made a face at her, and she winked.

"If you think you can manage a little bit of a workout, we can go see one of the underwater volcanoes. That way you know what they look like above and below."

Jacob's eyebrows drew together, and he leaned back a little. "How far are we talking?"

"Not too far, but it is deep," Sevencea warned.

"How deep, exactly? Humans can't go all that far underwater without getting screwed up from the pressure." Jacob glanced upward at the surface. It seemed so far away, a distant light, distorted by the motion of the waves. How long would he last before he started to get sick from being down here?

"Oh, that won't be a problem." Sevencea waved her hand, dismissing the issue.

"Because…?" Jacob folded his arms.

"It's part of my magic." Her tone implied it was obvious. Jacob nodded. Maybe it ought to have been.

"So I can breathe and swim as deep underwater as I want?" Jacob clarified. He might already be pretty deep underwater and breathing just fine, but he was still a skeptic at heart.

Sevencea laughed. "Of course. The magic is designed to allow humans to reach our clan if needed."

"That makes sense." Jacob sucked in a deep breath. He couldn't feel the water entering his lungs, and he was getting better at not letting his ability to breathe underwater distract him. He shoved the salty tang on his tongue to the back of his mind and set his gaze on Sevencea. "The volcano it is, then. Lead the way."

Chapter Fourteen

The swim to and from the closest underwater volcano wasn't long in Sevencea's mind. Jacob, however, was panting when they arrived.

"Sorry." Sevencea winced. Her eyes went to Jacob's heaving chest. "I didn't think—that was probably a long swim for you."

"It's fine," Jacob huffed, waving her off. "I'm not out of shape, I just don't swim a lot. It'll take some practice." He inhaled deeply, then exhaled, the slight shifting of the water capturing the motion.

His words brought a lightness in Sevencea's chest. She joined their hands. "I could get used to that, helping you practice."

Jacob's face went pink, but he maintained eye contact. "Me too."

"I'm still sorry I wore you out. I hope the effort was worth it." Sevencea gestured forward to the crater. Jacob didn't seem to have noticed it yet. As far as she knew, this volcano wasn't a risk to anyone. It was simply a crater, a mound of earth beneath the waves. Deep shadows hinted at what lurked beneath, but it was still just a remnant of something that had yielded its massive power a long, long time ago.

"Wow."

Jacob made a whistling noise, his eyes darting around the impressive mound before them. It almost looked like it had collapsed in on itself at one point. Sevencea watched him evaluate the volcano, like he wasn't sure if he should be worried or not. "It's not active, right?" he asked warily.

"Not as far as I'm aware," Sevencea assured him. "It's just interesting, not dangerous."

He nodded, eyes still on the crater. "Mauna Loa—the volcano on the island I told you about—is still active."

Sevencea pushed herself forward with her tail and used her grip on Jacob's hand to turn and face him. She raised both her eyebrows.

"They let people go to this active volcano?" She tried not to sound accusatory. It wasn't Jacob's fault if humanity liked to take unnecessary risks. But if Jacob got hurt visiting an active volcano, that was another thing entirely.

Jacob squeezed her hand and shook his head. "It hasn't erupted in decades," he explained. "Humans do dumb things sometimes, but most of us aren't that dumb."

Sevencea allowed herself a laugh. She relaxed and drifted back into place at Jacob's side. "All right, fine. I can't say I approve though."

"I wish I could show it to you." Jacob glanced back at her. "Not to insult this crater, which is cool and all, but Mauna Loa is beautiful."

Sevencea met his gaze, drinking in its sincerity. "I'm sure the crater isn't insulted," she murmured. The idea of visiting land with Jacob, volcanoes aside, picked up her heartbeat to a pace he must surely hear. Was it echoing in the water? It was echoing in her ears.

"I'll bring you some photos," Jacob promised. He offered her a soft smile.

Sevencea nodded. Photos were a consolation prize. She wanted the real thing. An inkling of an idea bloomed in the back of her mind, and she set it aside to consider once she'd taken Jacob home.

She twitched her tail a little, and Jacob moved with her, seemingly in sync with her thoughts.

"Time to head back," he said. A statement, not a question.

Sevencea squeezed his hand. "No day lasts forever. I can help make this leg of our swim a little less exhausting though." She winked at him, then tightened her grip on his hand and pushed forward with a powerful flick of her tail.

Jacob made a surprised noise behind her, then she heard the swish of water as he began to kick with his flippers, pushing forward to catch up with her.

"You don't have to tow me!" Jacob protested. Laughter colored his tone.

Sevencea giggled, glancing back to see Jacob trying and failing to pull even with her. "I'm just showing you what the ocean looks like at my speed!" She tried for an innocent tone, but Jacob rolled his eyes at her and she broke into a full grin.

"I'm going to keep practicing," Jacob panted. "Eventually I'll be as fast as you down here!"

The petulant yet determined expression on his face did nothing to abate her laughter. She slowed briefly, allowing Jacob to drift closer.

When his face drew even with hers, she whispered, "I'll hold you to that."

Jacob's expression lit up. He matched her grin with one of his own.

Sevencea put on a burst of speed and went back to dragging Jacob along behind her. A startled laugh bubbled out of the human.

"For now," she called over her shoulder, "I'm here to help!"

It wasn't too much of a challenge to get back to Jacob's beach, but as they drew close Sevencea regretted the shortness of the journey. It was harder than she'd expected to pull Jacob back above the surface of the water. Showing someone her world, sharing all those pieces of her life—she didn't want to stop. Jacob pushed his head above the water, flipping his head back to get the mass of wet hair out of his eyes. He took a deep breath of air and met her gaze, a similar sentiment reflected in his eyes. No one was ready to say goodnight.

They waded together toward shore, neither in much of a hurry. When they did finally reach the edge of the waves, Jacob dug his fingers into the black sand, lifted up a handful, and let it drop back to the beach.

"Home," he murmured. "It feels weird to be back." He looked at her again, something almost painful hiding behind his eyes.

"This is only goodnight," Sevencea assured him. The words were just as much for herself. "Believe me, I'm returning you reluctantly."

Jacob laughed and shot her a grateful look. "I enjoyed spending time in your world."

The pink and orange-hued sunset bathed the sky above them. Sevencea followed Jacob's gaze to the sky, gasping softly at the magnificent sight. It was a shame neither of them had their cameras.

"I enjoyed having you there." Sevencea didn't disguise the longing in her voice. "We'll share worlds again, I promise." Leaning forward, she pressed a soft kiss to Jacob's cheek. "Goodnight, Jacob."

His face pinked up a little. "Does that turn off whatever your magic turned on this morning?"

Sevencea laughed. "No, I told you before, you're magic-free as soon as you breathe air again, remember? This was just for me."

His blush deepened, but he laughed too. He leaned forward and returned the kiss on her cheek. "Then that one's for me." He got to his feet and strode to the gear he'd abandoned on the beach that morning. He picked up a towel, waved at her, then collected his belongings and walked back toward his home.

Sevencea watched him leave. Her chest felt tight, even though she knew she'd see him soon. Being together was an all-encompassing adventure of the heart and mind. Being apart just made her wonder how long it would be until she could see him again. That must be its own kind of magic.

Sevencea pushed off the beach and into the water. The idea she'd had before drifted back to the forefront of her mind. What if there were a way for her to see Jacob's world? It wasn't fair if she could only share her own. Jacob deserved the chance to show her his volcano, and the other wonders on land. But how to manage it? Her magic didn't work that way, but perhaps someone else could help.

Sevencea swam toward home out of habit, making a mental list of the merfolk in her clan and their magic. Most couldn't be helpful even if they wanted to be. Sevencea muttered names to herself, then froze. "Athys!"

Her brother's magic was so broad, surely it could help her. The real question was whether he would. Sevencea thought back to their last conversation. Had his demeanor implied disapproval of Jacob? Teasing her was one thing, but would Athys actually be willing to help her get on land?

Sevencea honestly wasn't sure. "Only one way to find out."

She put on an extra burst of speed. It was getting darker and darker, but Athys was often up late. Hopefully she wouldn't be disturbing him. A tightness overshadowed the tingling place in her chest where Jacob had begun to reside. She took a few deep breaths, focusing on her goal. Athys would help. If he didn't, well, at least she hadn't gotten Jacob's hopes up. There wasn't anything to lose by asking—other than her own dreams. If she could never join Jacob on land, it wouldn't matter.

They'd still find a way.

Feeling a little calmer, Sevencea slowed to a steady glide as she approached her home. It wasn't too late, so a few merfolk still milled near the communal table. The sight of it caused a rumble in her belly. She made a mental note to get something to eat after she found her brother. Athys kept a workshop full of ingredients for his potions. If he hadn't gone home yet, that's where he'd be. She'd only passed the place, never sought it out. Sevencea swam to her right, glancing at the opening of each cave as she passed. Other than a few luminescent fish and some curious merfolk who happened to catch her eye, there was nothing to see. Glancing ahead, Sevencea sighed in frustration. Had she gone the wrong way?

"Sevencea?" Athys's voice called from behind her. Sevencea whirled, pushing her fin back swiftly to try and stop her momentum. She'd passed right by his little cave without noticing. Only his head—easily identified by the reddish hair that matched his tail—drew attention to the opening. His workshop was a small cave, not really large enough for her to follow him inside. There were grooves worn into the wall, all of which had been filled with ingredients. In the center of the space was a smooth stone Athys used as his workstation. It was scattered with shells, human coins, a few plants, and a grinding stone. He retreated into the cave, settling back into place beside the stone and raising an eyebrow at her, waiting for her to explain her presence.

"Good, I found you." Sevencea swallowed her nerves and straightened her shoulders. "You said before you were here for anything I needed. Is that still true?"

Something flashed in Athys's eyes, but it wasn't surprise. He actually relaxed, like he'd been expecting her. "Of course. How can I help, sister?"

"Your magic…" Sevencea paused, trying to phrase what she wanted. She fidgeted with the pearls around her neck. Floating just outside the cave entrance felt awkward.

Athys held up a hand. "I can guess why you're here." His lips twitched, and he folded his arms across his chest. "Did you bring your human underwater?"

Sevencea fought hard not to blush. "Yes."

"And now you want to be able to do the opposite. Go to him, that is." Athys watched her carefully. He didn't look opposed to the idea.

She nodded once. "It doesn't seem fair to be limited to my world only. I want him to be able to show me his."

Athys continued to watch her, remaining quiet for a moment. "You aren't just seeing a human, then." One corner of his mouth tilted up, then his expression returned to neutral.

That was hard to answer. Any sort of declaration seemed dramatic, given how briefly she'd known Jacob. But to pretend their relationship was nothing—that would be wrong. Her tail flicked back and forth as she struggled with the right words.

Her silence must have been the correct answer.

"I've been there," Athys admitted. "Not with a human, obviously, but I know this look." He waved in her direction. "It's too new to describe. It's not definable yet, but far too much to be ignored. Am I close?"

Sevencea's pulse picked up. She took a deep breath before she could speak. "Will you help me?"

Athys laughed. "I must be a romantic at heart." He let out a long-suffering sigh, then shot her a wink. "I've never done exactly what you want before, but I'm sure I can. It's going to take some trial and error though, and it's not free."

That much Sevencea had expected. Everyone who performed a service did it in exchange for something. Often it was another service, though she wasn't sure what she could offer her brother. Her skills were limited to exploration and photography. "What do you want?"

"I have an apprentice these days. I don't know if you knew." Athys turned to his workstation, tidying the items left out from whatever potion he'd been working on.

She hadn't, but that wasn't a surprise. The apprentice was probably someone with magic similar to Athys's, or something complementary.

"All right."

"His family went on a crossing and won't be back for a bit. If you fill in for him while he's gone, I'll make you what you want." Athys glanced up and rolled his eyes at her expression. "It's nothing difficult, sister. I'll mostly have you running errands for me."

"I can do that." Sevencea moved forward a little and extended a hand to her brother. "I'm grateful, Athys. Truly."

Athys copied her motion, and the siblings grasped each other's forearms. "I'm glad you asked."

Chapter Fifteen

❀

Day 7

After a brief breakfast of toast, Jacob made his way down to the beach with a genuine spring in his step. Sevencea wasn't there yet, but it wasn't the first time he'd beaten her. His ever-present worry was soundly defeated by his growing confidence of the reality of the past few days. Jacob set up his beach chair out of habit and settled into it, content to wait.

Waking up with a smile every day was new and different. It was nice feeling, getting out of bed with excitement. Sevencea gave him something to think about other than his settled, impending sense of doom. Jacob gave the ocean a fond look. Perhaps he could believe the future might be real again. He'd given up on planning more than a day or two ahead. It would be nice to think about a future that included goals and dreams for himself.

Jacob scanned the water for signs of a pink fin and started humming to himself. He was starting to hope again. Before, he'd stopped hope from knocking; having it back felt like having an old friend drop in. The niggling doubts persisted, but Jacob was better at ignoring them. Or, more accurately, Sevencea's presence beat them back. She'd brought hope with her. If nothing else, Jacob was grateful for that.

The water was still today, like a pane of patterned glass concealing all the wonders it held beneath the surface. In a single day, Jacob had seen a shipwreck, visited a volcanic crater, and been brought underwater by an actual mermaid. What more could he see with additional visits? His flippers hung in a bag behind his chair, just in case. Any time Sevencea wanted to take him into her world, he wouldn't say no.

Of course, that brought to mind a more pressing issue. Jacob didn't have any magic of his own. How could he ever hope to bring Sevencea to see any of his favorite parts of the island? Or introduce her to his father? He gnawed on his lip, examining the calm sea in hopes that the mermaid would pop up and distract him.

Nothing.

Jacob pushed away his worries and focused on his toes in the sand. Sevencea still had plenty of time to show up.

"She must have been busy." Jacob spoke out loud to the water. It hadn't stirred with a hint of blonde all day. He nodded to himself, packed up his beach chair, grabbed his bag, and headed up the hill toward home. Tension had built in his chest throughout the day, strengthening with each hour Sevencea did not appear. He forced himself to take a deep breath and avoided the temptation to turn back and look at the beach one last time.

He'd left her alone on that beach. Once.

She'd waited for him.

He could wait for her.

"She'll be here tomorrow." He repeated the words under his breath as he walked, alone. "The beach is black. The sky is orange. It's nearly dark." He paused, trying to think of other things to ground himself in reality. He didn't have any reason to panic yet. "Sevencea will be here tomorrow." He put as much conviction into the sentence as possible. It still didn't feel like a fact. Jacob closed his eyes and sighed heavily.

"Tomorrow," he said again. "She'll be here tomorrow."

Chapter Sixteen

A thys had been floating over Sevencea when she awoke that morning. She'd let out an embarrassing screech of terror. He'd laughed and claimed he was just making up for lost time as a big brother. Then he'd dragged her to her new job.

Somehow, when she'd agreed to this the night before, Sevencea hadn't realized she wouldn't be able to go to the beach at all.

"I have to tell Jacob I'm busy or he'll think I've abandoned him!" she protested in the middle of Athys's list of errands for her.

Her brother huffed and waved off her concerns. "He'll be fine. The sooner you help me, the sooner you get your solution and get to go say hello properly." He waggled his eyebrows at her. She threw a handful of sand at him. He just laughed again.

Athys's errands were mainly hunting down ingredients, delivering finished products to other merfolk, and collecting orders for new products. When he'd handed her the deliveries, Athys had been very adamant that there was a difference between the potions, the tinctures, and the serums. What that difference was, Sevencea had no clue. Most of his creations were contained within bottles humans had left to the sea. Some had corks, others had screw-on lids, and a few he stoppered with clumps of seaweed. They would be fascinating if she wasn't in a rush.

"Here you are, ma'am," Sevencea inclined her head and passed over a stoppered bottle filled with an odd assortment of ingredients.

A wrinkled, white-haired mermaid accepted the bottle. She unstoppered it immediately and dumped the contents into her mouth, chewing loudly on the crunchier ingredients.

Sevencea screwed up her nose, wincing at the noise. Why did Athys even call them potions, serums, and whatever else if they weren't liquids? Sure, there was a bit of ocean water in there, but it was just a bottle full of random stuff. She glanced at the bag of deliveries her brother had given her. Yeah, none of the ingredients were what one might call blended.

The older mermaid made a satisfied smacking sound and grinned toothily at Sevencea. "Thank you, dear!"

Sevencea glanced back up, startled. The mermaid's previously white hair floated around her in a dazzling shade of lavender. "Uh… you're welcome!"

While she appreciated getting an idea of what her brother did for their community, apparently being Athys's new errand girl came with its share of customer condolences.

"Ah, well, I'm glad you've got something to do, but that Athys, he's a busy one! You won't have a spare moment, I'm sure!" One of the clan's elders chuckled at her as she gave him his delivery. He didn't consume it in front of her, so she had no idea what it was for.

Many of Athy's customers repeated that sentiment. They all liked him, but were sure she'd be far too busy for a breather. It was said as a joke, something she should even be grateful for, being kept busy. For Sevencea though, it only meant one thing.

She wasn't going to be able to slip away to see Jacob.

It was early evening when Sevencea finished everything Athys had asked her to do. Still, she wasn't giving up. As soon as Athys set her loose, she set out for Jacob's beach. Perhaps she could catch Jacob before it was fully dark.

She breached the surface when she was within sight of his beach. The black sand stretched before her, barren of life except for a small white bird. Sevencea looked up, toward Jacob's house on the hill. A light glowed faintly, too far away for her to get Jacob's attention. She stared up at the house anyway, trying to will Jacob to look down and see her. Had he waited for her? She could picture the way his face sometimes pinched when he was troubled. Leaving him without warning had certainly not been part of the plan.

Sevencea turned away, muttering about all the dark things she'd like to do to Athys. Tomorrow, she *would* find time to slip away.

Chapter Seventeen

Day 8

It only took an hour of sitting alone on the beach for Jacob to start having trouble breathing. The tightness in his chest was back, followed by a rebellious staccato in his heartbeat. He felt like a child without object permanence. Just because he couldn't see Sevencea didn't mean she wasn't real. He gripped the arms of his beach chair and focused on taking a deep breath. Inhale. Exhale. He'd been so close to certain that it was all real—that she was real. Close enough to be willing to set aside his fears in favor of hope.

Last night, sleep had been hard to come by. Maybe that's all this panic was. Lack of sleep.

If only he could convince himself of that.

"My imagination has never been that good," Jacob declared. Only the ocean was listening, and the empty waves lapping at the beach didn't care. His words felt like the truth. How could he have come up with such an amazing person by himself? If his mind *was* turning on him, he had a lot more creativity than he'd ever given himself credit for.

Jacob had been told his father's illness might be hereditary mere seconds after being told his father was sick. Yes, he'd spent the last year allowing that concern to fester, but he'd started to give just a little bit of credit to the voices in his life arguing for his sanity. His father. Dr. Wilcox. His mother.

Sevencea.

A rock settled in the pit of Jacob's stomach, growing by the minute. Its weight seemed intent on dragging him through the sand until he reached the center of the earth.

Was any of it real?

Surely it was real; he didn't have any other symptoms. Jacob picked at what was left of the hem seam of his shorts, his fingernails down to nubs after he'd worried at them yesterday with his teeth. It was unnecessary. He was working himself up over nothing. It was still early. The sun had some distance to travel before he could be sure that a mermaid wasn't coming.

Unless she was real.

She had to be real.

Chapter Eighteen

Day 13

"Athys!" Sevencea hurled a handful of oyster shells at her brother. He neatly dodged them, giving her a disparaging look while they sank to the ground. Sevencea fumed. She snatched a clam shell off his work bench and chucked that at him for good measure.

The clam shell glanced off his side, leaving a small welt. "Hey!" Athys snapped. "What did I do?"

"It's been *days*. I just need a few minutes! What if he thinks I don't care anymore?" Sevencea's pulse hammered in her ears, and she took a deep breath to calm herself. She focused on the swishing of their tails, backing out of the cave's opening and away from Athys's ingredients to avoid the temptation to throw anything else.

The memories of Jacob questioning whether she was even real plagued her dreams. She needed to see him, but she had yet to complete any work for her brother with enough time left to reach the beach before Jacob went home. If he was still going to the beach. All the joy of her idea had faded. What was the point in joining Jacob on land if he no longer wanted to see her?

Her brother's reddish tail gave a powerful flick, pushing her back a little further. "Calm down, sister. I'm almost done with your potion. I told you I'd never made one like this before. It's difficult, which means I need a lot from you. Do you have such little faith in your human?" The words might have been teasing, but they sounded genuine. She glanced at him, surprised to see his eyebrows drawn together and a firm set to his lips.

Sevencea paused, watching Athys for a moment. Was it right to tell him things Jacob had shared with her? "I think he questions things more than most."

Athys studied her, then nodded. "All right. I'll do my best not to keep you much longer. Perhaps I'm taking advantage of your time. A little. But I'm not trying to keep you from him on purpose, Sevencea. I'll admit I'm obnoxious; I'm not cruel."

Some of her earlier frustrations faded, and Sevencea's anger wilted. Her shoulders slumped. "I know. I'm not mad at you. Well, I'm a little mad at you."

He chuckled. "I don't think I could be your brother without making you a little mad at least."

"I'll hold you to that promise though, Athys. Not much longer." Sevencea glanced toward the open sea, in the direction of Jacob's beach. A chill rippled through her bones, though the water felt as warm as ever. "I'm afraid something's already happened."

Athys swam toward her, reaching out and squeezing her shoulder. "I'll get you to your human, sister. I promise. Trust me, all right? Half the delay is me wanting to make sure this potion actually helps you and doesn't turn your top half into a squid."

Sevencea reared back, her lips curving downward. "Can that happen?"

Athys shrugged. He held up a bottle he'd stoppered with a

bunch of yellowish ingredients and shook it. "It hasn't happened yet, but who knows? Here, your next delivery."

Sevencea accepted the bottle with a heavy sigh and swam away. Hopefully the force of her tail spoke for her.

Chapter Nineteen

Day 15

The twisting in Jacob's gut started before he even reached the beach. The purples and pinks of the sunrise barely registered. He only had eyes for the empty ocean. At this point, it felt like he was just doing his due diligence to check that she wasn't there. No matter what he told himself, sometime over the past few days hope had slipped away.

The ocean gave no sign it intended to reveal a mermaid. It caressed the black sand. The soft noise grated on Jacob's nerves, and he clenched his fists tightly. Everything that once gave him peace just served as a reminder of how foolish he was. How gullible. The beach grew blurry, and Jacob hastily wiped at his face and turned back toward the house. With downcast eyes he marched up the hill, his lips set in a firm line.

If there was any silver lining to this whole situation, it was that he had a contingency plan. He'd once called it his "in case of crazy" plan. His father had tried to tell him this was unnecessary. Well, a plan to handle a declining mental state is only unnecessary until you hallucinate a mermaid.

Jacob snorted as he unlocked his front door. His father had spent so much time trying to reassure him that nothing was wrong with him. Now, though, Jacob had proof. Undeniable proof. He was exhibiting symptoms. Dr. Wilcox had agreed to accept him as a patient if and when that ever happened. The doctor had also made it clear he never expected that to be necessary. Still, he'd agreed. Having Dr. Wilcox in his corner, however reluctantly, was the biggest part of Jacob's contingency plan.

Step one was packing a bag. Jacob shoved anything he might need into a duffel bag. A toothbrush, any clean shirts he could find, deodorant, and a few pairs of comfy pants were first on the list. His camera bag was hanging by the door where he'd last left it. He eyed it briefly, but it was impossible to look at without thinking of Sevencea. In the end, he left it where it was. Maybe someday he could use it again. Right now it was just a reminder of what was wrong with him.

Step two would be driving the hour and a half to the east side of the island to Mana'o Treatment Center. If he was going to seek treatment, of course he was going to stay close to his father. No one knew more about whatever condition Gerald, and now Jacob, had than Dr. Wilcox.

Jacob stood in front of his door, bag in hand, and took a deep breath. It was so different to inhale and feel nothing but real air. He could still taste the saltwater from his adventures underwater. No, of course he couldn't. That was an illusion. A vivid, detailed illusion, but an illusion nonetheless. Jacob closed his eyes for a second, reopened them, grabbed his keys, and walked out the front door.

He ignored the beach completely and moved to his car. He threw the bag in the backseat then slid into the driver's side. A small, bumpy, private road brought him to the highway. He'd always valued the privacy. Now, that small road just made him wonder how much of his insanity was due to isolation. He drummed his fingers on the steering wheel in time to a nonexistent song. He felt like a bolt of electricity was contained within his body—turning on the radio would just make it worse.

The highway, once he reached it, stretched on quiet and traffic-free. Normally that would be a blessing. His breath hitched. Today the silence felt lonely. He should have insisted on being under observation. Something, anything to keep this from happening. His grip on the steering wheel tightened, and he fought against the moisture pricking his eyes.

Why did he feel like he'd lost something? His heart beat irregularly, like it was trying to compensate for a hole. Jacob sucked in another shaky breath. This was ridiculous. Once he got to Mana'o, they'd help. They'd get him treatment. Maybe since he'd caught the symptoms early, he had a chance of getting better.

Nervous energy continued to prickle under his skin. Every few seconds his eyes flicked to the rearview mirror. All the glass rectangle showed was his life fading into the distance with each passing moment.

The drive felt like it took exponentially longer than normal. Jacob pulled into the clinic parking lot and breathed a heavy sigh of relief. It was nice to be somewhere familiar, even if the reason was less pleasant. He found a spot, turned off his car, closed his eyes, and sat there in silence.

Was he brave enough to go through with it? Sevencea's smile intruded on his thoughts, her eyes bright and teasing like they'd been when she kissed him. Jacob jerked his bag from the back seat with a shiver. That sealed the deal.

Jacob still couldn't remember the name of the receptionist, but she looked up with recognition then surprise. "Hello, Mr. Pearson." Her eyes darted to his duffel bag, then back to his face. "Are you here to see your father? I'm afraid we weren't expecting you today."

"I'm actually here to see Dr. Wilcox," Jacob explained. He offered an apologetic shrug. "Sorry, I don't have an appointment, but it's important."

The receptionist examined him over her glasses, twirling a pen between her fingers, then nodded and reached for her intercom. "Dr. Wilcox, Mr. Pearson is here for you."

Dr. Wilcox took barely a minute to emerge from the back. He strode into the room, his shoes clacking against the hard floors. He only stood an inch or two taller than Jacob, but he was much broader. As usual, too much gel slicked back his hair. His sharp blue eyes locked on Jacob's, searching for the problem that had brought him.

"Good morning," Jacob offered. His heart wasn't in it. The greeting fell flat between them.

"How can I help you, Jacob?" Dr. Wilcox's eyes narrowed when they fell on the duffel bag.

Jacob glanced sideways at the receptionist. "Can we talk in your office?" He didn't really feel like spilling his deepest fears and secrets in front of strangers.

Dr. Wilcox nodded and gestured for Jacob to follow him. He moved back into the heart of the building. Jacob knew the way; he'd been in that office multiple times for meetings about his father. He walked into the oak-paneled room and, out of habit, dropped into a leather chair facing the desk.

Dr. Wilcox lowered himself into the chair behind the large

desk. Even behind the giant piece of furniture he was imposing. "So. Jacob, tell me what happened." If Dr. Wilcox was anything, he was solid. That was why Jacob had insisted on his cooperation when forming his contingency plan.

Jacob sighed. He could say anything to get himself admitted, but he didn't have to. The funny thing about truth was that it was often stranger than fiction. Jacob fixed his eyes on the doctor, folded his hands, and stated his case. "I spent a week with a mermaid. We went on underwater adventures, and I may have been falling in love."

Dr. Wilcox blinked, then reached for his notepad and pen. "All right, start at the beginning."

Chapter Twenty

Day 16

Sevencea breached the surface with a gasp, her head tilted back to keep her hair out of her face. The sun already blazed high in the sky. She basked in its warmth for a moment, then lowered her gaze to the beach.

No Jacob.

A frown creased Sevencea's brow. She shouldn't attach too much significance to his absence. It had been over a week since she'd first gone to Athys. After that long, she might have given up too. Her eyes went from the beach to the house at the top of the hill. All the windows reflected the scenery. She couldn't see inside, at least not from down here.

Sevencea took a deep breath. So, she wouldn't get to share a dramatic reveal with Jacob. She'd known that was a possibility. Every time she'd managed to get to the beach, Jacob was already gone. Unless ... had he stopped coming to the beach entirely? On some of her visits she *thought* she could see where his chair had been—four divots in the sand, created by the weight of a human sitting, waiting. But sometimes the tide had come and she couldn't even see that much. Her gut twisted as she looked at the empty beach. She shoved the feeling down. All she had to do was go up the hill and knock on the door. Jacob would forgive her for being gone so long. It would all be fine.

She wanted to blame Athys, but it wasn't really his fault. He'd told her from the start he'd never tried anything like this before. And he had come through—eventually. The bottle she clutched in her hand was evidence of that. An odd, greenish-pink concoction with a little bit of a glow filled the misshapen glass bottle. Unlike many of her brother's potions, this one was a liquid. Or maybe "a sludge" was a better term for it. Sevencea held it up. It looked intriguing in the direct sunlight. She shook it a little, wary of actually taking a sip. She trusted Athys, but she also had no personal experience with his magic. What if it didn't work?

If it didn't work, she wouldn't get to experience Jacob's world with him, let alone apologize for her absence. Sevencea huffed, shaking the bottle again and rotating it in the light. "This better work."

Sevencea opened the bottle and sniffed the mostly-liquid substance. "Here goes nothing." The mermaid took one small swallow and grimaced at the unusual taste. She didn't have a word for the flavor, but it wasn't nice. According to Athys, if the potion worked correctly, she'd have enough for a month.

Sevencea watched her tail intently, digging one hand into the black sand beneath her. The other hand clenched the bottle tightly.

Nothing happened.

After a few seconds, Sevencea began to scowl. There would be hell to pay if Athys was just messing with her. He knew how important this was!

Her tail seized up. Sevencea collapsed backward, narrowly keeping hold of the bottle. A sharp, tearing pain ripped its way up her tail. Sevencea looked down and cried out. An actual split had formed in her tail. Her fin spasmed, then seemed to retract. That part didn't hurt, but it was so disconcerting that Sevencea thought she felt the pain of it anyway. She tried to flick her tail and felt a curious sensation instead. Blinking, Sevencea stared down at her lower half. Legs. She had legs! A mass of wet fabric buried the new appendages, the shallow water rippling the cloth.

Sevencea placed her hands down in the sand and pushed herself up. Slowly, reluctantly even, she shifted her weight to her new feet.

"Whoa!" Sevencea wobbled and thrust her hands out for balance, barely managing to avoid crashing to her knees. She had knees! She straightened and adjusted her stance a little, trying to decide how to distribute her weight. Without the effortless way the water hugged her body, she felt far too heavy, like the earth was trying to drag her down. The wet fabric fell around her, clinging to her skin and forming a misshapen skirt. It brushed her knees in front, but draped down to her ankles in back, rippling with a discordant mix of textures and colors.

Sevencea tentatively touched the fabric. Athys may or may not have intended to give her some modesty along with the legs, but Sevencea was grateful, nonetheless. She looked closer and grinned. The pinks, purples, blues, and teals in the skirt echoed the scales she'd just given up. Her tail was still with her, just in a more human way.

Human. She was human! At least, for all intents and purposes.

Sevencea's hands went to her hair. Had anything unexpected changed? Her damp curls seemed normal, and the pearl headdress still hung in place. Her other pearls draped around her neck beneath the strap of her camera. She caught the glint of further pearls affixed to the new fabric encircling her waist.

"Not bad, Athys." Sevencea smiled down at herself. Given all possible outcomes of drinking a magical potion, this one was pretty satisfactory.

She took an experimental step on the beach and grinned as her toes squished in the damp sand. Toes! What tiny, marvelous little things. She didn't move any farther for a few seconds, too preoccupied with her feet in the sand. A small wave washed over her foot, smoothing away several clumps of sand. She giggled, then reluctantly pulled her attention from her new feet to look up the hill toward Jacob's home. It wouldn't do to spend all her time on the beach when Jacob was probably worried about her. It was time to surprise him with her new limbs. Sevencea took a deep breath, then began to walk toward the hill.

Her equilibrium was a lot better than she'd expected. That is, she hadn't collapsed yet, and walking seemed natural. Athys had promised she wouldn't be helpless, but it was still a relief to find that she wasn't stuck on the beach flailing her legs around.

She reached the path to Jacob's home and paused. She didn't have shoes. Jacob always wore shoes with a Y-shaped strap. Now she understood why. Sevencea eyed the dirt, plants, and rocks that made up the path. Sand was kind to her. The path seemed like it might have a bit of an attitude.

There weren't any materials she could fashion into protection for her feet, nor was there an alternate path up the hill that promised fewer potential injuries. Sevencea winced and stepped onto the path anyway. It was the only way to get to Jacob—she could handle being uncomfortable for a few minutes. Her hands went to the camera to keep it from bouncing around too much, and she began her hike up the hill. The incline wasn't severe, but she'd never walked up a hill, and the burn in her calves wasn't pleasant. After a few rough steps, she learned what to step on and what to avoid. Dirt was fine. Not as pleasant as sand, but not painful. Rocks were the enemy, and plants were often deceptive.

At least if she did damage her legs it wouldn't be permanent. Like most merfolk magic, the potions her brother fashioned weren't meant to last forever. The next time she immersed herself in the ocean, she'd revert to normal. Another swig of the potion, and she'd be back in Jacob's world.

Sevencea turned and glanced back at the ocean from her new vantage point on the hill. Below, the water sparkled in the midday sunlight. It was a clear day, not a cloud in sight, which seemed like a good sign. She'd never seen her home from so far above before. Sevencea could understand why Jacob wanted to live here. She grinned at the view, then down at her legs. "Worth it."

"Just remember, Sevencea—" Athys's voice cautioned in her memory. *"The potion does have one potentially fatal side effect..."* Sevencea shrugged the memory off as she started walking again. She wasn't worried. Athys had told her that if she stayed on land for too long without refreshing herself underwater, the potion could permanently damage to her body. She needed to return to the water roughly once a week. It was a small price to pay. She had no intention of letting the potion become a hazard to her health. Once she found Jacob, everything would be fine.

Jacob's house up close wasn't that different from Jacob's house at a distance. It was all windows, reflecting the scenery back at Sevencea. Her own reflection distracted her as she approached. Light glinted off her jewelry, and her skin seemed almost too pale. She was human though! Her legs were more fascinating than ever now that she had a better idea of how other people would see her. How Jacob would see her.

Sevencea knocked on the door and waited with her breath held. No one came. She exhaled. Was Jacob not at home? That possibility hadn't even occurred to her. She tried the handle. The door didn't open. There was a lock on the door, similar to old treasure chests, though much smaller. She didn't have much experience with locks, but knew how they were supposed to work. Sevencea pursed her lips and scanned the ground for a good place to hide a key. Did humans hide keys near their homes? Or did they keep them on their person? If Jacob had taken his keys with him, she had no hope of getting inside his home.

The small garden didn't reveal anything interesting. The mat in front of the door was scratchy against her toes, but revealed no key when Sevencea moved it. She folded her arms and glared at the scene before her.

"There has to be a key somewhere," she informed the ground. She glanced up at her own reflection, her nose wrinkled in annoyance. Sevencea bent to take a closer look at the rocks and natural plants along the edges of the door. One rock seemed a little bigger than the others, and she picked it up.

"What...?" Sevencea's brow furrowed. She could feel the edges of a small hinge on the bottom of the rock. Finding a depression in the rock, she applied pressure. A small door sprang open. "How bizarre!" She retrieved the key the door had revealed, but continued studying the rock. Humans really were strange creatures. She couldn't wait to have Jacob explain his secret rock to her.

She redirected her attention to the door. After three attempts to insert the key, she figured out the right angle. With a slight turn, the door opened.

Jacob wasn't home. No one came to greet or challenge the un-invited guest in the little home by the sea. Sevencea stood in the open doorway, waiting. She glanced around, hoping for signs of life, but the house was silent. The earthy scent that met her was unmistakably Jacob's though. What she could see of the main room seemed like him, practical and not elaborate. She didn't have any other human homes to compare it too, but Sevencea was confident in her assessment of Jacob so far. She gingerly stepped foot inside, and her eyes caught on Jacob's camera bag, hanging on a peg by the door. Why had he left that?

Sevencea reached for it, unzipping the main pocket and pull-ing the camera out. She'd rarely seen Jacob without it, but she was grateful to find a piece of him.

Turning on the camera, Sevencea pressed the button to see the stored photos. A smile lit up her face as she saw herself, in the ocean, looking at Jacob. It was a beautiful image. A comforting certainty settled in her chest. Surely her feelings for Jacob were mutual. She only needed to find him!

Sevencea turned the camera back off and placed it in the bag, leaving it where it hung. She continued through the house, scan-ning for anything that might tell her where Jacob was. The house wasn't large, but it was very open. The windows and the natural light streaming through them constantly drew Sevencea's gaze.

There were a lot of things in the house she didn't understand, but plenty of things whose purpose she could guess. The front room, food preparation room, and room for relieving oneself were all easy enough to figure out. Sevencea reached the bedroom door-way, and her heart seized, then sank, settling in her stomach like a pit. The closet door stood open, with large gaps where clothes had been removed. Several drawers hung half open. The swim trunks she'd seen him wear lay cast aside in a corner of the room. Jacob wasn't just away from home; he was gone. The scattered items reminded her of when her father created whirlpools inside structures. Things flew all over the place. This room was a mess, but it was a calculated mess. She could see an element of its normal organization, cast aside by a need to pack things and go.

"He left," Sevencea murmured, testing the words on her tongue. They tasted as bad as her heart expected. She pivoted slowly, dragging her eyes across the evidence of Jacob's absence, before moving back toward the front room and all the windows.

"He left," she repeated. She caught sight of her reflection again, this time in the shiny exterior of one of Jacob's appliances. Now her legs mocked her, an obvious sign of failure. Her deal with her brother had taken too long; she'd driven Jacob away by leaving him.

Sevencea collapsed on Jacob's couch, her skirt fanning out around her. "What am I supposed to do now?" she demanded of the windows. The ocean dominated the scenery—another mockery.

"I'm not going home," she told the water. "I didn't become Athys's errand girl for nothing."

The house was quiet. She couldn't even hear the water from inside this structure that didn't contain the one thing she needed it to.

Sevencea let the silence dominate the room and evaluated her surroundings again. By the time her eyes hit Jacob's camera bag, she'd gathered her resolve. She turned back to the windows and wagged her finger at the ocean. "I'm going to find him."

She had no experience finding a missing human, but she could figure it out. Hawaii was only an island. Jacob could have left the island, a small voice in the back of her mind reminded her. She shushed it. He was still on the island. She could feel it. Or, at least, she would have felt something if he'd left. They had a connection.

Sevencea relaxed into the couch. She'd stay here until morning. Maybe Jacob would come home, and save her all the trouble of hunting for him. If he didn't, she'd try and find some wearable shoes in his closet and go after him tomorrow. One way or another, she wasn't going back to the ocean before she got a chance to show Jacob the legs she'd worked so hard for!

Chapter Twenty-One

❀

Today may have been his first full day at Mana'o, but Jacob was as set in a routine as could be expected. He'd assumed once admitted he'd be handled like a patient, but that hadn't been the case so far. Dr. Wilcox had agreed to let him stay and undergo some testing and therapy, but it was clear the man didn't believe Jacob had his father's illness. He'd actually floated several alternative theories as soon as Jacob told him what had happened. Including calling him a hypochondriac.

Normal, healthy people didn't invent relationships with mythical creatures. Was the mermaid not enough? The underwater adventures, the tail, the ethereal whirlwind romance? Those weren't clear symptoms? Apparently not, according to Dr. Wilcox. Or his father.

"You aren't sick, Jake." Gerald had shrugged and looked at his son over a pair of reading glasses. "If anything, you're probably lonely. I don't have an explanation for the mermaid thing, but what you've described is a far cry from my symptoms."

After checking in yesterday, Jacob had secluded himself in his room. He didn't bother to change his clothes, didn't get up to eat, and answered any questions directed at him with grunts. Only after he heard a staff member murmuring that Jacob had suffered a heartbreak did he get up and take a shower. It was impossible to suffer a heartbreak when the object of your affections wasn't real. Logically, it should have been reassuring that no one believed he was sick. But no one had seen what he'd seen. No one had experienced what he'd experienced. If they had, no would question his concerns.

"...it could be hereditary..."

Those words had shaped so many of Jacob's choices over the last year. Dr. Wilcox could throw around words like hypochondriac all he liked, but the truth was that no one could tell Jacob for sure that he wasn't going to get sick. The fact that no one else found the uncertainty of his father's illness as terrifying as he did was mind-boggling.

That morning, Jacob had thrown himself into life at Mana'o. The routine of the place was mostly based around mealtimes. Other than eating at mandated hours and having to follow the rules regarding television and internet usage, Jacob was mostly left to his own devices. He wasn't even required to surrender his cell phone, which made the limited internet rule moot. Jacob used the center's computers once to update his freelance photography website with a notice that he was on hiatus. He hadn't had any active jobs before he'd left home, but it seemed irresponsible to let people think he was available for hire.

Jacob had always been good at entertaining himself, but something about being locked in a treatment facility made boredom much easier to come by. He could spend time with his father, but Gerald had a much more consistent schedule of treatments and testing. If Jacob couldn't spend all day with his father, the only thing left was messing around on his phone. That got old fast.

So, he could definitely blame boredom for the impulse that led him to actually answer his phone when it rang. "Hi, Mom."

"...Hello, dear." The surprise in her tone was clear. It jabbed at the guilt Jacob usually chose to ignore. He hadn't answered her calls in a long, long time.

A chill worked its way through his body, and Jacob adjusted his grip on the phone. Why had he answered? "What can I do for you?"

She cleared her throat, apparently also out of practice at the whole mother and son thing. "Well, I saw that your website was updated to show you were taking a break. I'm concerned."

An impulse to laugh bubbled up in his chest, but Jacob swallowed it. Insulting his mother wouldn't help matters. "I'm fine, Mom. So is Dad, by the way. You know, in case you cared." All right, maybe he couldn't help insulting her a little. He'd fed his bitterness toward her for too long to keep it quiet.

Meredith Pearson was in control of most situations, but her harsh exhale of breath didn't sound intentional. A tense silence held the line for a few heartbeats.

Meredith's tone was careful when she spoke. "That isn't fair, Jacob."

Jacob exhaled, his fingers moving to rub at the space between his eyebrows. "Sorry." The word was more instinct than intent.

"Are you?" His mother sighed. "We haven't spoken in so long, Jacob. I know you're angry, but you're going to have to listen to me someday."

A few weeks ago, Jacob might have hung up just to prove a point. Today he worried at his bottom lip with his teeth, considering her words.

"I get it, Mom. I know you, so I know all your whys. But—you don't think before you do stuff." He paused, his brow furrowing. "No, that's not right. You think too much, just all in your head, not your heart. I know the *why,* Mom. It's the *how* I can't understand."

It was the most he'd said to her in the last year. Any emails he'd answered were with perfunctory details about his photography and his father's treatments. He'd refused to have this conversation. The agitated thumping in his chest was just part of his reasoning.

Meredith was briefly quiet, like she was really thinking about his words. For the first time in a long time, Jacob wished he could see her. It was so much easier to read his mother when he could actually see her face. His father's emotions were always clear in his tone. Meredith was another animal entirely.

"Sorry," Jacob said again under his breath. Still habit, but a little genuine this time. He often felt furious when he thought of his mother, but he didn't actually want to hurt her.

Meredith laughed gently, the sound far more musical than her normal demeanor suggested she was capable of. "It's all right, Jacob. At least you got the words out. I imagine you've wanted to say them for a while."

Jacob grunted, but didn't deny it.

"You told me once that we didn't understand each other," Meredith continued, "but I don't think you give yourself enough credit. You're absolutely right that I live in my head. It's served me well. Your father lives in his heart. Always has. It's why we're good together. You're a better balance than either of us though. You view the world with your heart, but you operate in it with your mind." Meredith chuckled a little, the sound softer than before.

"Huh." Jacob didn't like his mother's use of the present tense when she talked about her marriage. If she and Gerald were so good together, why had his father been hallucinating his mother not even two weeks ago? That episode had been heartbreaking, but it probably wasn't his place to bring it up. And this didn't seem like the time to mention it.

Meredith cleared her throat. "So, why the hiatus from your photography?"

Jacob suppressed a snort. Of course she wouldn't let it go. He gnawed on his lip again, releasing it before he could break the skin. "I, well, I'm…" He bowed his head, taking a deep breath. "I'm showing symptoms, Mom." Bitter tears welled up in his eyes, and he blinked them back rapidly.

"You aren't," she snapped. Old frustrations reared in her tone. "We've been over this, Jacob. Your father's illness is his own."

"And yet I spent a week falling in love with a mermaid," Jacob spat out through gritted teeth. His fingers clenched around the phone. "I don't care how many tests told you I'm probably not sick, Mom. These kind of symptoms don't lie." His vision was still blurry. He cursed under his breath, rubbing at his eyes.

The line was silent, save for some heavy breathing from them both. He must have actually shocked her.

"You're actually hallucinating?" Meredith finally asked.

Jacob took a deep, shaky breath. "Yeah, Mom. It was so vivid I fully believed it. As soon as I was out of it, I drove straight to Mana'o."

Well, more or less. He'd sat around for a week and a half waiting for it to come back first, but he wasn't going to tell her that. If the ache that kept him up nights was any indication, his heart hadn't yet figured out what his head knew. None of it was real.

"You're with your father?" Meredith sounded surprised.

"Yeah. His doctor is going to work with me to figure out a

treatment plan, all that good stuff." At least, he would once Jacob convinced him he actually had his father's illness.

"All right," Meredith murmured, maybe more to herself than him. "All right," she said again, "thank you for telling me. Please, keep me apprised. Can I call you again?"

Jacob rubbed his eyes. His face was probably blotchy. "Yeah, Mom. You can always call me, even when I don't answer."

There was a pause, but he was almost sure his mother was smiling. "All right, dear. I love you. Promise."

He was saved from having to decide how to answer when his mother ended the call.

Chapter Twenty-Two

❀

Day 17

Sevencea awoke with a swell of hope, which came crashing down in disappointment. She was still alone. The sun streaming through the windows had woken her. A quick glance around the room confirmed that Jacob hadn't come home. Sevencea rolled off the couch with a groan and made her way to Jacob's room to find something to wear.

The footwear she found didn't fit, but the Y-shaped strap kept the floppy black shoes in place, so they would do. She threw a black and gray checkered shirt on over her bodice, relaxing under the feel of the soft fabric. She ducked her head and took a deep breath. It smelled like Jacob—earthy with a hint of sea spray. Taking another look around, she picked up a bag from the floor. Sevencea selected a few more of Jacob's shirts and placed them in the bag. There was no way to know when she'd be back here.

"It's just a new adventure," Sevencea reasoned with herself. She walked back to the main room and gave the front door a speculative once-over. She didn't know where to go, let alone how to track one human on an island filled with them, but she could figure it out. Sevencea was her father's daughter. He'd raised her to be resourceful, not to mention determined.

Her stomach growled. Sevencea nearly dropped the bag. Her eyes went wide, and she stared at her middle. She knew what hunger felt like, but the rumble of her stomach had never sounded like that before! Had it merely sounded different underwater? Sevencea shook her head and went into the room she'd assumed was for making food. She wasn't entirely sure what human food looked like, but surely she could find something edible. She opened the door of the tallest machine. The inside was cold, but empty shelves greeted her. If it was meant to store food, Jacob must have cleared it out.

Her heart seized. All food went bad over time, right? If Jacob intended to be gone for a long time, it would make sense for him to have cleared his home of perishable things. Sevencea tightened her grip on the machine's door and closed her eyes, then relaxed her hand and allowed the door to fall closed. He wasn't returning.

She needed to leave Jacob's home and go searching for him. That desire grew with each passing moment. Sevencea turned on her heel, examining the other possible storage options for food. Finally, she found an unopened bag on a shelf that had a picture of seaweed on the label. When she opened it, she discovered it was full of dried seaweed.

"New and familiar," Sevencea murmured. "How apt."

Slowly, she placed one of the dried pieces in her mouth, bit down, and tilted her head. It was an odd texture, but at least a flavor she recognized. Until she knew what anything else was, this was probably her best bet.

Once she'd devoured the contents of the bag, she folded the

crinkly packaging and set it on the counter. It was likely disposable, but where Jacob disposed of his waste wasn't clear. This would have to do for now.

"All right, fed and packed. What else do I need?" Sevencea rolled her eyes at herself for continuing to speak out loud. Perhaps it was a consequence of how lonely her heart felt.

Sevencea picked up her packed bag, and her eyes fell on Jacob's camera bag. She pulled it off the peg by the door and slung the strap around her neck. Her own underwater camera was nestled within her bag of supplies.

"This is an island. How far could he have gone?" Sevencea asked the window. She caught a glimpse of her reflection in the glass. Her hair looked matted, and her bodice and skirt were rumpled from sleep. She turned back into the house and moved toward the room for relieving oneself. She wasn't going on an adventure in the human world until she felt a little more human herself.

While she didn't know what human explorers looked like, Sevencea felt like she was doing a pretty good imitation. She'd discovered a string while trying to tame her hair and used it to secure her curls over her right shoulder. Hopefully it was enough to keep it from getting too unruly. Her hair had never been fully dry before, and the wavy mass was becoming a bit of a nuisance.

Traveling away from Jacob's home was easy—until Sevencea discovered the massive gray snake with the yellow lines down the center. She rested her bag on her hip and studied the hard, gray pathway. She'd been hoping for some kind of guidance as to what direction Jacob had gone. This gave her nothing.

"Well," she mused, looking from side to side, "what direction should I choose?" Picking the wrong way would be a massive waste of time. And her time on land was limited.

With a heavy sigh, Sevencea turned left and began to walk. "At least I get to test the new legs." Who cared if there was no one around to hear her? For the first time, she was truly on her own. If she needed the encouragement of her own voice to keep her going, that was her own business.

"So," she continued, "I'm going to find people who can help me make a plan. This is a big island. If someone can help me figure out the lay of things, then maybe I can find Jacob."

Sevencea nodded, feeling more resolved and less adrift. Actually forming that plan was a more daunting task. She'd ignore it for now.

A low roar sounded behind her, growing steadily louder each second. Sevencea's heart seized and she lurched away from the sound. A large blue contraption came hurtling into view.

A car. Sevencea took a deep breath. She knew about cars, of course, but knowing they existed was completely different from being nearly flattened by one. A belated honk sounded, like it was chastising her for being in its way.

"Note to self," Sevencea muttered, "do not walk on the gray paths." With a shudder, she shifted further onto the side of what she now realized was the road. Seeing a road from the water was very different from walking on one. Well, at least she'd already learned something. She was *not* a fan of cars. At least, not the noises they made. Maybe if Sevencea stayed out of their territory, they wouldn't try and crush her again. A small red car missing its top sped down the road going the other way. Sevencea scowled at it, but the driver and passenger didn't seem to notice.

She walked in peace for the next few minutes before another car approached. Unlike the others, this one slowed down. It was driven by a young man, probably about the same age as Jacob, in a very small and sleek-looking car.

"You need a ride, *wahine*?" he asked. His skin was a rich, dark tan, and his teeth glinted when he smiled.

"No thank you," Sevencea replied, with as much force as she could muster while still sounding polite. Even if she was interested in experiencing a car, it seemed unwise to accept a ride from any young man who looked like he wanted to eat her.

The man rolled his eyes and gestured for her to come closer. "I don't bite. Get in!"

Sevencea took a few steps back. How quickly could she run in her borrowed shoes if the need arose? The aggressive look on the man's face indicated it might be a skill she needed to practice sooner rather than later.

A larger vehicle pulled up behind the man. It was gold, with two doors on either side and another door on the back. The gold car began to honk—a long, loud noise, far more aggressive than the car she'd had honk at her.

The man turned, flashed a scowl at the honking vehicle, then pulled back onto the road and tore off, his tires making an awful screeching noise.

The honking stopped, and the window of the gold vehicle rolled down to reveal a woman. Some giggling, like the sounds of young children, came from behind her, but Sevencea couldn't see anyone else through the darkened windows.

The woman leaned across the empty seat next to her to look out the window. "Oh my goodness, miss, are you okay? I didn't mean to startle you, but you looked so freaked out, and I didn't want that man to do anything…" She trailed off with a grimace. "I'm sorry, was that all right? Did you know him? I was just trying to help."

A smile formed on Sevencea's lips and she held up her hand. This was a human she liked. That last man … not so much. She laughed softly. "Please, don't apologize. I was walking, and he pulled up and was kind of intense. I didn't know what to do, so your rescue definitely saved me!"

Maybe if she'd been human for more than a day, she could've handled it. But Sevencea was still a stranger in a strange land. She was more than willing to take any help she could get.

The woman relaxed, a warm smile replacing her look of concern. "Oh, that's good. I normally wouldn't do something like that, but you really did look scared. I'm sorry, I keep babbling. Do you need a ride?"

Sevencea gave the woman a quick once-over. She was tan, like the aggressive man had been. Her hair was blonde, but not nearly as light as Sevencea's, and it looked darker at the roots. More importantly, she seemed friendly, and the noise level definitely implied children in the car. If she was going to ride with anyone, this seemed like the safest bet.

Plus, she'd been walking long enough to realize that civilization was not close by. Her feet were beginning to protest so much use. Was that normal? Maybe she just didn't have enough practice. "Only if it's no trouble," she finally said.

"Not at all," the woman assured her. "You seem a little lost, and I'm not in the habit of letting people wander the island helplessly." She hit a button on her vehicle, then leaned across the seat again and pushed the door open. "Climb in. I'm Caroline, by the way."

Gripping the door for leverage, the mermaid stepped into a

vehicle for the first time. She glanced around, taking in the new environment. Did all cars have so many buttons? And the wheel in front of Caroline, was that similar to a ship's wheel, or did it serve another function? There was no way to ask without making things more complicated, so instead she smiled at Caroline. "Sevencea," she offered. She glanced behind her and waved at the three children in the back. They were all staring. "Hello, there!"

"Are you a princess?" The little girl asked, her eyes wide. She had darker skin than her mother, and a large body of curly hair held in place with a bright pink headband.

Sevencea smiled, feeling her cheeks flush. "I'm afraid not." The mermaid leaned closer and asked in a conspiratorial whisper, "Are you?"

The little girl lit up and ducked her head. "Nah," she murmured. She snuck a glance up at Sevencea and smiled.

Two young boys sat in the back, who looked so identical they must have been twins. They were younger than the girl, little more than babes, but they stared at Sevencea with the same fascination as their sister.

Caroline pulled back onto the road and the car slowly accelerated again. She glanced sideways at her new passenger. "So, are you from around here?"

"Nearby," Sevencea evaded. She didn't want to lie, but she was pretty sure the truth would be difficult to swallow. "I'm not from this island though, so I don't really know my way around."

"That would explain why you were hiking on the side of route eleven," Caroline said wryly. "Parts of this highway are really busy, but it depends on the time of day. We're only out and about because Lily has a doctor's appointment." She glanced up at the mirror and smiled fondly at her daughter.

"Where do you live?" Sevencea asked, her curiosity piqued.

Caroline jerked her thumb over her shoulder. "Back that way. My husband works at the reserve." She waved her hand in the general direction of an expansive area of greenery just visible from the road. "We live with him in housing near his office, but most of what we need is in Kailua-Kona, which is where we're headed now. Is that where you need to go?"

Sevencea shrugged. "It's as good a place to start as any."

Caroline's eyebrows rose. "Start what?"

"I'm looking for someone," Sevencea explained. She liked Caroline too much to try and come up with a false story. "I went to his house, but he had left. I think he gave up waiting on me, but I did come. I need to find him so I can tell him that I didn't abandon him." Was that enough detail? Did it even make sense? Sevencea glanced over at Caroline. Something in her face suggested that Caroline understood just fine.

"Paul—that's my husband—and I had a fight once," Caroline said. Her voice carried a tone of nostalgia. "He kept having to leave for work trainings, and I was trying to explain that I didn't want to be without him anymore. I didn't say it right. He thought I was trying to say that I was done dealing with his absences and with him." She shot a sad smile at Sevencea.

Sevencea let out a soft gasp. "That's awful! What happened?"

"He stormed out and headed for the airport to catch his flight." Caroline rubbed the edge of the wheel with her thumb, then added, "His training was in California, not here on the island, or it wouldn't have been so bad. Anyway, I raced after him, but my car was almost out of gas, and by the time I'd filled the tank and made it to the airport, he was already halfway through security." She chuckled and shook her head.

Sevencea only understood parts of what she was being told, but she could guess the general meaning. "What did you do?"

Caroline snorted. "I yelled at him across a huge line of people, telling him I loved him, that he was stupid to believe for a second that I didn't, and that I'd meant I wanted to come with him, not for him to leave me behind forever."

"Wow," Sevencea breathed. Just imagining that kind of a declaration, in front of dozens of people no less, made her stomach lurch and her heart race in tandem. "What did he do?"

"He abandoned his luggage with a very twitchy TSA guard, jumped over two barriers, and immediately got down on one knee to propose. He'd been seconds away from taking the ring out of his pocket to put it in the little tray so he could go through the metal detectors!" Caroline laughed and shook her head. "The whole security line cheered for us. They let Paul get right back in line once we'd had a moment to say goodbye. It was wonderful."

Sevencea had no idea what a TSA guard was, or the nature of the ritual Caroline was describing, but she understood the implications. "That sounds amazingly romantic."

"My point," Caroline continued, "is that there's always a chance to fix something that's been messed up. Sometimes it doesn't work, and sometimes it takes a lot of effort, but sometimes it's as easy as trying. If you really want to find this guy, then go get him!"

"Thank you, Caroline." Sevencea offered a warm smile. "I hope it goes as well for me as it did for you."

Caroline shot Sevencea a speculative glance and made a thoughtful noise. "You know, I might know someone who can help you out. Do you have a place to stay, or a job? Or did you just show up on the island with a bag and a quest?" Her lips twitched into a smile.

"I think I'm quest driven," Sevencea admitted. Caroline's eyebrows climbed again, and Sevencea ducked her head.

"In that case, I'm going to drop you off at The Makai," Caroline announced.

Sevencea shrugged. "Okay."

Caroline huffed a laugh. "Let me put it this way: The Makai is a place that helps visitors." She glanced back at her daughter who sat quietly petting the hair on a doll. "You holding tight back there, Lily?"

"Yes, Mommy." The little girl gave a shy smile. Her eyes darted to Sevencea, who smiled back. The twin baby boys appeared to have fallen asleep.

"You're being very patient, sweetheart." Caroline's eyes flicked between the road and the mirror. "I'm very proud of you, okay?"

"Thank you, Mommy." Lily ducked her head again, barely hiding her wide smile.

Sevencea faced the front of the car again, unable to hide her own smile. "She's precious."

"The most precious of gifts," Caroline agreed. Her eyes went once more to the mirror.

An ache gripped Sevencea's heart. She remembered that look on her own mother's face. It was beautiful. Wonderful. And she missed it more than she could put into words.

Chapter Twenty-Three

❀

D r. Wilcox sat in his office chair, watching Jacob.

Jacob watched him back.

They'd met a few times since Jacob had checked himself in, and both of them viewed the meetings very differently.

Jacob considered this his chance to convince Dr. Wilcox that he was actually experiencing the symptoms of his father's illness. This was his best hope at getting help.

Dr. Wilcox seemed to think this was the time to convince Jacob of the perils of not keeping a regular social life.

In the short time Jacob had been at Mana'o, they'd already fallen into a pattern of beginning their sessions in silence, watching each other.

Them meeting at all was a little unique. Dr. Wilcox, while trained to conduct therapy sessions, was not a therapist. Dr. Wilcox carried enough specialties related to the brain that Jacob wasn't sure what kind of doctor he technically was. Still, he wasn't a therapist. He just knew Jacob better than anyone else in the building, other than Gerald. It's why they had their deal. The deal that Dr. Wilcox wasn't treating as seriously as Jacob wanted him to.

"You keep acting like there could be a ton of reasons I might hallucinate. Does that seriously happen to people? They just invent entire relationships and there isn't an actual disease behind it?" Jacob finally asked, not bothering to conceal his skepticism. He rested his head in his hand, his elbow propped on the arm of his chair.

"That depends on what you mean," Dr. Wilcox replied. He fiddled with a pen on his desk, tapping it at odd intervals. "Do people hallucinate for no reason? Generally, no. Do people hallucinate for reasons other than degenerative brain diseases? Reasons that are completely non-harmful? Yes, Jacob. Far more often, in fact."

Jacob scowled at him. "My hallucination wasn't an acid trip, and I'm genetically at risk. Why aren't you taking this more seriously?"

"You know the answer to that," Dr. Wilcox chided gently. The man's slicked back hair was less well-behaved than normal. A stray piece curled up near the crown of his head.

Jacob's eyes drifted to the misplaced hair, taking a little satisfaction from the chink in Dr. Wilcox's otherwise well-put-together manner. "Because you don't believe me. You think I'm crazy. Just, not the right kind of crazy."

Dr. Wilcox shook his head. "You know we don't use that word here, Jacob. It's disrespectful." His lips twisted into a frown that was more disappointed than angry.

Jacob sighed heavily and waved a hand. "Sorry, but you know what I mean, Dr. Wilcox." He gnawed on his lip, resisting the temptation to bite down. He'd met his father's doctor a year ago. They knew each other pretty well by now, for men with only one major thing in common. Dr. Wilcox had never called Jacob "Mr. Pearson," unlike the rest of the staff. The doctor knew a lot about Jacob, knew what it meant to him to be Gerald's son. Jacob couldn't quite bring himself to address Dr. Wilcox by anything but his title, but if he asked, he was pretty sure he could get away with a first name basis. Their relationship, and the fact that it wasn't enough for Dr. Wilcox to just believe him, was what kept Jacob's stomach in knots.

"I do know what you mean." Dr. Wilcox leaned over his desk, his gaze intent on Jacob. "I don't think your father's illness is hereditary, Jacob. I've told you this many times. The fact that I can't prove it definitively is the only reason we keep having this conversation. What you've described to me sounds like a vivid daydream, not a hallucination. Or, a sensory disturbance, as they can be called. I don't think you're losing your faculties, developing an illness, or going senile before you're legal to drink. Jacob, I think you're lonely."

It wasn't the first time he'd said it, or even the second, but the words still made Jacob flinch.

"You didn't answer my question though," Jacob pointed out. "Is that even a thing that happens? People imagining entire romantic encounters with mythical creatures? Because they're *lonely*?" He practically hissed the last word, hating how it felt.

"You act like daydreaming isn't a totally normal phenomenon." Dr. Wilcox chuckled. "Jacob, lots of people invent things in their minds. Sometimes those scenarios and characters never leave their dreams. Sometimes, they write books and make movies."

"So, you're saying I'm just really creative?" Jacob injected as much derision into the question as possible. He didn't like the sympathetic expression Dr. Wilcox sometimes had when he looked at him. That was the hazard of trying to get therapy from someone who already knew you. If Dr. Wilcox thought he was actually sick he would've assigned his case to someone else. It was the professional thing to do. This evidence that Dr. Wilcox didn't believe him should have rankled, but Jacob didn't care. He was too relieved to not have to deal with a stranger.

Dr. Wilcox leaned back in his chair, studying Jacob's expression. "Jacob, have you ever heard the word hyperphantasia?"

Jacob blinked.

The doctor chuckled. "I suspected not. It's a word for people with, to stick to simple terms, overactive imaginations. Those who can create extreme, visually intense, mental images."

Jacob narrowed his eyes. "That doesn't sound like a thing."

"It is absolutely a thing," Dr. Wilcox countered. "It's one of those instances where, as the world has become more and more connected, and more and more research is being done, we've discovered that not everyone visualizes in the same way. Some, like those with hyperphantasia, are good at visualization to a dramatic degree. Others, who have what we call aphantasia, can't visualize anything at all."

"Huh." Jacob mulled over that concept. Was there an explanation for his experience other than his father's illness? Something that could actually be diagnosed? That was the biggest hurdle with his father's illness—they couldn't name it. They couldn't say for sure what it was or how it would morph over time. Or if it was hereditary. This thing had a name. It wasn't even technically an illness, the way Dr. Wilcox described it. He almost made it sound like a good thing.

"I know you dislike when I say this, Jacob, but in all my time knowing you, I've seen far more evidence that you're simply a hypochondriac than I've seen evidence of you developing your father's illness."

A furious scowl developed on Jacob's face.

Dr. Wilcox held up his hand. "Again, I know you dislike being labeled as such. Given your recent experience, I'm willing to look at other explanations with you. I may not believe you're dealing with Gerald's illness, but that doesn't preclude the possibility of something else going on. We'll find an answer, Jacob. You just need to recognize that it may not be the answer you expect, or perhaps want to hear."

Jacob gnawed at his lip. "I don't *want* to hear that I've got whatever Dad has. I don't. It's just ... One of the first things I ever knew about his illness was the chance that I could have it too. I need to know, Dr. Wilcox. Living with this uncertainty might be the thing that kills me." He sucked in a breath. That last part had escaped before he could think better of it.

Dr. Wilcox's expression softened. "I understand. But Jacob, you may not ever know for sure whether you're at risk of developing Gerald's illness. I know it's awful to not know, but I can't promise we'll ever be certain. And I don't believe you should allow that uncertainty to dominate your life."

Too late, Jacob thought, but he merely nodded and offered Dr. Wilcox a small smile. "Well, maybe there's another explanation." He tried to sound hopeful, but he wasn't sure if it worked.

"We're almost out of time for today, but I can get a test together for our next meeting." Dr. Wilcox stood, adjusting his shirt.

Jacob's head snapped up. "You can test for this thing? For hyperphantasia?" Something fluttered in his chest. If it was the hope he'd been searching for a second ago, he was going to put it away and not look at it until after the test. He didn't actually want to hope yet, not consciously.

Dr. Wilcox waved his hand. "Sort of. It's not like getting a diagnosis, Jacob. Hyperphantasia isn't a bad thing. It's just a name for a phenomenon—a state of reality for part of the population. If you have it, then what's happening to you is likely a combination of your self-imposed isolation and a lack of diversions available to your mind."

"Still. You can test for it." Jacob stood as well, rubbing his hands against his pants.

"Yes. We can test for it."

Jacob exhaled, then nodded once. "Good."

Chapter Twenty-Four

❀

The Makai turned out to be a narrow, three-story building with a roof covered in straw. Sevencea stared at the odd structure in utter confusion.

"It's not actually thatched." Caroline leaned out her car window. Sevencea now knew the vehicle was called a minivan, thanks to Caroline's patient explanation. The young mother gestured to the straw. "There's a real roof under there, but a previous owner thought the thatching would make it look more island-y. Heaven only knows what that man thought he was doing. Maggie Iona owns it now, and she's done a good job cleaning up after the guy. I'm sorry I can't stay. Just go inside and tell Maggie that Caroline sent you to her for help." Caroline offered an encouraging smile, then rolled up her window and turned her vehicle back toward the road.

Sevencea gave the building another once-over, her lips pursed. "I'm in over my head." She sighed heavily. The signs seemed to indicate that the building was a place for people to stay, but that was just a guess. So much about humanity was turning out to be new and strange. It was a wonder she hadn't scared Caroline off with her ignorance.

The front door opened and a young man, definitely younger than Sevencea, stuck his head out. "Maggie says to come inside or leave, but you can't just stand in the middle of the parking lot. It's weird." He flushed bright red and pulled his head back inside.

Sevencea laughed out loud. Maybe everything would be fine. She might not know humans all that well, but straightforward and no-nonsense she could handle. Steeling herself for the inevitable onslaught of stuff she didn't understand, Sevencea walked up the front steps and opened the door.

The interior was warm and smelled floral, which drew away some of Sevencea's tension. The walls were wood-paneled, and a gigantic pink hibiscus rug covered the floor. Caroline had pointed out the same flower earlier, on a sign when they reached town. It was beautiful, and Sevencea stared at it, awed by its sheer size.

"Was that Caroline I saw dropping you off?" a deep female voice spoke. Sevencea's head snapped up. The speaker sat behind a counter with a few decorative bowls on it, reclined in a position that gave her a clear view out the windows. She wore a loose orange top and blue pants. For some reason her chair was a little taller than the counter. It didn't seem practical, which distracted Sevencea enough that she answered the question a beat late.

"Yes, I met her on the road. She thought you could help me. Assuming you're Maggie, that is." Sevencea paused. She didn't really know what else to say.

The older woman nodded, blatantly looking Sevencea up and down. Her deep brown eyes were piercing, like they saw more than Sevencea intended. Maggie's hair was black, long, and unbound, with a little bit of a wave to it. A streak on either side had gone gray, and it accentuated the sharpness in her eyes and the strength in her square jaw. Her skin was darker than Caroline's, in a way that suggested she spent a lot of time outside.

"Can I get you something to drink, ma'am?" The youth from before stood to Sevencea's left, half-poised to walk to a drink cart in the corner. He trembled a little, his eyes darting around the room, but never making eye contact.

"Water would be nice, thank you." Sevencea swallowed. Her throat was dry. Another new sensation!

"What did Caroline think I could help you with?" Maggie prompted, ignoring the boy. Her stare shifted to the camera bag at Sevencea's hip, lingered for a moment, then moved back to Sevencea's face.

Sevencea shrugged. "I'm not completely sure, to be honest. I'm looking for someone, and she seemed to think you were the person to talk to."

"Your water, ma'am." The youth, who was more bones than boy, handed her a plastic cup, then scuttled out of the room.

Maggie watched him go and rolled her eyes. "I swear, Jim's a sweet kid, but he's terrified of his own shadow, never mind a pretty girl. No matter. He's only seventeen. He's a hard worker, which is all I care about." She turned back to Sevencea. "So, Caroline thinks I'm a bloodhound now?"

Sevencea blinked. What was a bloodhound? Something in her face must have shown her confusion, because Maggie's eyebrows rose a little and her eyes took on a curious gleam.

"You're a stranger in a strange land, aren't you." It wasn't a question, either in tone or expression.

"Not from the island, no," Sevencea agreed, hoping to avoid specifics. "The man I'm looking for though is from here. Or, he at least lives here."

Maggie leaned forward in her chair, clasping her hands together and jutting her index fingers out at Sevencea. "So, you met a man, lost him, and need help finding him? *Kama Lei*, that's what personal ads are for." She waved a hand toward a stack of papers covered in black text.

Sevencea sighed, shifting her weight back and forth. This wasn't going well. Caroline had been so sweet though, and so sure that Maggie could help.

"The man I'm looking for, we haven't known each other long. I was away for a while unexpectedly, and when I came back he was gone. I don't know the island at all, and I don't know where he went, but I think he's under the impression I abandoned him." She sighed, her hand coming up to fidget with her pearls. "I don't know anyone, I have no currency, and no clue where to start. I need help, but I couldn't even tell you what kind of help." Sevencea threw her hands up and took a deep breath, blinking to rid her eyes of the moisture they'd begun accumulating.

A slow smile graced Maggie's face for the first time since Sevencea had walked in. The older woman sat up and folded her arms, nodding slowly. "I might not be a master of hunting down missing men, but helping lost souls is something I've done a time or two."

Pushing herself out of her chair, Maggie came around the corner and stood in front of Sevencea. She was just barely shorter than the mermaid, but her presence dominated the room by no small margin. "Let's get you settled."

Sevencea studied Maggie as the older woman walked her around the building, giving her an informal tour. If she'd had any expectations when Caroline dropped her off, Maggie would have defied them all. Sevencea's initial impression of her had been that she was a quiet, intense type. Intense was right, quiet less so. Maggie could dominate a conversation if she was passionate about the subject. When Sevencea asked about the building's history, Maggie's expression let her know she was in for an earful.

"The old owner was an idiot," Maggie declared. "He decided to 'Hawaii' up the place for tourists. It's a lovely old building, but he made it the tourist trap from hell! Trust me, if I could get rid of that stupid roof, I would." She muttered something indecipherable under her breath, probably a profanity. In the brief time she'd spent with Maggie, Sevencea had learned many new words.

"Moron's the one who decided to call this place 'The Makai,'" Maggie fumed, coming to a stop to emphasize how irritated that made her. "That's not how language works!"

"I'm confused," Sevencea admitted.

Maggie shot her an annoyed look. Sevencea offered an apologetic shrug.

Maggie exhaled and closed her eyes, then reopened them. "'Makai' is a Hawaiian word, but it's a word you use to describe something else, most of the time, and it's more of a phrase. Like, if I said this building is *makai*, I mean that it's by the sea, or toward the sea. Putting an English article in front of it just shows you don't understand Hawaiian." She huffed and waved her hand. "Not that it matters. I've tried fixing it, but there's too much marketing invested in the name. Even the locals call it 'The Makai' now."

"I'm sorry?" Maybe Sevencea couldn't handle straightforward and no-nonsense. "So what exactly is this place?"

Maggie shrugged. "It's a hotel that's been marketed as a bed and breakfast because, as I may have mentioned, the old owner was a moron. Like I said, my attempts to update the marketing have been less than successful."

Maggie conveyed most of the history of the building while showing Sevencea around, so when they returned to the lobby, Maggie became strictly business.

"How are you at cleaning?"

Sevencea hesitated. Presumably cleaning on land was a lot different than cleaning underwater. "I'm capable of learning quickly," she hedged.

Maggie pinned Sevencea to the wall with her eyes, then nodded. "Fine. That's good enough for me. If you're going to work in the building, I can't afford to pay you *and* let you stay here. You'll have to pick one."

"Somewhere to stay is my bigger priority, I think." Money would be helpful in tracking down Jacob, but somewhere safe to stay would be harder to come by. She could have stayed at Jacob's house, but it was too far from civilization to be helpful. Maggie seemed trustworthy. Sevencea would worry about money later.

"Fair enough." Maggie led Sevencea back to the counter where they'd started. "I'll introduce you to everyone. They're a helpful bunch. You already met Jim, who does a little bit of everything. Keisha is our housekeeper—you'll work with her the most. And then there's Frank, who runs the kitchen. He doesn't talk much. We all do our part to keep this ship afloat. You'll get the hang of it soon."

Sevencea bit the inside of her lip. How should she broach her concerns? Maggie was a force of nature, and she hadn't yet figured out how to navigate this particular storm. "I appreciate you helping me, but I still don't know how to start looking for Jacob."

Thankfully, Maggie didn't look insulted in the slightest. "Jacob what?" she prompted. She moved behind the counter and approached the silver machine perched on it.

What? Sevencea squinted at the older woman, her head tilted. The pearl she'd almost forgotten was there rolled a little, and she abruptly remembered her first meeting with Jacob. "Pearson," she blurted.

Maggie frowned, her brow furrowing as she tapped her fingernail against the edge of the silver machine. "It's not exactly a unique name." Her tone was apologetic. "Hawaii's not that big of an island though, population-wise at least, so I'll see what I can find. What else do you know about him? Where would he go?"

That was a harder question. Sevencea mentally dug through everything Jacob had ever told her about himself, searching for something helpful. "His father is sick." She gestured toward her head. "He lives somewhere on the island, at a special place for his mind."

Maggie arched an eyebrow, but didn't inquire further. "Last I checked we've got three different facilities for brain-related illnesses on the island. I think a couple are for dementia and Alzheimer's, but at least one is a mental health facility." She began pressing the buttons on the bottom half of her machine, then nodded at the top half. "Yeah, one care facility here in town, the mental health place is north of Waimea, and another care facility on the opposite side of the island, in Hilo."

Seeing the blank look on Sevencea's face, Maggie's expression softened. She turned the machine around so Sevencea could see the map she was looking at. "The good news is that it doesn't take longer than an hour and a half to go west to east or vice versa from here. The bad news is that your best bet will be taking a cab. Cab fare plus tips to all three facilities is going to be pretty spendy."

"I don't really know anything about money," Sevencea admitted. Merfolk mostly exchanged things or did favors for each other.

Some clans used a currency, but most didn't. The concept of money she understood, but actually earning and using it wasn't something she had any experience with.

"I figured," Maggie said wryly. "Don't worry about that. I'll try and find something you can do that'll generate more of an income. You could always sell that jewelry, if you're desperate." Maggie nodded to Sevencea's pearls. Sevencea hesitated, her fingers going to the strands around her neck. Maggie smirked, then shook her head and kept talking.

"You're welcome to stay here as long as you earn your keep. I might loan you some money to go shopping though." Maggie looked pointedly down at Sevencea's ill-fitting sandals. "You could use more of a wardrobe than that bag is capable of carrying, not to mention shoes that fit."

Sevencea nodded, offering a grateful smile. The pearls were a hand-me-down from her mother. If there was another way to pay for finding Jacob, she'd take it. There was so much she didn't know, but that didn't matter. She understood Maggie was offering her a significant gift. All she had to do was accept. "Thank you, Maggie."

Maggie scoffed and waved her off, smiling as she did so. "*A'ole pilikia.*" After a beat, she added, "I think the investment will pay off."

Chapter Twenty-Five

Day 18

I'm not very good company today, Jake," Gerald warned.

Jacob paused in the doorway and smirked. "It's all right, I'm used to it." He took a seat opposite his father, hiding his grin at Gerald's outraged expression.

"Impudent spawn," Gerald muttered. His eyes twinkled. "I mean it though, I had a rough night, so I'm not all here."

Jacob's eyebrows drew together. He leaned forward and the amusement left his expression. "What do you mean? What happened?"

Gerald sighed, running a hand through his hair and slouching back against his seat. "I couldn't remember something at dinner."

"Right." Jacob nodded. He'd been there for that part. "Weren't you trying to remember something you watched on TV last week?"

Gerald nodded slowly. He stared at the wall, not making eye contact with his son. "I think so. It's such a small thing, but I hate when I can't remember. I should be grateful that the important things aren't gone, but I hate feeling like small details don't matter because my brain just chews them up and spits them out."

Jacob listened with a sympathetic wince. If he'd understood Dr. Wilcox and some of the other specialists correctly, his father's memory issues weren't like some of the more common degenerative brain diseases. The memories weren't gone, they were just scattered, inaccessible. Gerald's mind would re-decide on an hour-by-hour basis what was important, and sometimes that meant small details just vanished. It sounded confusing, and Jacob didn't envy his father the frustration.

"I know what you're thinking," Gerald grunted. His gaze shifted to Jacob's face. "My memories aren't actually gone, they're just hiding from me, right?"

Jacob shrugged. That's exactly what he'd been thinking.

Gerald sighed heavily, rolled his eyes, then threw up his hands. "Well, what good is it having them if I can't get at them? They might as well be gone!"

Jacob scooted his chair a little closer and leaned forward again, resting his elbows on his knees. "This isn't exactly new for you, Dad. What was so bad about last night?"

"Well, after we said goodnight, I was still upset. Cranky, I guess you could say. Dr. Wilcox has warned me about this before, sometimes my emotions can trigger the ... well, you know."

"The hallucinations," Jacob finished.

Gerald shuddered. "Yeah. Or, what's that other phrase? The fancy-sounding one?"

Jacob fished back in his own memory, trying to remember the phrase Dr. Wilcox had used. "Sensory disturbances?"

Gerald snapped his fingers and nodded. "Yes, that. It makes me sound less..." he paused, his expression betraying reluctance.

"Dr. Wilcox isn't here, Dad. I won't tattle." Jacob chuckled a little.

"Crazy." Gerald winced. "I know I'm not supposed to use that word. Old habits die hard, I guess. I'm sick, not crazy. I get it. And you know I don't want to insult anyone else who lives here. It's just… how am I supposed to feel when my senses betray me and my memories play hide and seek?"

"I get it." Jacob ducked his head, blinking a few times to avoid his own emotions betraying him. While he'd sympathized with his father before, his own situation had given him an even greater ability to empathize.

Gerald stared at the wall, idly drumming his thumb against his knee. When he blinked, his gaze returned to Jacob. He cleared his throat. "Anyway, the reason I wanted that other term was because I had auditory disturbances last night, not visual ones. Made it hard to sleep."

Jacob looked up again, examining his father's expression. "Are you all right?" Auditory hallucinations were arguably more common than visual ones, so Jacob wasn't surprised, but he tended to focus more on what his father saw that wasn't there. Somehow that seemed more outside of the norm.

"Yeah." Gerald's response was sincere, and Jacob relaxed slightly. "I'm just tired, which is becoming the new normal." He waved his hand dismissively. "What did you do with the rest of your evening?"

Jacob bit his lip and ignored his father's question. "You don't have to bear it alone, Dad."

Gerald glanced up, narrowing his eyes. "What do you mean? Aren't we sharing and caring now?"

Jacob's lips twisted into wry smile. "You can tell me what you hear. What you see. You keep so much of it to yourself. You're not going to scare me off, and you don't have to protect me." He let out a heavy sigh and ran his hands through his hair. "You're not alone."

There was a long stretch of silence as Gerald looked at him, his expression unreadable. "Jake. All it took was the suggestion from your mother that my illness might be hereditary, and you put your whole life on hold. Imagine how I feel, knowing that I have the power to increase that fear so drastically? All I'd have to do is mention a symptom that's a little too similar to something you've experienced, or think you've experienced, and you'd assume you were doomed. Letting you dig into all the treatment information with the doc is one thing, but giving you ammunition to detonate your life? I'm not doing it, Jake. I'm not. My visual hallucinations are just ridiculous enough that I can usually play them off as funny. They aren't funny. I know they're not, but they're not something you could mistake yourself as having. At least, I didn't think they were. I still think there's another explanation for your mermaid. But the auditory hallucinations, those are much more … insidious, I guess. You might think you'd experienced them. You might think you were sick. And you aren't, Jake. You aren't."

Gerald stopped speaking, his chest moving a little too fast. He sucked in a deep breath, and closed his eyes for a brief second. He opened them again, focusing on Jacob.

Jacob felt numb. He wasn't sure what expression was on his face, but it felt like one of horror. There was an awful tightness in his chest. He struggled to pull his thoughts together. He'd known his father, really both of his parents, didn't agree with his concerns about his own health. He'd even been questioning his worries himself before he imagined a mermaid. But to know that his father had been weathering the storm of illness alone out of a fear that he might make Jacob's concerns worse?

"Dad." Jacob exhaled sharply, his hands twisting in his lap. He stretched mentally for the right words. "I'm so sorry."

Gerald raised an eyebrow. "What for?"

Scoffing, Jacob dragged his hands down his face. How was he supposed to fix this? "I knew you thought my concerns were unfounded. Which is fine. I had no idea you were … I don't know, suffering in silence? I'm not made of glass, Dad. If you told me you hallucinated birdsong in the middle of the night or something, I'm not going to assume every time I hear birds that it's a symptom. I checked myself into Mana'o because I manufactured a romance with a mermaid. I'm cautious, not paranoid. Dr. Wilcox may think I'm a hypochondriac, but if that was true, I'd have found a reason to get myself here a long time ago."

He huffed and leaned back in his seat. Until he'd said it out loud, he hadn't realized how true it was. He didn't want to be sick. There were just too many unknowns with his father's illness for him to be anything other than cautious.

Gerald's expression softened. "I don't think you're crazy, Jake." His lips twitched at the corners.

Jacob rolled his eyes, folded his arms, and gave his father a pointed look. "Just not rational enough to hear the ugly truth about your symptoms?" He winced. That sounded harsher out loud that he'd meant.

Gerald chuckled. "Sometimes it is ugly." He shrugged. "It's not wrong to point that out, Jake. You aren't going to hurt my feelings."

"It's not exactly what I meant though," Jacob admitted. "I just don't want you to feel like you can't talk to me. For any reason! But especially not because you think sharing what's going on will make my subconscious convince me that I'm sick too. I'm a pretty logical person, Dad."

Gerald held up his hands. "You're right. I didn't mean to insult you. I do feel like my concern is legitimate though. It's not like you had a factual basis to be worried about your own health, but you put your whole life on hold anyway. It's like you were waiting to get sick."

Jacob opened his mouth to argue, then closed it. Is that what he'd done? He had his freelance photography career, but it was nothing like the business he'd hoped to build after leaving school. He had a home, but his bills were taken care of by his mother, a silent apology. He had friends too, even if they hadn't talked much since graduation. They still counted, didn't they?

Gerald nodded and inclined his head toward Jacob like he'd agreed out loud. "Maybe you didn't do it on purpose. But I wasn't going to be part of the reason you stopped living your life, Jake."

"I'm going to have to think about that." Jacob rubbed at his chin, the roughness scratching at his hand. He hadn't shaved since arriving at Mana'o.

"That's okay." Gerald looked him over, then sighed and admitted, "I was hallucinating voices. Mumbling, mostly inaudible voices. It's pretty common."

Grateful they were no longer discussing his own issues, Jacob leaned forward again. "I can see why that would keep you up. It's not people you know, or discernible speech though?"

"Almost never."

"Still," Jacob murmured, "I'm sure it's hard. Voices keeping you awake."

"I'm just tired," Gerald said. He was slumped enough in his chair that it was easy to believe he could get some much-needed rest in that position. "I told you I wouldn't be good company because, well, you know what I'm like when I'm tired." He offered an apologetic smile.

Jacob slowly grinned, some of the tension from their conversation draining out of him. He did know. He was the same way. And his mother was grouchy when she was tired. He came by it honestly.

The brief thought of his mother brought to mind something he hadn't yet shared with his father. He gnawed on his lip, then straightened. "I meant to tell you, I talked to Mom."

Gerald's eyebrows shot up. "On purpose?"

Jacob stuck his tongue in his cheek to avoid laughing and nodded. "Yeah. She called, I answered, I told her I was here."

"Wow." Gerald let out a low whistle as he mulled that over. "I mean, that's progress, for sure. I've been telling you that you need to talk to her for ... what, has it been a year already? I know why you've been upset, but it's not your battle, Jake. If anyone has a right to be angry, it's me, and I'm not."

Jacob scowled. "You might not be angry, but the day you hallucinated Mom? To me, you sounded heartbroken. I feel like I've got a right to be angry about that."

Gerald pursed his lips. "You know my ... sensory disturbances ... can be over the top. Whatever I really feel was probably amplified ten-fold. I love your mother, Jake." He held up his hand. His wedding band caught the light. "This means as much to me today as it did when I put it on. I appreciate your concern, but I do *not* appreciate your disrespect. If there's an issue to be had with Meredith regarding my situation, it's for me to have, not you."

Jacob didn't fully agree with that, but he wasn't in the habit of outright disobeying his father. "Yeah. Okay, Dad."

"Good." Gerald adjusted his position in his chair and fixed his eyes on Jacob. "So, did you berate your mother during this conversation, or did the two of you actually talk?"

"We talked," Jacob admitted. "I may not have been one hundred percent respectful, sorry, but I wasn't a total—"

"Language!"

"I didn't say anything!" Jacob protested. The unuttered profanity wilted on his tongue.

Gerald smirked. "I know you, Jake."

Jacob rolled his eyes, hiding a smile. "Honestly, it was probably the most civil conversation we've had, verbally at least, since she told me she'd sent you here."

"Well, good. I need to know you two have each other. Just in case." Gerald rubbed awkwardly at his neck.

Jacob narrowed his eyes and pinned his father with a glance. "You aren't dying, Dad."

"We're all dying, Jake. Someday something will take me out. Maybe it won't be my disease, but it'll be something. And statistically, men die younger than women. You'll probably have your mother longer. Just humor me and try to repair your relationship, all right? You shouldn't have detonated it so thoroughly in the first place."

Disappointment showed in Gerald's expression. Jacob could practically see his father remembering that fatal graduation ceremony, even though Gerald hadn't actually been there. He'd known for a long time that his parents were still talking regularly, no matter how bewildering he thought that was. How frequently they spoke and what the tone of the conversations were, he had no idea. Jacob assumed his father knew the details of the fight, but he'd never asked. If he did know, Gerald wasn't holding it against him. He only offered him a gentle push toward reconciliation from time to time.

Sometimes Jacob did feel guilty about that fight. Most of the emotions that had led up to it were still present, but he regretted the way he'd blown up at his mother. He just hadn't figured out how to fix it.

Gerald knew that, if the look on his face meant anything.

"She said she would call to check in, sometimes," Jacob said slowly. "I'll try to fix things with Mom, all right? I promise." If nothing else, this was shaping up to be a time when he needed the support.

Gerald watched his son closely for a moment, then nodded. "That's good, Jake."

Chapter Twenty-Six

First thing in the morning, Maggie began Sevencea's training. As it turned out, little of Sevencea's knowledge from life underwater translated to cleaning a building on land. But Sevencea *was* a quick learner. She honestly felt relieved that she hadn't been lying. Cleaning, while not something Sevencea could say she enjoyed, was not challenging.

Although, was it normal to be tired so quickly? Walking on legs had come easily to her. Walking up and down the stairs of The Makai while carrying cleaning supplies was exhausting.

Sevencea finally took a seat to catch her breath. Maggie watched her from the counter, eyes dancing with amusement and a smidge of sympathy.

"You're not technically an employee," Maggie pointed out. "Don't let me run you ragged. Take a break, then find Keisha when you're ready, and she'll let you know what she needs help with."

From what Sevencea had gleaned so far, The Makai had a small, motley crew of staff that worked together to do pretty much everything. Keisha was the full-time housekeeper, but the Makai was a deceptively large building. Sevencea had wondered how one woman managed to keep the entire thing spotless on her own.

"During the busy season we've got some part-timers that help out," Maggie had explained.

Apparently they hadn't quite reached the busy season. Other than Maggie and Keisha, the only other current employees were Frank, who ran the kitchen, and Jim, who ran for whatever Maggie told him to.

Sevencea eventually pulled herself to her feet and sought out Keisha. She'd only met her in passing so far. Actually, she'd most-ly heard Keisha, not seen her. The woman's dominant personality trait was being just as loud as Maggie. Maggie had starting the morning's instructions by showing Sevencea how the building's in-tercom worked, but she and Keisha both bellowed up and down the staircases to get people's attention.

Sevencea finally located Keisha on the second floor collecting trash and singing to herself. "Hello, Maggie told me to find you?" Sevencea greeting came out more as a question.

Keisha glanced up from her cart of supplies with a quick smile. "Oh, right! You can help with the bathrooms. There aren't many; it'll be quick." Even when she wasn't smiling, Keisha's whole face radiated joy. She was a lot younger than Maggie, and had much darker skin. She also had a more muscled physique that Sevencea assumed was a result of how much the woman seemed to run up and down the stairs. Keisha's warm caramel eyes set Sevencea at ease right away, and were perfectly framed by her deep laugh lines.

The more humans Sevencea met, the more amazed she was by how varied people were on land. Hair, skin, body shape, personal style—all of it could look so different. There was variety under the sea, of course, but not nearly as much within Sevencea's clan. And it wasn't like she'd gotten to explore much of the world yet.

As Sevencea learned the ins and outs of cleaning a bathroom, she also learned the hazards of cleaning while having a lot of hair. After the second time Keisha witnessed Sevencea trying to keep her hair from falling forward into the toilets she was trying to scrub, the older woman passed her a piece of patterned cloth. A similar piece tied up her own hair.

"Get it in a braid, a bun, or something, or it'll be in your face all day," Keisha instructed. Sevencea studied the older woman's hair. Her mound of black coils was secured on top of her head, spilling out like a fountain.

"Thank you," Sevencea said fervently. She wrestled with her tangled mass of hair, attempting to contain it twice before finally managing to tie it up out of the way.

Keisha glanced at Sevencea's handiwork and chuckled. "Well, it's not neat, but it'll work."

That ended up being a fairly accurate statement about most of Sevencea's first day on the job.

"How'd you get to be grown without knowing how to clean a bathroom?" Keisha stood over Sevencea with her hands on her hips, both eyebrows raised and lips twisted in an expression that might have been amusement.

"I'm learning now," Sevencea countered. She grunted and stood from the crouched position she'd been stuck in. "I'm doing all right so far, aren't I?"

"You're not awful." Keisha pursed her lips, evaluating the job Sevencea had managed so far. The older woman sighed and gestured for Sevencea to leave.

Maggie had apparently instructed Keisha to give Sevencea enough odd jobs to make her part-time. It was still a little bit of a mystery what her daily schedule was going to look like, but that was okay. Sevencea was grateful for the flexibility, especially since she wasn't sure exactly how to start looking for Jacob yet. It sounded like some days she might be needed for a few concentrated hours, and other days would consist of random tasks throughout the day. Everyone assured her she'd have plenty of time to learn all the new tasks she was being given. Everything about having this job was new and interesting, even cleaning the toilets. Although Sevencea was grateful there hadn't been many. The Makai only had a few guests at the moment, so the task hadn't taken long.

The best thing about working was the distraction. When she worked, Sevencea didn't have time to think about Jacob, and how she wasn't already out searching for him. The pinch in her chest felt an awful lot like guilt, but she pushed the feeling away. If she didn't work, she wouldn't have anywhere to stay. If she didn't have anywhere to stay, how was she supposed to find Jacob? Him leaving was her fault in the first place. If she hadn't left him, he wouldn't have left her.

Well, she still had some of the day left. Maybe she could start working on a plan to begin looking for him.

Since the bathrooms were done, Sevencea took a moment to stretch. She felt ready to take a break, but decided to track down Keisha first. Three stories was enough to lose a person in. Sevencea came around the stairway banister to the third level and spotted Keisha's mound of curls. The woman was down on the ground, using an attachment on the vacuum to get after something under one of the decorative tables in the hall.

Sevencea cupped her hands around her mouth to project her words over the racket of the vacuum. "What do you need me to do now?"

Keisha shrieked and sat bold upright, brandishing the vacuum wand like a sword. She let out a growl and relaxed at the sight of Sevencea, then smacked the vacuum's power switch.

The noise stopped, and Keisha laughed. "Go check and see if there's any work to be done in the kitchens. And never scare me like that again!"

Hiding her smile, Sevencea headed back down the stairs. The vacuum started up again. Sevencea jumped, her grip tightening on the banister to keep from stumbling. Lots of odd items made crazy sounds on land, but so far she was least fond of vacuums and cars.

The kitchen on the first floor was Frank's domain. He was a grizzled man that Sevencea hadn't heard speak yet, though so far she'd met him only briefly. He was older than Maggie by at least ten years and had mastered the art of pointing at things he wanted. Sevencea had no idea if he was silent by choice or not.

"Frank?" Sevencea ducked the long hanging strand of garlic in the kitchen doorway. The kitchen itself had very little decoration. The garlic was an anomaly in an otherwise pristine room. No one answered her call, which was unsurprising. She rounded the refrigerator and found Frank, bent over a mixing bowl full of batter. As soon as she spotted him, he thrust his right hand toward the sink, pointing at a pile of dishes.

Sevencea sighed, but followed the unspoken instruction. She didn't have much practice cleaning dishes, but she did want to be helpful. Starting in on a bowl with something yellow congealing in it, Sevencea eyed the back of Frank's head. What would she have to do to befriend the silent kitchen man? Her lips twitched as one of her siblings came to mind. The magic of mind reading would definitely be handy.

Frank glanced her way, observed her scrubbing, and gave a single nod of approval.

Well, it was a start.

There was something oddly comforting about working in silence. It was a little too easy for Sevencea's mind to wander. Still, the quiet of the kitchen was companionable, not awkward. Despite knowing almost nothing about him, Sevencea felt confident that she liked Frank. He reminded her, in a small way, of Jacob. Except Jacob talked, of course. Still, he was hardly a chatterbox. Jacob communicated so clearly without needing to speak. He said everything with his face. Frank was more stoic in his silence, but she couldn't help making the comparison.

Cleaning dishes was a very repetitive task, and Sevencea lost herself in it until suddenly the sink was empty. "I'm done, Frank," she announced, turning toward the man. He was still bent over whatever he'd been working on when she arrived. He waved a hand dismissively in her direction.

"You sure?"

Frank nodded.

She felt a soft twinge of disappointment. There was still work to do, but it was a shame she wouldn't be doing it in the pleasant quiet of the kitchen.

The hand wave became a little more insistent, then Frank pulled his hand back and refocused on his work.

A small grin crossed Sevencea's face. Yes, she was pretty sure she liked Frank.

Making her way out to the lobby, she spotted Jim standing in the middle of the room, looking lost. In the few times Sevencea had interacted with Jim, she'd figured out that the younger man's default state was just a little scatterbrained.

"You all right, Jim?"

"Nancy!" Jim jumped as he turned to face her.

Sevencea squeezed her eyes shut for a moment. At least he wasn't trembling in front of her like yesterday. One step at a time. "It's Sevencea, Jim. Are you all right?"

"I was going to look for you. Maggie said I could ask you to help me carry all the luggage upstairs?" His hazel eyes were wide, like he thought Maggie might have lied to him for some reason.

Sevencea peered around him. A pile of the new guests' baggage sat in the parking lot. She laughed "Of course! I'm not going to make you carry—" she paused, counting the mound of luggage in her head, "—twelve suitcases and four backpacks by yourself."

Jim almost wilted with relief. "Thank you, Celia!"

She rolled her eyes and didn't bother to correct him. She stepped outside and picked up a suitcase. What was Jacob like at Jim's age? Surely not as skittish around women? Sevencea hadn't met enough adolescent men to know if that was normal for the age, or if Jim was just special. It was fun trying to picture Jacob's features as a younger man. His hair was already a little long. Had it been longer when he was younger? It curled a little, and Sevencea liked the idea of a young Jacob with a bouncing head of curls. There must be pictures somewhere, but she'd have to find Jacob to ever see them.

"What did these people pack?" Jim gasped out from in front of her. He struggled with a larger bag. He glanced at Sevencea, saw her looking at him, and immediately flushed bright pink.

Sevencea suppressed her grin and chuckled quietly to herself. The bright color in the young man's cheeks reminded her of Jacob too, though Jim's blush was much more obvious. She missed seeing the way Jacob's cheeks grew rosy when they were close. It was fun to see how different humans could be, just within the small world of The Makai, but she missed *her* human. It felt wrong learning how to be human without him.

Chapter Twenty-Seven

❀

Day 19

I don't need anybody!" Jacob groaned. He knocked the book on the perils of loneliness off his nightstand. Another gift from Dr. Wilcox. They hadn't had their next session to test for hyperphantasia yet, and Jacob was getting antsy. He sighed. Dr. Wilcox had plenty of responsibilities at Mana'o, and technically Jacob was still not a real patient. Plus, their last session had only been two days ago.

The perception of time within the walls of Mana'o was really messing with Jacob's head. Objectively, he knew he'd come to the treatment facility just five days ago. Though he tried not to think about Sevencea, he knew he'd last seen her almost two weeks ago. Thirteen days, to be exact. And yet, since arriving at Mana'o, he could swear months had gone by. Nearly every day had contained its own emotional battle.

Jacob missed the quiet of home. Going to the beach every day, his camera in hand ... He craved the comfort and routine of his lonely life. Wait—lonely? He scowled. He wasn't lonely! Spending most of his time alone didn't mean he was lonely. It didn't.

Jacob gnawed on his lip, his eyebrows drawing together. This was just Dr. Wilcox getting under his skin. He'd lived alone for a year without incident, and he'd been fine.

Then again, he'd spent the four years before that surrounded by his classmates. Maybe he'd only been comfortable living alone because it was his first time ever doing it.

Jacob glanced down at the book Dr. Wilcox had gifted him. The cover stared back from the floor where it had landed. It looked a little like it was mocking him. He looked away with a sigh, pinching the bridge of his nose. The doctor was just trying to help. He could appreciate the gesture.

Loneliness though? Was that really all this came down to?

It sounded like an insult. It was possible to live alone and be perfectly happy, thank you very much. Really, it was just rude of everyone to assume he'd invented a mermaid purely out of loneliness. And the fact that his father agreed with Dr. Wilcox—that felt like a betrayal. But his father's concerns were all from a place of love. Jacob couldn't stay mad at his father for long.

So, he understood. That didn't mean he agreed. A couple books about loneliness in young adults and how to make friends lay scattered around his room, all from Dr. Wilcox. Jacob was *not* going to read them, no matter how petulant that made him look.

Jacob's phone buzzed, distracting him from his irritation. He answered it without looking at the caller ID. "Hello?"

"Oh! Hello, dear. I didn't expect you to answer so quickly." Meredith's tone implied she'd questioned if he'd answer at all.

"I told you you could call," Jacob reminded her. Although, her surprise wasn't unwarranted. He hadn't promised to answer. He rubbed at the spot between his eyebrows and sat down in a chair with a huff.

Meredith paused. "Are you all right?"

"Just frustrated. Dr. Wilcox thinks I'm suffering from a combination of loneliness and an overactive imagination. I'm annoyed he isn't taking this seriously." Jacob spat out the issue before he could think better of it. Although, his mother was an outsider to all of this. Maybe she would be the one person to actually listen to him.

"Dr. Wilcox is an excellent doctor, Jacob. Why don't you give his theory a little credit?" Meredith sounded tentative, but a bit of her "mom voice" snuck in anyway.

Jacob opened his mouth to argue, then the first part of what she'd said hit him. "Wait, you talk to Dr. Wilcox?"

Meredith scoffed. "Really, dear? I know what you think of me, but just because I'm not on the island doesn't mean I'm not fully apprised on all aspects of your father's treatment. I talk to Dr. Wilcox regularly. I've stayed up to date on what's working and what isn't."

"Why?" The question slid out before Jacob could pull it back. He winced. He hadn't meant that the way it sounded. Or maybe he had. It was hard to tell anymore.

Meredith was quiet for a moment, then she let out a small sigh. "Jacob, I love your father with all of my heart. Just because I don't express it in the same ways you do doesn't mean it isn't true."

Tears pricked at Jacob's eyes. He blinked rapidly, fighting the impulse. "I know that, Mom."

"Do you." It wasn't a question, just a sad statement.

He rubbed at his eyes, now actively wiping away moisture. "I do. Look, I'm..." he paused, exhaling. Taking a deep breath, he forced the next words out before he could change his mind. "I'm sorry for what I said at graduation."

Meredith inhaled sharply. For a moment, the line was quiet. "Thank you. I'm sorry for how I told you. I was trying to be practical, not cruel."

Jacob could see the memory clearly. He wore his cap and gown, his boarding school career behind him. He stood in the reception area, looking for his parents. Only his mother was there. She'd flown in from Hawaii, after checking his father into Mana'o. He hadn't even known anything was wrong back then. In a room full of celebrating teenagers and their parents, his mother had let him know that his father had a degenerative brain disease, and would be living in a treatment facility while she continued to run their company.

Jacob hadn't handled it well. That's what he said so he didn't have to tell anyone he'd raged against his mother in a room full of people. He'd called her selfish, heartless, and several profanities that he shouldn't have used, let alone levied against his mother. In retrospect, the fact that she'd been willing to subsidize his move to Hawaii and help support him was far more than he deserved. But he'd never thanked her. He was too busy being angry. He'd only spoken to her in emails, arranging all the tests necessary to confirm he didn't carry any risk of inheriting his father's illness. They all showed he was healthy, but of course, no one knew for sure if the illness was hereditary. She'd been satisfied. He still wasn't.

He'd been quiet for too long, but Meredith hadn't said anything either. Clearing his throat, Jacob asked, "Why didn't you ground me for life?"

Meredith actually laughed out loud. "You were eighteen, Jacob. Did you think I was going to just lock you up while I worked? You were ready to live your life. If it wasn't going to have me in it, well, at least it would have your father. I didn't think it would be forever.

A year was a bit longer than I'd expected we'd be at odds, but…" He could picture her shrugging on the other end.

"I was…" Jacob mulled over a few choice words, but didn't feel comfortable saying any of them to his mother. "I was a real jerk," he settled on.

"That's one way to put it." Meredith chuckled. "Still, I understand. I won't sugarcoat it, Jacob, I was heartbroken, but I still understood why you were angry."

"Once I knew Dad wasn't angry at you, I should have let it go." Jacob sighed, running his fingers through his hair. "I felt like he should have been, and since he wasn't I had to be angry for him."

"Your father is a remarkably forgiving person," Meredith mused. "More than that, he understands me very well. I may not have done what was best for him, I'm not sure, but I did what seemed best for him in the moment. That's all I've ever been capable of doing."

"Yeah." Jacob nodded and gnawed on his lip. "I get it. He gets it. Although…"

"What?"

Jacob gritted his teeth, then let the words go. "There's something you should know. A couple weeks ago, Dr. Wilcox asked me to come in because Dad was having a really bad hallucination."

Meredith hummed. "Yes, Dr. Wilcox told me about it. He said your father was conversing with someone, and you helped bring him out of it. I understand it was worse than usual, but he's been all right since then. When I spoke to Gerald, he said it wasn't a big deal."

Jacob blinked, surprised she'd already talked to both of them about it. "Well, yeah. Except, Mom, Dad was hallucinating you."

Meredith didn't reply.

"He kept asking you why you didn't still love him," Jacob admitted, a little hesitantly. "He never talks about you like that, but he thought you were there and he was … Mom, I thought he was going to start sobbing. It was awful."

A small, choked noise was the only reply.

"I think he misses you, Mom. You call, sure, but you've never visited. I know you're busy, but he misses you." After a beat, Jacob screwed up his face and muttered, "*I* miss you."

A soft sound of pain came from the other end of the phone. "He doesn't call me Merry anymore," she murmured. The words sounded distant, like she didn't know she was saying them.

"He did when he was hallucinating," Jacob admitted. "You should come, Mom. For all of us."

There was another beat of silence.

"I'll try, Jacob." Meredith took a deep breath. "Thank you for telling me. For talking to me."

"We're all pretty messed up, huh?" Jacob grunted. He closed his eyes and leaned his head back against his chair.

Meredith chuckled a little. "Well, maybe this is how we fix that."

"See you soon?" Jacob cracked his eyes open.

There was another pause. "I'll do my best, dear."

Chapter Twenty-Eight

Sevencea came down the stairs to the lobby, ready to hear her assignments for the day. Maggie was waiting for her, standing by the front desk. Before Sevencea even stepped foot into the lobby, the older woman held out a few $10 bills. Sevencea accepted the money automatically and tried not to examine it too obviously. She only recognized it as currency because of how much time she'd spent on the computer since Maggie showed her how to use the device. She counted the bills quickly. Maggie had handed her thirty dollars. It was the most money she'd ever held, though that would be true of any amount.

"What's this?" Sevencea raised one eyebrow.

Maggie smirked. "A loan. You can pay me back later. I'm working on finding you a way to earn a little cash. In the meantime, you need to get yourself some extra clothes. Take the day and do some shopping at the mall. I'm sorry it's not more, but hopefully it'll be enough to give you a bit more flexibility." She cast a pointed eye at the outfit Sevencea had been attempting to mix up every day.

Clothing was not on the forefront of Sevencea's mind, but she knew better than to refuse a gift. "Thank you!" It didn't sound like enough gratitude, but Maggie got grouchy when you compliment-ed her too much. Of all the things she'd learned since getting on land, what she'd learned best was how to speak to Maggie.

Maggie shifted her weight and scoffed under her breath. "Yeah, yeah. I'm sending Jim to run errands on that side of town, so he'll drop you off. Call the lobby phone when you need a ride back. The customer service desk should be able to loan you a phone."

"Okay. I can do that."

Maggie had taught her how to use the phone early on, citing it as a safety skill. Maggie really didn't push Sevencea about her lack of knowledge. Sevencea would have been more curious about that if it wasn't working out in her favor.

"Oh!" Maggie snapped her fingers. "I forgot to tell you, I made a few calls for you. I reached out to all three of the facilities you think that man of yours might be at."

Sevencea's eyes widened. "You did?" Despite having just learned how to use the phone, the thought of calling the places Jacob might have gone hadn't occurred to her. It seemed like such an obvious first step.

"Don't get too excited." Maggie warned. "I figured no one would give out any information, which is exactly what happened. I only bothered because I'm a lot more intimidating than you are. If I got some information, it might have saved you time. Unfor-tunately, you're going to have to resort to visiting each location in person to play the distraught girlfriend."

Sevencea shot her an annoyed look, and Maggie smirked.

Going to each location was the extent of the plan Sevencea had come up with, but she hadn't been planning to "play" any sort of part.

"Thank you for trying." Sevencea paused and drew her eyebrows together. "And I can be intimidating!"

Maggie laughed out loud. "I'm sure you can, *Kama Lei*. But I put myself in that role for everyone I care about. You may be new here, but we're adopting you for as long as you need somewhere to be." A fond smile spread across her face.

Warmth bloomed in Sevencea's chest. She'd never expected to feel at home anywhere other than below the sea with her father and the familiarity of her clan around her. This was only her fourth day on land—a process she'd expected to be a great challenge without Jacob's help. And yet, she'd already found humans willing to welcome here and offer her a place. She smiled back at Maggie and felt a twinge in the corners of her eyes.

"Ready to go?"

Sevencea started. She hadn't heard Jim come up behind her. She blinked rapidly, chasing away any oncoming tears. "Oh! Jim, yes, thank you." Turning back to Maggie, she added, "Really, Maggie, thank you for this. For everything."

"Go on, get out of here." Maggie shooed them off, but didn't bother to hide her smile.

The mall was huge. Sevencea wandered around the main halls for almost half an hour before she actually got up the nerve to step inside a store. The first place she tried was small and brightly colored, but the article of clothing she picked up had too many zeros on the tag. She turned around and left, resuming her exploration of the mall.

One of the big halls opened into a large store with a big red star adorning the doorway. Intrigued, Sevencea wandered in. She came to a dead stop. So many rows of clothes! So many shirts, pants, skirts, dresses, and articles of clothing Sevencea didn't even have names for.

"*Aloha*! How are we doing today? Can I help you find anything?" A young woman with a name tag appeared at Sevencea's elbow, startling her out of her clothing-induced trance.

"I need shoes." Sevencea was certain of that one thing. Now that she had a better idea of how humans dressed, she knew wearing sandals meant for men wasn't a practical choice. "Maybe more clothes too. I don't have a lot of options at the moment." She glanced down. The skirt she'd come out of the water with was holding up well, but she'd only brought a few of Jacob's shirts and they were all too big. She *could* just wear her bodice by itself, but it was a little more revealing than everyone else's work clothes at The Makai. She was starting to question how long the process of finding Jacob would take. If it took too long, she was going to need a larger human wardrobe.

"Sure, sure." The girl nodded and spun on her heel. Her black hair fanned out around her as she evaluated the store. "Do you have a particular style in mind? Or a budget you'd like to stick to?"

"Oh." Being wise with the money she was gifted seemed like the most important factor. "I've only got thirty dollars," she blurted.

The girl's expression twisted with sympathy. "Oh, girl, come here." With a light grip on Sevencea's arm, she steered her away from the door and started whispering. "Look, I'm not supposed to say stuff like this because I work here, but if you want to get a good deal and not spend a lot, you really need to get yourself to Goodwill."

Seeing Sevencea's blank look, she added, "It's a store of stuff that's been used, so they have good clothing deals. You can get a lot more without busting your budget. The local one is like ten minutes from here, right up route nineteen."

Sevencea bit her bottom lip, considering. "How long would it take me to walk that?"

The girl winced. "An hour, maybe. You don't have a way to get there?" Her gaze roved over Sevencea, her eyebrows doing an odd dance as she took in different pieces of the puzzle Sevencea presented.

"The friend that dropped me off is already gone," Sevencea explained. "I'm okay to walk though, if you really think that's the better shopping option."

The girl sighed and rubbed at her forehead with her thumb. "All right, call me crazy, but I get off in about twenty minutes. I had the stocking shift this morning, so thankfully I don't have to stand around and look pretty all day!" She grinned and made a kissing noise. "Anyway, if you're cool to hang out for a bit, I'll drive you up there. I live that direction anyway."

Sevencea beamed at her. "That would be wonderful! I'm sorry, I don't even know your name."

The girl pointed to the small name tag affixed to her shirt. "Kasey."

"I'm Sevencea. You're very generous, Kasey."

Kasey waved her off. "Don't worry about it. I'm pretty sure you aren't an ax murderer, and it would be super unethical of me to talk you into wasting all your money on some useless top covered in sequins." She rolled her eyes and winked at Sevencea. "Just meet me here in twenty and we'll head to my car." With that, she strode back toward the center of the store.

Sevencea rocked back on her heels. Where should she wait? She quickly surveyed her surroundings and settled for a chair near one of the rooms where people were trying on clothing. Every so often a middle-aged man would walk past and give the occupied chair a disappointed look. Otherwise, she was left alone.

All the different people ebbing and flowing through the store fascinated her. If nothing else, she was becoming convinced that she needed a style upgrade to have any hope of blending in with humanity.

Twenty minutes went by a lot faster than Sevencea expected. She was surprised when Kasey walked up to her, sans name tag and wearing a different shirt. The girl looked different than anyone Sevencea had met so far. Her skin had a more rosy undertone, and her eyes were small but pronounced. Her eyebrows moved a lot when she talked, as did her hands.

"Entertaining yourself?" Kasey adjusted the purse slung over her shoulder and smirked at Sevencea.

"People interest me." Sevencea shrugged and stood to her feet. She followed Kasey out of the store. Kasey's car sat at the very back of the parking lot. It was the smallest car Sevencea had ever seen, and it was bright green, making it impossible to ignore.

"So," Kasey began as soon as they were both in the vehicle, "are you seriously trying to build a whole wardrobe with just thirty bucks?" She backed out and pulled toward the main road.

Sevencea shook her head. "Not exactly. I've got a few different tops and these sandals, but I took all of them out of a man's closet, so they don't exactly fit. I have one set of my own clothes, but I can't wear those every day." The world whizzed at a rate far exceeding either of the other times Sevencea had been in a vehicle. She didn't like it. How fast could a car go? How fast was a car supposed to go?

Kasey snorted and glanced into the mirror before moving

lanes. "What, did you steal clothes from your boyfriend because you didn't have any?"

"Sort of." Sevencea smiled at the idea of calling Jacob her boyfriend. It wasn't the merfolk term, but since she still had legs, the human term was fine. Maggie had used it this morning too. She was kind of starting to like it.

Kasey shot her an odd look and opened her mouth to comment, then closed it again. She shrugged and glanced over with a wry smile. "Well, whatever, at least you found me. We'll get you taken care of." She hit her turn signal, exited the main road, and turned onto a new street. Kasey waved toward the Goodwill. "There it is. Told you it wasn't far."

Sevencea looked up in surprise, then smiled at her new friend. "I really appreciate it."

Kasey pulled into the parking lot. She gave Sevencea an appraising look, then turned her car off. "Screw it, I'm coming with you. I don't have anywhere to be anyway."

"Why?" Sevencea's eyebrows flew up. She inclined her head a little to see Kasey's face better.

Kasey laughed. "Be honest. You have any idea how to shop for yourself?"

"Oh. Well, no." Sevencea shrugged and ducked her head.

Kasey rolled her eyes. "That's what I thought. You're super weird, but it's none of my business. I just want to make sure someone else doesn't take advantage of this whole Bambi thing you've got going on. C'mon, girl, let's go get you some clothes."

"I really do appreciate this," Sevencea said. They got out of the car and began walking toward the store.

"Don't worry about it, honestly. I love shopping! Let's see what kind of style makeover we can give you." Kasey grinned and picked up her pace, gesturing for Sevencea to follow.

Goodwill was much easier to navigate than the large store. Everything was organized. Clothing for women had its own section, and the types of clothing were separated out already, and clearly marked by sizes.

"Anything you know you like?" Kasey asked. She rushed a rack of shirts.

"Uh..." Sevencea didn't know how to answer that. What would Jacob like? She wished he was here, so she could ask him. What would he think she looked pretty in? Sevencea's face heated a little. She knew the answer to that. Jacob would find her pretty in anything.

"Thinking about the boyfriend you stole from?" Kasey leaned against the rack, watching Sevencea with a grin.

Sevencea ducked her head again. "Is it that obvious?"

Kasey snorted. "You're lost on him, I can so tell. Do you want to dress up for him, or are we trying for practical?" She held up her hands for each option, raising and lowering her palms like her words had weight.

"Well, I know he really likes this." Sevencea held up her skirt. The strips of fabric in the tones of her scale was the closest thing she had to an outfit she felt comfortable in—the closest thing to her true style.

Kasey took a closer look at the skirt and nodding. "All right, I can work with that. Let's find you some things in those colors, then you can mix and match. Sound good?"

Sevencea shrugged, feeling helpless. "You're the expert. I'm going to trust you!"

Chapter Twenty-Nine

Jacob knew he was fidgeting, but he didn't try and stop himself. He'd been distracted ever since hanging up with his mother, but hadn't even told his father what was bothering him. Mostly because nothing was bothering him, exactly.

"Jacob." Dr. Wilcox's voice was patient, but with that tiny edge of annoyance. He didn't try and disguise it as much with Jacob as he did with other patients. He probably didn't think of Jacob as fragile. Though Jacob still disagreed with Dr. Wilcox about several things, he was grateful the doctor didn't treat him with kid gloves.

"Yeah." Jacob examined his fingernails in an effort to still his hands. They could stand to be filed.

Dr. Wilcox sighed, leaning forward on his desk. "Would you like to tell me what's got you so distracted? I was under the impression you'd be focused on the test I promised you."

Jacob nodded slowly. "Right. The test. I am interested in that, I swear. I just…" He didn't know how to express his thoughts. How did you explain that you'd sort of repaired a relationship you'd torn to shreds a year ago? Had he even repaired it, or just slapped some duct tape on it? He'd felt relieved when he'd hung up with his mother, but tension had been building in his chest ever since, and he didn't know why.

"Sounds like we've got something else to address first." Dr. Wilcox's brow furrowed, then smoothed out. His hair was fully slicked back today, no flyaway hairs to focus on.

Jacob took a deep breath. "I've been talking to my mom. Or, well, we've talked twice."

Dr. Wilcox's eyebrows shot up. "You haven't spoken to her in a year, correct?"

Jacob bit the inside of his cheek. Figured his father would talk about everything in his sessions. "Yeah. After she agreed to help me move out here to be close to Dad, I stopped answering her calls. We just emailed."

"All right. So, why answer her calls now?" Dr. Wilcox started taking notes. He didn't normally do that when he and Jacob spoke. Interesting. Maybe sharing and caring would actually get them somewhere.

Jacob tilted his head and considered. "When she first called, I was bored, so I answered. It was like, what have I got to lose by answering, you know?"

Dr. Wilcox nodded. "What, indeed. So how do that first call go?"

"I was a bit of a brat." Jacob smiled faintly. "But I told her I was here, and she didn't argue I was fine the way you and Dad do."

A brief scowl crossed Dr. Wilcox's face, but he repressed it quickly. "You know why we push you on this subject, Jacob. Still, I'm glad your mother offered you support."

"Then she called again, and I … I apologized." Jacob tilted his head back, still a little shocked by that. "When I graduated she came alone, to tell me Dad was sick and she'd just dropped him off here. I lost it. I called her every name I could think of, and I did it in front of kids, parents, staff, everyone." Jacob winced, the memory as sharp and bitter as ever. Except now he knew she'd forgiven him. He still hadn't fully processed that.

"Wow." Dr. Wilcox made a low whistling noise. "You've never struck me as particularly combative, Jacob. I'm surprised."

"You've mostly seen me with Dad," Jacob pointed out. "Dad's... well, he's not a pushover, but he's relaxed, you know? He'll fight you if you're doing the wrong thing, but he's otherwise content to let someone else lead. He's not combative, or argumentative, or anything. He's easy to get along with."

"Ah," Dr. Wilcox said. "So the combative side is brought out by your mother?"

Jacob snorted and ran his hand through his hair. "Yeah. Mom's a powerhouse. She and Dad ran the company together because they made a good team. He's the easy to make friends with type, and she's the one who won't let you get away with anything. Together, they made solid deals with people. But I always felt it was her way or the highway, you know? Like, I blamed her for abandoning Dad. I know he doesn't think of it that way, but that's how it always looked to me."

"So, because your father usually doesn't express anger over the situation, you felt like you needed to do it for him." It wasn't a question, though Dr. Wilcox studied Jacob with one raised eyebrow.

Jacob nodded. "Pretty much. I always forget that she doesn't really think emotionally. Like, she had no idea I would be furious about Dad until I got angry with her. She told me on the phone she was trying to be practical, not cruel." He winced a little at the memory of her words. He'd never wanted his mother to believe he thought her cruel.

"So, how did she react when you apologized?" Dr. Wilcox scribbled something with his pen.

"She said thank you." Jacob sighed heavily. "We might be in the best place we've been since I graduated, but it still feels…"

Dr. Wilcox nodded. "You've had one conversation. That won't heal a major rift, Jacob. Think of it more as the first few stitches on a wound. Your relationship with your mother is on its way to healing, but it isn't done yet. It'll get there."

"Huh." Jacob rolled that idea around in his head. Maybe that was the source of his agitation. When you're a kid, you're told that sorry makes it all better. But that's not always true. Was he putting too much weight on one apology?

"You're taking the right steps, Jacob." Dr. Wilcox assured him. "Seriously, this is great progress for your overall mental health. I don't know how far it'll help with the reasons you're in my office, but healing often is aided when outside challenges are resolved."

"So, what you're saying is that I should keep talking to my mother," Jacob's lips twitched into a smile, "whether or not it resolves my hallucinating-romantic-partners problem."

Dr. Wilcox grinned back. "Basically. Although we still don't know for sure that that was a hallucination. I've got the quiz materials to test your mind's ability to visualize, but I think we should give it a few days. This evolution in your relationship with your mother is its own achievement. Focus on that. We'll come back to your mermaid, I promise."

Jacob eyed the doctor for a moment, raising an eyebrow at him in challenge, but ultimately nodded. "Fine. I'm not forgetting why I'm here though."

"Sure," Dr. Wilcox agreed easily. "I'm only saying you may be here for reasons beyond what you initially thought."

Chapter Thirty

When Sevencea made it back to the Makai, she was penni-
less again. She *did* have two different pairs of shoes, three
shirts, a pair of pants, and one dress to add her to fashion rotation.
Kasey had done a good job of finding colors similar to Sevencea's
skirt, and her wardrobe now looked almost intentional. Slowly but
surely, Sevencea was getting the hang of this human thing. Hopefully these skills would translate into being able to find Jacob.

Maggie looked relieved when she walked in, but was swift to
interrogate her about her day. She chastised her for getting into a
car with someone she didn't know.

"I didn't know Caroline," Sevencea protested, "and that worked
out fine."

Maggie pursed her lips and fumed. "At least now you'll look a
little less like an urchin I scooped off the street," she muttered.

Sevencea retreated to her room and traded the shopping bag in
for her camera bag. She returned to the lobby with it, unzipped the
bag, and pulled out the camera. She presented it to Maggie. "Do
you have a way for me to take photographs off this and save them?
It's been warning me that there's no space left." She'd taken some

time each day to practice with Jacob's camera. The Makai had a garden out back, and while on land taking photos of flowers was the closest she could get to taking photos of coral. Besides, using the camera made her feel closer to Jacob. Until she could find him, she'd take what she could get.

Maggie gave her a curious look, then motioned Sevencea around the corner. "Sure, you can back up photos on the computer. The card reader lives in this drawer, with the cord to plug it in. Here, I'll show you how it works." She retrieved the pieces of technology out of the drawer.

Sevencea watched over Maggie's shoulder as the older woman connected the card reader. She surrendered the camera to Maggie, keeping a careful eye on each step of the process. It seemed simple enough to access the memory card and remove it, but Sevencea was still learning how to use the computer. She might delete everything by accident.

Maggie slid the card into the reader and pulled up the folders. She evaluated the many photos stored there. "You've got a good eye, *Kama Lei*," she mused, sending Sevencea a fond smile over her shoulder.

"The first half of those are Jacob's," Sevencea explained. "I don't want to take those off the camera."

Maggie hovered over one of the images near the beginning of the folder, her eyes narrowing. She didn't click on it though. She moved back to the section Sevencea had indicated as hers. "All right, whatever you say. Here's how to save them."

Sevencea breathed a sigh of relief. If Maggie pulled up the photo of her as a mermaid, she didn't know how she could explain. She directed her attention to the folder the older woman was creating on the desktop titled 'Sevencea.' Drag and drop. That was easy enough.

Maggie hummed to herself as she popped the SD card out of the card reader and inserted it back into the camera. She returned the camera to Sevencea. "You know, I sell photography prints and homemade postcards here in the lobby. If you want, I can get some of your photos printed out to sell in here. It might not be a steady income, but it's something."

Sevencea's face lit up. Could using Jacob's magic help her to find him again? "Yes, of course! Thank you, Maggie!"

Maggie huffed and waved her off, muttering something under her breath in another language. "You're welcome. Go get some rest now. You've got work to do tomorrow."

Sevencea went with good grace, keeping the rest of her gratitude to herself. "Have a good afternoon!" she called as she left.

She darted up the stairs, clutching Jacob's camera. She couldn't suppress her grin. Finally, a way to earn some money for herself! She'd have to pay Maggie back, of course, but then she could use her earnings to get around the island and actually search for Jacob. She loved the people at The Makai, and she loved the funny old building itself. But learning how to be human was only a means to an end. She'd done all of this for Jacob, and he didn't even know it yet.

As she reached her room, a cramp spasmed in her calf. Sevencea caught herself on the doorframe and scowled down at her legs. Well, that warning was clear enough. It hadn't been a full week yet, but she'd been pushing herself. Apparently it was time to return to the ocean. She closed her eyes briefly. Four days on land, and she hadn't found Jacob. A fresh wave of guilt hit her, but she pushed it aside. In four days, she'd found wonderful people to help her, found a potential way to make money, gotten a few leads on where

Jacob could be, and made the start of a plan for how to find him. It was going to work out.

It had to.

Sevencea removed her shoes, adjusted her skirt, then traded out Jacob's t-shirt for her bodice. She didn't know if she had to be wearing the same outfit when she returned to the water, but better safe than sorry. After a moment's consideration, she grabbed her underwater camera too. Satisfied, she headed back downstairs.

Thankfully, Maggie wasn't in the lobby. Sevencea crossed the room barefoot. The hard floor felt cool on her bare skin. It was odd how used to shoes she'd grown, but she didn't want to risk losing Jacob's sandals in the water. The Makai had a beach nearby, so she wasn't concerned about damaging her feet on the way to the ocean. Sevencea slipped out the back and exhaled with a smile. No Maggie, Jim, Keisha, or Frank. No one to wonder where she was going. These people had accepted her easily, and Sevencea refused to lie to them anymore than was necessary.

Then again, she *could* always tell them the truth. Sevencea had considered it, especially with how accepting Maggie had been about her ignorance. But Jacob had disappeared in part because she was a mermaid. That had to be the case, especially with what he'd told her about his father. He'd run off somewhere because he thought she wasn't real. What if the somewhat motley family she'd found were freaked out by the truth too?

The smell of the ocean grew stronger, and Sevencea smiled. Maybe one day she'd tell the other humans who she was, but restoring her relationship with Jacob came first. She reached the edge of the beach and paused, her soul soaring at the sight of the water. The beach itself was crowded, children laughing as they played in the sand and the waves. Sevencea couldn't help but compare it to

Jacob's beach. The sand here was a dusty yellow, and the water didn't seem as clear. Still, it was home. Sevencea's bones urged her to simply walk into the waves and swim away. No matter how comfortable she became on land, some piece of her would always rejoice in returning to the water.

She buried her toes in the sand as she walked forward. Some of the tension eased out of her shoulders. Her legs felt like they had their own pulse, one that grew stronger as she approached the water. While returning to the water was a necessity of the potion, Sevencea still felt her heart flutter at the prospect of submerging. Or, half of her heart. The other half was still focused on Jacob. She was going back to the ocean with nothing to show for her efforts. No, that wasn't true. She'd accomplished a lot in a short time. Her thoughts drifted to the warm look in Maggie's eyes whenever Sevencea got excited to learn something new. Or the effortless grin Keisha tossed her whenever Sevencea made her laugh. Frank's fond, sometimes exasperated glances. And even Jim's awkward, slightly awe-struck friendship. Those people all mattered. She'd come to care deeply for them all already.

Still, she'd come on land with a single goal. Find Jacob. What if he was miserable, locked in a room somewhere, convinced that their relationship had been a lie? A figment of his imagination? She couldn't let him suffer. Keeping herself healthy was important too though. Once she came back from this rejuvenation trip, she would throw herself into finding him.

She closed her eyes as she drew closer to the water. Her toes hit wet sand, and her eyes popped open, adrenaline flooding her at the sensation.

Glancing around, Sevencea kept an eye on where all the beach patrons were, making sure no one was too close. What would happen if somebody saw her tail? According to Athys it would come back seconds after she immersed herself in the water. A few people glanced her way as she stepped toward the waves. She wasn't wearing a swimsuit like most of the beach-goers. Sevencea put her hand to her chest, pressing lightly. Yes, the potion bottle was securely tucked beneath her bodice. No more delaying; it was time to return to the sea.

A large wave rolled toward the beach. Sevencea took off with a run and dove into the water. She pushed hard with her legs, kicking away from shore. Swimming with legs felt wrong, but she made it work. The power in her arms helped compensate. No one followed her. Sevencea breathed a sigh of relief and pushed herself deeper and deeper underwater, eager to escape the potential for prying eyes.

Her legs jolted like she'd been shocked, snapping together as the transformation began. Her feet morphed back into the flexible pink fin she'd always loved. She used the extra power to swim farther out, laughing to herself. It was so much easier to move underwater! Effortless, even. Sevencea gasped as her skirt became suctioned to what had been skin. Her scales cascaded back into place, covering her from fin to bodice.

Sevencea spun in the water and evaluated herself. She hadn't realized how much she'd missed her tail. Was it vain to appreciate how pretty it was for a minute or two? She did a few twists, relishing the sensation of water across her scales. She hadn't allowed herself to miss the tail on land, but underwater it felt like she'd never left.

Sevencea's heart gave a dull thump. She grew still. No matter how much she loved the water, she'd left it for a reason. She loved more than one thing.

She'd have to spend at least eight hours underwater for her health, so she planned to make the most of it. She picked up speed, one hand holding her camera to keep it from bouncing. Sevencea fixed her keen gaze on her surroundings. What beauty could she capture? What photographs had the most potential to bring her closer to Jacob?

Chapter Thirty-One

Day 20

It was almost lights out when Jacob worked up the nerve to walk into his father's room. Gerald had been having a pretty good day. He looked up with an easy grin, one eyebrow raised.

"What brings you here so late, Jake?" Gerald made a show of looking around. "If an orderly catches you, we're going to be in trouble!" He sang the last word, still grinning.

"Someone's in a good mood." Jacob smiled back. His father's demeanor was a relief. "And the orderlies don't care if I'm in here. They don't know what to do with me, so they just leave me alone."

"Oh, so they've picked up on my parenting strategy." Gerald nodded sagely.

Jacob rolled his eyes. "Seriously, what kind of happy pills are you on today? I haven't seen you this chipper in a while."

Gerald waved him off. "I'm just messing with you. I haven't had any episodes today and I slept fine last night, so I've got more energy than usual. No obvious memory gaps either. Some days the meds help more than others. I can't say I'm getting better, but I'm not getting worse at the same speed, so that's something."

Jacob's eyes tightened, but he forced the smile to stay on his face. "That's good, Dad. I don't want to kill your buzz, but I wanted to talk to you about something kind of important."

"That sounds ominous." Gerald straightened a little and gave Jacob his full attention. "You can always talk to me, Jake. What's up?"

Jacob took a deep breath. "Okay, so I talked to Mom again, and I've been thinking ever since."

"Talked? Not fought?" Genuine concern peeked through the teasing in Gerald's tone.

"Yes, Dad, we talked. You know how I said I got mad at her, at graduation, when she told me about you? About this place?" Jacob gnawed on his lip, bracing himself. He'd always known his father knew more details than Jacob had revealed, but they didn't talk about it.

"Mmhmm." Gerald's acknowledgement betrayed nothing of what he was thinking.

Jacob cleared his throat. "Yeah, well, that graduation conversation was pretty bad, honestly. I was awful to her. But, this time when she called I apologized, and we talked. I've been thinking a lot ... about how I was raised, you know? You and Mom—I've been treating you like two separate people since you got sick, but you were always one unit when I was a kid. Remember how if Mom said 'no' and I asked you, I'd get in trouble and vice versa? Because trying and get around one of you was disrespecting the other." Jacob risked a glance upward, meeting his father's gaze.

"I remember." Gerald offered Jacob a soft smile.

"I was so mad at Mom when she checked you in here. I know you aren't mad, mostly, but I was. And I stopped thinking of going against her as disrespecting you. But … it is, right? Because you're both still my parents, and whether or not I'm angry with Mom shouldn't matter. Two wrongs don't make a right. Even if I was *sure* she was wrong about checking you in here or the way she told me about it, what I did was wrong too. And hurting her—that was hurting you too. So, yeah, I apologized to her, even though it took me a year. And I need to apologize to you too. Dad, I'm sorry." Jacob sucked in another deep breath. He stared at the ceiling, trying to keep back the tears.

Gerald stood, moved toward Jacob, and pulled him into a hug. "I forgive you, son."

A sob escaped Jacob's lips. "I'm so sorry."

"I know, Jake, I know. I'm sorry it took you so long to heal from that argument, to find a way to say all that out loud." Gerald rubbed his hand along Jacob's back, holding his son tight.

"Did Mom tell you, when it happened?" Tears raced each other down Jacob's face. He'd always assumed, but he had to know.

"We talked about it," Gerald acknowledged. "We both know what your arguments with her can be like. You two bring out the heat in each other. We assumed you'd reconcile a little sooner, but we didn't want to push it. You're an adult, Jacob. We weren't going to put you in time out until you apologized for yelling at your mother. She was more in shock than anything at the time." Gerald paused, releasing Jacob and guiding him into the second seat.

"She said something like that on the phone," Jacob admitted. His short laugh jostled free a few more tears. He quickly brushed them away.

Gerald chuckled. "We're very different people, but we're usually on the same page about you, kiddo. I know you've felt like you had to be angry on my behalf. I've tried to disabuse you of that notion, tried to do what I could to push you to reconcile with your mom. But you were going to have to make that choice on your own. Look, I've never blamed your mother for taking the steps she did. I hate that I never get to see her, and sometimes I do get lonely, but that is my struggle. That is a conversation I have with her, and have been having for a long time. I understand how busy she is. But that's part of marriage, part of love—working through the times when you aren't in the same place about everything, or where you've hurt each other unintentionally. It's our journey, Jake. Not yours. I love your mother so, so much. She loves me so, so much. And we both love you so, so much. You don't ever have to hold on to hate, and you never need to do it on my behalf."

Jacob nodded. "I know, I know, Dad. I'm so sorry I've been so…" He trailed off, not sure what word was strong enough.

"Stubborn?" Gerald smiled at him, his eyes soft. He reached up and brushed a stray tear from Jacob's cheek. "That can be a good quality, Jake. You're stubborn about things like your passions, your values. All that is great. I'm so proud of you for working through this with your mother. It's been hard on her, not talking to you."

Jacob hung his head and took a deep breath. "I turned my anger into a personality trait," he muttered. "I defined myself by being mad at her. I don't know why. I'm sorry. I'm sorry it took me so long to just…" he exhaled again. "To just talk to her!"

Gerald squeezed Jacob's arm. "I know why. You're your mother's son, Jake. That fire is one of the things I love about her. Just never let it take you over. You have a head and a heart. You have to use them both." He grinned, squeezing Jacob's arm once more.

Jacob stood and leaned over his father's chair to hug him. "Thank you, Dad, for everything."

"Always, Jake." Gerald murmured the words.

Jacob's heart seized. He wasn't "always" going to have his father, was he? At some point, either due to the progression of his illness or the end of his life, Gerald would be gone. "That's not a promise you can keep," Jacob choked out. His grip on his father tightened for a split second.

Gerald was quiet for a moment. "You're a part of me, Jake. You're a part of your mother. You'll have a little bit of both of us forever. No matter what happens, you can look in a mirror and remember that you look a bit like your dad, that you inherited his love of the arts and passion for life. You can remember that you have runner's muscles like your mom, that you inherited her tenacity and unwillingness to compromise. You'll always have us, Jake."

Jacob whispered into his father's shoulder, "Sure, Dad. Always."

Chapter Thirty-Two

Day 22

"Sevencea, come over here." Maggie perched on her normal chair by the counter, still far too high to be practical. She held out a white envelope between her fingers.

Sevencea took the proffered envelope and examined it. "What's this?"

"Open it." Maggie rolled her eyes. She sat back, folding her arms and intently watching Sevencea's face.

Sevencea warily opened the flap and peeked inside. "You're giving me more money?" She stared from the wad of green paper to Maggie.

"It's yours," Maggie clarified. "It's what you've earned so far from the prints I've been selling in here. They were cheap to have made. That's what you've earned minus production fees. It's about fifty bucks."

"How?" Sevencea's bewilderment hadn't vacated her tone yet. "You only asked me about selling my photos"—she had to think about it for a second—"what, two days ago? Fifty dollars seems like a lot."

"Three days ago," Maggie corrected absently. The computer made a dinging noise, and her attention shifted to it.

Sevencea tilted her head. It had been three. In the days since, pretty much everyone in her human family had praised her photography.

Keisha had been the first to say something. She ambushed Sevencea on her way to the supply closet.

"You're good with a camera, girl." Keisha brandished a feather duster in Sevencea's direction. "Keep it up and you might find yourself a career without even meaning to!"

Sevencea's lips twitched toward a smile, and she arched a mischievous eyebrow. "Who says I don't mean to?"

"Ha!" Keisha grinned broadly and pushed the feather duster into Sevencea's hand. "You tell 'em, girl. You're going places, just watch!" Gesturing upward, she added, "The second floor's your first stop; it could do with a spruce up."

Then, Jim had all but shouted, "I like your photos!" from the end of the third-floor hallway. He immediately scampered down the stairs to hide how red he'd gone.

Sevencea grinned at the empty hallway, took a deep breath, and yelled after him, "Thanks, Jim!"

Finally, while Sevencea did the dishes yesterday evening, Frank had thrust a thumbs up in her general direction. He'd even offered her a rare, albeit small, smile.

"I appreciate that generous compliment, Frank," Sevencea said, her tone and expression neutral. Her twitching lips almost ruined her attempted gravitas.

Frank exhaled a harsh breath through his nose, a sign of amusement.

"I'm glad we're friends," Sevencea added. Frank replied with a withering glare. She had ducked her head and smirked.

Sevencea brought her attention back to Maggie and cleared her throat. "Still, fifty dollars?"

Maggie glanced up again and grinned. "It's Hawaii, *Kama Lei*. I get to upcharge a lot. Besides, you're undervaluing your own work. People like good photography, and this place gets mistaken for a visitor's center all the time with that stupid roof. I get a decent amount of foot traffic in here. You're a hit." She shrugged, her expression smug.

"I'm impressed," Sevencea admitted. She thumbed through the money, still in awe that there was so much. Wait, she still owed Maggie money, so this wasn't all for her. Sevencea counted the currency and extracted three $10 bills. She offered them back to Maggie. "Here. Thank you for the money from before."

Something sparked in Maggie's eye, and she accepted the bills with a nod. "I appreciate it. I always say you get the measure of a person when you loan them money."

"Thank you, Maggie, for everything you've done. It's been so much more than I could've asked for." Sevencea's arms twitched at her sides; the urge to pull the woman in for a hug was strong.

"Don't thank me yet." Maggie handed a piece of paper over the counter with an address scrawled on it. "Twenty bucks might not be a lot, but it's enough to pay for a cab to Big Island Healing Center and back. It's the largest care facility on the island, and it's nearby. I'd have someone drive you since it's not far, but unfortunately nobody's free, and I didn't think you'd want to wait. I already called you the cab."

Sevencea looked to the front door in time to see a taxi pulling into the parking lot. She whirled back toward Maggie, bouncing on the balls of her feet. "What if I find him?" The words rushed out of her.

Maggie shrugged. "Then your quest is complete, isn't it? Don't get your hopes up though. Like I said, this is only one of three locations where your man's father could be. Plus there's no telling whether or not your man even went to his father."

Sevencea's enthusiasm was undeterred. "Doesn't matter. Progress is progress, even if I don't find him. I'll at least know for sure where he isn't!"

"Fair enough. Go on, get outside before the cab driver gets tired of waiting on you." Maggie waved her off with a grin.

Sevencea skipped outside and down the steps. She reached the taxi and slid into the back.

"Where to?" The driver met her eyes in the rearview mirror.

"Big Island Healing Center," Sevencea replied, examining the interior of the car.

She returned her gaze to the mirror and saw the driver giving her a wary look. Sevencea raised an eyebrow at him. Was this part of what made Jacob fearful? Possible judgment from strangers? No one deserved that, but especially not Jacob.

She just hoped she was right, and he'd gone to his father. It was her only theory, and she didn't know enough else about Jacob to make a new plan if this one didn't pan out. Once she found him, Sevencea had decided they should learn everything they could about each other, just in case they were ever separated again. She touched the potion hidden inside her shirt. If she found Jacob, she wanted to be able to explain everything right away.

"Whatever you say." The driver pulled out of the parking lot and hit the button to start the meter. Sevencea watched his motions, curious about how it all worked. She was getting better at figuring things out from context.

The drive was interesting. Sevencea was starting to gain a little familiarity with Kailua-Kona. The taxi took her back south, toward where Caroline had found her. They passed several resorts, all larger than The Makai. Greenery overwhelmed some of the buildings; she couldn't even tell what they were beneath all the plants.

While they weren't driving too far out of the area, simply traveling back south was enough to send Sevencea's thoughts back to where she'd started this journey. In some ways it felt like she'd been living on land for a long time, but there was still so much she hadn't seen. When she found Jacob, they'd have to go exploring together. Doing it without him didn't spark the same excitement within her. Once again, she cursed herself for not convincing Athys to give her the potion sooner. Although, for all she knew, Jacob might still have been gone.

"You visiting the area?" The cab driver's eyes darted up to examine her in the rearview mirror.

Sevencea nodded, then thought better of it and wagged her head side to side. "I live at The Makai." It was a true enough answer for a stranger. She glanced out the window again. So many structures had large balconies and open-air sections. And so many flowers! Everything they passed seemed to bloom under the streaming sunshine and the cool sea breeze.

"I hear good things." The driver shrugged. He inhaled like he was going to say something else, but no words left his lips.

Sevencea focused on the scenery flashing by her. What she wouldn't give to be able to take a good photograph while in motion. Maybe that was something Maggie's computer could teach her. Jacob's face emerged from her memory, casting disapproval on the idea of learning from the computer. She smiled a little. As if she'd pick the computer over Jacob's instruction. Still, the computer was helpful. She'd learned how to charge the camera's battery, which had felt like a miracle.

She was lost in her thoughts when the taxi turned off the main road and onto a side street, then pulled into a wide parking lot.

"Here we are," the driver announced. He put the cab in park. "You paying cash?" He turned in his seat, one eyebrow raised.

"How much?" Sevencea opened the envelope Maggie had given her, fingering one of her $10 bills.

"Nineteen dollars and eighty-seven cents." The driver inclined his head toward the meter's readout. Sevencea realized it was flashing the number at her.

"Really?" Sevencea's eyebrows flew up. Based on what Maggie had told her, she hadn't expected it to be nearly so much.

The cab driver huffed at her, giving her a once-over that now felt hostile. "Really."

Tentatively, Sevencea handed over the envelope with all of her money. "Keep the change," she said weakly. She moved to step out of the vehicle. The phrase was borrowed from Maggie, intended to be a kindness offered for a well-performed service. But in this case, all Sevencea could focus on was what was she going to do with thirteen cents anyway.

The cab driver grinned, the expression somehow darkening his features. "Thanks! *Aloha!*"

"*Aloha!*" Sevencea repeated automatically.

She climbed out, and the taxi immediately whisked away. She watched it leave with all her money, a sinking feeling in her stomach. Had she just been scammed? Did she look that naïve? She'd have to work on that. She could call Maggie for help, but she didn't want Maggie to know she'd been cheated, not on her first time using her own money out in the world. Obviously not everyone was as helpful as Caroline or Kasey.

Sevencea turned on her heel and switched her focus to the large building before her. She eyed it warily. Was this all it took? Could she just step through those doors and find Jacob? If he was here, maybe he had a car, and she wouldn't be stranded anymore. Sevencea took a deep breath and steadied herself. Like Maggie said, he might not even be here. If Jacob wasn't here, at least she'd know that much. Something was better than nothing.

Sevencea approached the glass doors. They slid open revealing a wide lobby. The room was all white, like the personality had been leached from it. It had none of the warmth and charm The Makai exuded. A few employees milled around, looking busy. A woman sat at the front desk, her hair pulled back into a sharp bun that did the rest of her features no favors.

"Can I help you?" The woman didn't even look up. She typed on the computer in front of her with a lack of enthusiasm equal to her tone.

"I'm looking for Jacob Pearson." Sevencea injected every ounce of confidence she possessed into the statement. Her hands tightened into fists, relaxed, then tightened again. Hopefully all other signs of her nerves were staying under wraps.

"Is he a patient? Are you family?" the woman droned, her inflection still on vacation.

"I don't think so, and no." Sevencea gnawed on her bottom lip, her confidence beginning to inch its way out of her. She had no idea how to deal with people at a facility like this. She was out of her element most of the time, but even more so here.

The woman's eyes lifted. They bypassed Sevencea's face and settled on the pearl on her forehead. A single eyebrow arched.

Sevencea flushed. She'd almost forgotten she was wearing her jewelry. No one at The Makai ever said anything about it. She wasn't used to it distracting people to the extent that they ignored the rest of her.

She cleared her throat and straightened her shoulders. "Ma'am, Jacob is important to me. I don't know where he is. His father is receiving care in a facility like this, but I don't know which one. I just need to know if he's here, or if his father is."

"Mmhmm." The woman shifted her gaze back to her computer. "I can't give out patient information. Have a good day."

Sevencea gaped at her. That was it? What did that even mean? It wasn't a yes or a no. She couldn't work with no information at all. "Please, all I need to know is if he's here. If he's not, I'll leave."

"I can't give out patient information," the woman repeated. "Have a nice day." She didn't even bother to look at Sevencea.

Feeling a little off-kilter, Sevencea moved back toward the doors. She exited in a daze and took a deep breath of fresh air to help calm herself. The sun was still shining, and the sky was still crystal clear, but an awful gloom seemed to settle over everything. What was she supposed to do now?

"What now?" she yelled the words at the sky, then scowled at the blue expanse. How dare it be so beautiful when nothing else was.

The doors behind her slid open again, and a young woman emerged. Sevencea's eyes snapped to her. She looked winded and wore an outfit with the facility's logo on it.

"Hey, I'm on break, so I can't talk long." She gestured for Sevencea to follow her, then led her away from the door and toward the corner of the building. "I know Meg comes off like a jerk, but it isn't personal. The name was Pearson, right? I'm usually in charge of scheduling family visits, and we don't have any Pearsons in our facility, visiting or staying. I shouldn't really be sharing that, but you seem worried about this guy. Telling you he isn't here doesn't break confidentiality rules in my book."

The woman looked around to make sure no one was watching, then darted back toward the doors. She offered Sevencea a small wave and vanished inside.

Sevencea had read about whiplash, but she hadn't understood what it meant before. The woman had thrown out a few terms she didn't understand, but she'd comprehended the most important part just fine.

Jacob wasn't here.

She took a deep breath, evaluating that. Okay. So he wasn't here. That was still helpful information, wasn't it? She'd said as much to Maggie. This was still progress.

Her eyes pricked with tears anyway. She'd known he might not be here, but she'd still hoped. Her heart thudded against her ribs. Why? Was she really that upset? Maybe she'd been lying before, when she'd told herself it was okay if she didn't find him today. She gnawed on her lip again, something she'd seen Jacob do, then took a deep breath.

There were still two more facilities to search.

She had a way to earn money now.

This was not the end.

Sevencea took another steadying breath, then faced the road. First she had to deal with the no taxi, no money problem. She could still call Maggie.

She should probably call Maggie.

Sevencea considered for a moment, sighed, and reluctantly walked back into the building.

"Excuse me," she asked the unhelpful woman at the desk, "do you happen to know where the closest ocean access is from here?"

Chapter Thirty-Three

Dr. Wilcox adjusted a stack of papers on his desk and glanced up at Jacob. "Are you ready?"

"To find out if my imagination is as good as you think?" Jacob asked dryly. "Born ready. How does this work?"

The doctor's lips twitched. "This is easy, Jacob, really. I will ask you to picture some things with your mind's eye, and you describe to me what you're picturing. It's that simple. I'm not going to give you too much information up front, because I don't want you over or underselling whatever it is your brain is doing. We'll do about fifteen of these, all right?"

Jacob closed his eyes and nodded. "Whatever you say. I'm ready when you are."

Butterflies were going wild in his gut. They were eager to see what the outcome of this test would be. The rest of him was as shut down as he could make it. If he didn't have this hyperphantasia thing, then he likely *was* inheriting his father's illness. He'd been certain for the past year that it was inevitable, but now, sitting across from Dr. Wilcox, he hated believing it could be true. Of course, he'd already lost Sevencea, whether because he was sick or had dreamed her up. Just a couple weeks ago thinking about her made his heart race. Now, thoughts of her formed a deep ache in his chest. How could he miss someone so much when they'd never even existed?

Dr. Wilcox seemed to sense Jacob was distracted. He shuffled his papers, then cleared his throat. "All right, I want you to picture the sky first thing in the morning."

Immediately Jacob's mind went to his beach, the black sand in gorgeous contrast with the sunrise. The sky was often in soft orange hues, with pinkish tone and some red if it was feeling feisty. Jacob nodded.

"Explain what you're picturing," Dr. Wilcox prompted. There was a soft noise as he picked up a pen.

"Sunrise on my beach." Jacob paused, tilting his head a little, his eyes still closed. "How am I supposed to know how well I'm visualizing?"

Dr. Wilcox clicked his tongue. "That's my job. You said sunrise. Are you picturing a sky full of color?"

Jacob nodded.

"How many colors are you picturing?"

Jacob's brow furrowed. "Three. Ish. Mostly orange and pink, but there's some red, and they blend in places, so you could argue for more."

Dr. Wilcox made a few notes, his pen scratching softly. "All right, good. Would you describe what you're envisioning as vivid?"

"Sure," Jacob agreed. It wasn't hard to imagine a sunrise, not after having seen so many.

"Is it just as vivid if you were looking at it in real life?"

Jacob hummed, considering. He shook his head. "No. It's clear, and the colors are bright, but it doesn't look quite real." His stomach knotted a little. "Is that bad?"

"Jacob." Dr. Wilcox waited until Jacob opened his eyes again and matched his gaze. "No answer to this test is bad. No outcome to this test is superior to any other. Some people can't visualize anything at all. That's fine too. We are all unique individuals. All this will tell us is if you visualize more than the average person. Some of the things on this test you'll visualize more easily than others. For a few of these questions, I even have pictures so you can point out what is closest to what you see. Relax, please. This isn't a test you can fail."

Jacob exhaled slowly and nodded. "Right. I know that." He did. It just didn't matter. There was a wrong outcome to this test for him. He focused on his breathing. Relax. Focus. "Okay, go ahead."

"Close your eyes again." Dr. Wilcox said. Jacob obeyed. "Picture an apple."

Jacob's lips twitched. That was simple enough.

"You've got it?"

"Yes, I'm picturing an apple," Jacob smirked slightly. He wanted to take this seriously, but it felt silly.

Dr. Wilcox rustled some papers. "All right, open your eyes." He held a card in front of Jacob. It held several images of apples, some faded, one a little pixelated, and one that looked like a photograph. "Which of these is closest to what you pictured?"

"Well, I was picturing a green apple and these are all red, so…" Jacob shrugged.

Dr. Wilcox hit him with his "not amused" face. Jacob winced apologetically. That was fair. He was only going to get out of this what he put into it. He leaned forward, inspected the options, and settled on the image right before the photo-realistic one. It was a little pixelated, but close to the real thing.

"Good, let's move on."

Over the next hour, Jacob pictured animals, furniture, landscape scenes, shapes, and a hamburger. Though Dr. Wilcox had yet to render a verdict, Jacob wasn't oblivious. The pattern was clear. He was good at visualizing, especially animals and outdoor scenes, and pretty good at inanimate objects. His imagination was good, but not better than normal.

Jacob fidgeted while Dr. Wilcox reviewed his notes. He wasn't nervous. What was there to be nervous about? He knew the answer already. He couldn't be apprehensive. He was a normal guy who'd inherited a degenerative illness. He'd known that. All of this was just a diversion to sate Dr. Wilcox's strange theories of loneliness.

"All right, so based on your answers, you have a pretty standard imagination," Dr. Wilcox announced. Jacob slumped in his chair with a nod. The doctor frowned at him, then continued, "You have no trouble visualizing, though the degree of detail varies depending on the subject, which is absolutely normal. You don't fall into the parameters for aphantasia or hyperphantasia."

Jacob gave a slow nod. He gnawed at his lip. This wasn't a surprise, and he was going to keep control of himself. He was too worn out from his last emotional outburst to have another one.

Dr. Wilcox leaned forward, his hands folded in front of him. "So, this theory didn't pan out. While there may be other factors at play in what you experienced, Jacob, I still hold that there is no evidence you carry your father's condition."

Jacob huffed a laugh. "I know you don't believe me, but eventually you'll run out of alternatives. I have my father's condition. There isn't another good explanation." He tapped his fingers against the arm of the chair, then stilled his hands. "Is that it for today?"

Dr. Wilcox leaned back with a resigned sigh and nodded. "For today, yes. Don't worry, Jacob. We'll figure this out. When I agreed to let you come here for your contingency plan, it was because I hoped I could give you peace of mind. That's still my goal."

Despite his frustrations, a small, fond smile crossed Jacob's face. "I know. Thanks."

Chapter Thirty-Four

Day 25

Work, photography, and moments of pining filled Sevencea's next few days. From what Maggie had told her, her next adventure to seek Jacob would be a lot further away. She saved every dollar from her photography sales. It wasn't exactly making her wealthy, but it would be enough. The most frustrating thing was knowing that the facility might not tell her anything. She'd gotten lucky at the first place. She couldn't expect that to happen again.

Sevencea also needed to make sure she had a good way back to The Makai in the future. She'd walked into The Makai lobby sopping wet. Maggie's bewildered expression, funny though it had been, begged questions Sevencea wasn't ready to answer. Besides, based on her research on the computer, her first taxi had absolutely taken advantage of her.

Sevencea spent all day running up and down the stairs to fetch and deliver things for Keisha. After work, Maggie greeted her in the lobby with another envelope. This one was much thicker than normal.

Maggie released the envelope into Sevencea's waiting hands. A broad grin dominated the older woman's face. "Seems I'm not the only one who recognizes your gift!"

Sevencea opened the envelope. Her eyes went wide as she tried to count the stack of bills. "This is all from my photography?"

"That's all from one person," Maggie clarified, still grinning. She retrieved a small card from the counter and handed it over.

"Janet Woodbury, local interest, Hawaiian Shores Today?" Sevencea read the card aloud. She raised an eyebrow at Maggie. "What is this?"

"About a year ago, this lady," Maggie gestured to the card, "did an article on our humble hotel for her website. Hawaiian Shores Today is a local interest website. It's got articles, blogs, photography, et cetera, all about the island. They publish a physical magazine twice a month, which you can usually find in grocery stores. Anyway, she comes by to check in every so often, and she was blown away by your photos." Maggie winked and returned to the counter, taking her seat in the tall chair.

Sevencea was still confused. She held up the card again. "Okay, that's great, but what does it all mean?"

"It means," Maggie drew out each syllable, "that Janet wants to talk to you about publishing some of your photos. She bought a copy of pretty much everything I had out of yours. If you take her up on it, it would be a lot more money for you."

"Whoa." Sevencea looked down at the card again. The implications were a little staggering. Maybe, like Keisha had joked, she had found herself a career without meaning to. She hadn't been planning to become a businesswoman when she'd started her hunt for Jacob. Then again, she needed money to look for him, so this did seem like a blessing. Would a job elsewhere mean she couldn't stay at The Makai? She glanced up at Maggie. "I like it here, though."

Maggie clicked her tongue. "I'm not kicking you out, *Kama Lei*. You're welcome here any time. Once you get famous, I'll let you rent your room for money instead of labor, how about that?" She chuckled.

"Thank you, Maggie. For everything." If Sevencea had a dollar for every time she'd said those words, she'd could afford to fly to the mainland and back. Well, that might be a bit of an exaggeration, but Maggie had truly been very generous. "How do I reach this woman?"

Maggie rolled her eyes and pointed to the phone on the wall. "I don't know the full scope of what you don't understand, but I know I already showed you how the phone works."

All it took was a phone call and an email. With a single conversation and an email full of attached photographs, Sevencea seemed to have secured herself a career. Janet Woodbury sounded like a delightful person, and Maggie trusted her, so Sevencea was allowing herself to be excited. Jacob had shared his magic with her, and now she would get to share it with the world! Or, at least this island. She couldn't wait to tell him.

Which, of course, required her to make some progress in her quest.

With the money from Janet's purchases, Sevencea could more than afford to visit both mental health facilities left on her list. The closest was Relaxation Cove, not to be confused with Relaxing Cove, which was a resort. According to their website, this facility dealt mostly with mental health and trauma, so it didn't seem like the kind of place Jacob's father would be. Then again, Sevencea didn't know if trauma had played a hand in the man's condition. She couldn't eliminate any options.

. Sevencea fingered her stack of bills. She wanted to rush right over, but she was due for another trip home. She'd technically returned to the ocean after her trip to Big Island Healing Center a few days ago, but she'd swam straight back to the beach closest to The Makai. She wasn't sure she'd been under for even an hour. So, not counting that trip, it had been a week already.

Did she go back underwater, or did she search for Jacob? She sighed. Ultimately, the battle between her head and heart was irrelevant. If she wanted to find Jacob, she needed to take care of herself. That meant going back to the ocean for a bit. If she was careful, she could have her cake and eat it too. That was one of her favorite idioms she'd learned so far.

Day 26

First thing the next morning, Sevencea dressed in her bodice and skirt. When she'd been forced to swim back to The Makai she'd discovered that outfit was apparently attached to the potion. She hadn't been wearing her bodice when she'd jumped into the water, but it had returned along with her tail, showing up under the shirt she'd been wearing. When she got back, it wasn't with her clothes at The Makai. Apparently that was all part of Athys's magic. So really she didn't need to dress in her bodice and skirt specifically. Still, if she wore just those into the water, she didn't have to worry about hauling around extra wet clothes that weren't impacted by magic.

Sevencea went out the back door, through the garden, and down a few blocks. There it was—the beach in all its early morning glory. It still wasn't as pretty as Jacob's, and it was rather small, but it would get her home and secure her health once more.

Only a handful of tourists were on the beach so far. A few people ran past in workout gear, ignoring her entirely. A few people cast curious glances at the way she was dressed like before. Kasey had tried to convince Sevencea to buy a swimsuit while they were at Goodwill. The memory made her grin. She hadn't had the heart to try and explain exactly how unnecessary a swimsuit was!

Sevencea dove in the way she had before, waited for her tail to reform, then surged deeper into the sea. She allowed herself to drift after a while, flicking her tail in disinterest. Knowing she had the money to search for Jacob was a powerful distraction. The eight hours Athys's potion required her to be underwater were an inconvenience this time. Sevencea had a plan and resources now. Returning to the ocean just felt like a waste of time. She sighed heavily and tried to relax in the water, to feel the current move her. Sevencea flicked her tail again, counting the seconds. She couldn't handle being down here for the full time, not today. It would take forever. Also, she didn't know what time Relaxation Cove closed. If she waited too long she might miss her chance altogether.

Sevencea did her best to focus on swimming for two hours, then gave up and made her way back to the beach. Once she found Jacob, they could enjoy a good, long swim together. As soon as she was within range of the shore, she surfaced and swallowed the potion, moving toward the sand without hesitation.

She didn't notice anyone watching her as she emerged from the water. Her legs felt okay; she'd surely be all right for an extra few days. Besides, she'd spent a bit of time underwater when she'd had to swim back to The Makai. Between the two trips, everything should be fine. It was time to call a cab and head to Relaxation Cove.

Sevencea's damp hair hadn't taken on its usual curl, but the rest of her was mostly dry when she walked back into The Makai.

Maggie glanced up from the counter, evaluating Sevencea with a knowing look in her eye. "Welcome back."

Sevencea nodded and headed to her room to change. She glanced over her shoulder as she went. How much did Maggie know, or how much had she guessed?

Chapter Thirty-Five

No matter what Gerald would have everyone believe, Jacob was not moping. He wasn't skipping around Mana'o in a chipper mood, but he wasn't moping. He'd just been spending a lot of time on his own reading. That was normal for him. Well, normal would have been doing it at home. The rules of his contingency plan with Dr. Wilcox were clear. Jacob could go home whenever he felt like it.

He didn't feel like it.

"Jake, you've been reading the same page for six minutes." Gerald leaned over his son's chair from behind.

Jacob blinked. Nothing on the page looked familiar, which unfortunately proved his father's point. He'd been sitting in one of the common areas for a few hours, trying to relax. Jacob sighed, shut his book, and twisted to look at Gerald. "Can't you let me not-read in peace?"

Gerald moved into a chair facing his son. He watched Jacob's face intently. "You want to tell me what's bothering you?"

Nothing was bothering him. Jacob screwed up his nose, evaluating his father's expression. Gerald's furrowed brow, puppy dog eyes, and firmly set lips were all a dead giveaway. His father was genuinely concerned. Jacob sighed. He couldn't weasel out of this conversation. That was the downside of checking himself into the same facility where his father lived.

"Out with it." Gerald raised an eyebrow, his expression morphing from concerned parent to stern parent.

Jacob shot his father an exasperated look, but nodded. "I'm feeling a little helpless is all. Nothing's happened, I'm just stuck in my own head."

Gerald nodded. "Because the imagination test didn't tell you anything?"

"It's not the test, it's just—there aren't any other options. No one believes I've got your disease, but no one has a good explanation for the *mermaid*." Jacob's lips twisted, like the word hurt to say. "So I'm stuck." He ran his hand through his hair and sagged a little. "I just don't have a plan yet. Hence the helplessness."

"There are some other possibilities for your mermaid." Gerald leaned forward, resting his elbows on his knees. His graying hair fell forward, and he pushed it back automatically.

Jacob narrowed his eyes. "Like what?"

Gerald grinned a little sheepishly. "I've never asked you this before. You know I love you no matter what, right, Jake?"

"Where is this line of questioning going?" Jacob demanded.

Gerald shrugged. "I don't want to insult you or anything. I was just curious if you might have done any experimenting that could have led to … well, adventures that weren't exactly real?"

Jacob blinked at his father, his jaw hanging open. "No!" he blurted. "Dad, I've had the same six-pack of energy drinks in the fridge for six months because I was afraid of what I'd be like if I drank them. And you think I might've decided to find out what an acid trip is like?"

"I was just checking!" Gerald protested, biting back a grin. "Good call on the energy drinks though. You're a pain when you're hyper."

Jacob shot his father a withering glare and dragged his hand across his face. In spite of himself, he chuckled. "You're right, no one even asked me if it could've been drug related. Do I look that clean cut?"

Gerald gave his son a once-over and shrugged again. "Yes."

Jacob snorted. "All right, whatever. You said possibilities, plural. Now that you've confirmed I'm not a druggie, what other theories do you have?"

"Maybe she was real."

The words were said with such genuine openness, Gerald's eyes gentle and his smile encouraging. Jacob tensed in his chair, tearing his eyes away from his father's face and hunching in on himself. His head shook in a slow motion. "No."

A disappointed look crossed his father's face.

"How would you feel if I suggested your hallucinations were real?" Jacob clenched his fists, then sighed and released them.

Gerald rolled his eyes. "I know you don't think it's different, Jake, but it is. When an otherwise healthy nineteen-year-old says he saw a mermaid, I have to believe there's a logical explanation. Maybe the mermaid part is made up—you could've had a weird dream—but why should that automatically mean the woman herself isn't real?" He crossed his arms, his expression daring Jacob to argue with him.

Footsteps sounded in the doorway, and Jacob glanced over his shoulder, relaxing when he spotted an orderly. His back was to the door, which made him feel exposed. He'd been jumpy ever since Sevencea disappeared. Who was he kidding? He'd been jumpy for a year, just waiting for his fears to come true.

"I don't get out much, Dad. Where would I have even met her to come up with this dream you think I had?"

"You said you met her on your beach, right?" Gerald's eyebrows drew together into the thinking face he and Jacob shared.

Jacob nodded. "She just swam up and started talking to me." He could picture her, draped over the rock she'd used as a perch. Why was that memory so clear?

Gerald tilted his head slightly. "I know your beach is private property, but someone could find their way onto it. Maybe you actually met a woman on the beach. As to the rest, well, I know you hate the loneliness theory, but…" He trailed off and offered an apologetic half-smile.

Jacob took a deep breath, trying to give the theory genuine consideration before rejecting it out of hand. He shouldn't let irritation or anger be his initial reaction. "I hate thinking of myself as lonely." He flinching as he forced the words out. "I don't feel lonely."

"That's because you've always been fine to be on your own," Gerald pointed out. "But being good at being on your own, or even recharging by yourself, doesn't mean you don't still need other people."

"I know that." And he did. He'd had friends in boarding school. Initially he'd hated being sent off to school, but being stationary had eventually been a blessing. When he'd moved to Hawaii, he'd allowed those connections to wither and hadn't replaced them. Since he'd bitten his mother's head off, all he'd had was his father.

Jacob dropped his head into his hands. "Oh no."

"What?" Gerald leaned forward, trying to catch Jacob's eye.

"I'm a hermit," Jacob muttered. He could see his father from the corner of his eye, but didn't feel like looking up. How had he refused to acknowledge how sequestered he'd made his life? Maybe in the privacy of his own home he'd been able to lie to himself, but his father and Dr. Wilcox had been chipping away at the lies he'd constructed since he got to Mana'o. He'd never been forced to self-reflect so much in his life. For a brief moment, he missed the comfort of his home, where no one made him look at himself. That wasn't actually true though. Admitting it to himself hurt, but it was necessary. He'd isolated himself. Maybe unintentionally at first, but he'd still done it. Now he needed to figure out how to fix it.

Gerald made a sympathetic noise and patted Jacob's knee. "I've been trying to tell you that for a year, Jake."

Jacob finally laughed. He rubbed his hands across his face and lifted his head. "Yeah, you have. I've just been living in denial, I guess."

"Denial is a powerful thing," Gerald acknowledged. "But you see what I mean. When you've sequestered yourself the way you did, your mind may have tried to compensate for you. That doesn't mean you're getting sick."

Something, maybe a predecessor to hope, sparked in the back of Jacob's mind. He refused to pull it forward and look at it too closely. So, he'd had an epiphany about his mental health. His concerns about inheriting his father's illness could still be valid. Or they might not be. Jacob had no idea how to voice that, but Gerald smiled, like he understood.

Jacob opened his mouth to speak. His father's eyes flitted toward the doorway behind Jacob, then went wide. Fear and hope struggled on his face.

"Jake," Gerald whispered, "be honest. Am I having an episode?"

Jacob twisted in his chair, then lurched to his feet. From her suit dress to her heels, she looked exactly as she had the last time he'd laid eyes on her. Only her expression was changed. She looked more open and vulnerable than any time Jacob could remember.

For a heartbeat, Jacob clutched the chair, staring at her. Then he flung himself forward and wrapped his arms around her. Her arms came up, and she returned the hug with a fierceness he didn't expect.

Jacob squeezed his eyes shut and buried his face in her shoulder. "*Mom.*"

Chapter Thirty-Six

❀

Maggie didn't bat an eye when Sevencea ordered herself a cab. The older woman offered a farewell wave as Sevencea dashed out the door to meet the arriving taxi. Jacob's camera bag hung at her hip, her money tucked safely inside.

Sevencea slid into the vehicle. "Relaxation Cove," she instructed. She took a deep breath and attempted to find a level of calm. Just like before, if Jacob wasn't at this place, at least she would know. She closed her eyes, then turned her gaze to the window for a distraction from her dancing stomach.

Not overly familiar with the area, Sevencea didn't realize they were going the wrong way until she saw the sign declaring Relaxing Cove was just ahead.

"No!" she cried out. "I said Relaxation! Not Relaxing! This is the wrong place!" She winced. She wasn't normally confrontational. What if the driver grew irritated and just dropped her on the side of the road?

In the rearview mirror, the driver's eyes lit up with understanding. "Ah, you mean rehab!" He chuckled, made a u-turn, and headed back the opposite direction. "Sorry, miss. Most people going out that way don't take a cab. You understand."

Sevencea let out a breath as the tension eased from her shoulders. Well, at least he wasn't angry. She watched the road with a careful eye until she was confident they were going the right way. Studying maps could only get her so far, but she was slowly becoming familiar with the island.

The drive was longer than Sevencea expected, but her driver eventually delivered her to the correct destination.

"Want me to wait?" he asked, tallying up the bills she'd handed him.

"No, that's all right." Having a different driver on the way back wouldn't be the worst thing. Besides, she was comfortable calling her own taxis and hadn't been overcharged this time. Being human was getting easier every day.

Plus, it felt discouraging to walk into the building assuming she wouldn't find Jacob there.

Like the last facility, the doors slid open for her. A young man staffed the desk, smiling with a level of enthusiasm that didn't seem to correlate with his job. "Welcome to Relaxation Cove!" He spread his arms wide, like he'd just delivered a blessing.

"Hi." Sevencea bit her bottom lip, then released it and stood straighter. "I'm looking for someone."

The man sighed. "I've told everyone who's asked, and I'll tell you too. That guy in the sunglasses is the gardener, not Bono. I know he uses too much hair gel. Trust me, I've told him. But Ty doesn't listen to anybody, let alone me."

It had been a day or two since Sevencea had heard a sentence she didn't understand to this extent, but it wasn't about Jacob, so she ignored it completely. "No, I'm looking for Jacob Pearson. His father is getting treatment in a facility like this, but I'm not sure which one. Jacob and I lost contact a few weeks ago, and I haven't been able to find him."

The man typed rapidly and scanned his screen, then shook his head. He looked back up to meet her eyes. "I'm not technically supposed to give out information relating to patients, but we don't have any patients with the last name Pearson, so … We're probably not your place."

Sevencea exhaled slowly. She wasn't surprised, but fighting off the dark cloud of disappointment was more difficult than she'd been expecting. "Thanks for checking."

"Oh, sure, anytime!" The young man shot her another broad grin and offered a farewell wave.

Retreating back outside, Sevencea sucked in a deep breath, then released it. She repeated the process as she tried to settle herself. "Only one place left to try," she murmured. She squeezed her eyes shut. What then? What if Jacob wasn't there either? She couldn't get to the other side of the island before the last facility on her list closed for the night. That meant returning to The Makai. Empty handed. Alone.

No, not alone. There were people at The Makai who cared about her. Sevencea relaxed a little and evened out her breathing. She needed a phone to get a new taxi. Pivoting in place, her eye caught on a public use phone in the facility's lobby. Her shoulders slumped with relief, and she reentered the building.

Sevencea trudged through the lobby door.

"Struck out again?" Maggie offered a wince that might have been meant in sympathy.

"Only one place left I can check," Sevencea confirmed. She shifted the camera bag from her hip to her back and leaned against the counter with a huff. "Anything happening here that can distract me?"

Maggie shrugged. "Janet called again. Three of the photos you sent her are going in next week's magazine. It's last minute, but she said your work was worth the trouble. She sent you an email, too. She'd like photos to go with six more articles for the website."

"That's great!" Sevencea let the rush of success chase away the doom and gloom she'd been wallowing in. Having her own email address for her blossoming business was another thing Maggie had helped with. As usual, the older woman hadn't even questioned Sevencea's ignorance.

Sevencea gave Maggie a calculating look. "You should be my manager. You seem to have a gift for marketing me."

Maggie snorted. "I've got a job. At least half my time is spent just making sure my staff don't break everything."

Sevencea raised an eyebrow. "Did I miss something?"

"Nah." Maggie chuckled and shook her head. "Frank scared Jim this morning, but that happens at least twice a week. When Jim yelled, though, Keisha broke a glass, so honestly the kid was in more danger from her than from Frank." Maggie cast a fond glance toward one of the Employees Only doors that led into the back. Most of the main staff were probably home by now. Maggie, and now Sevencea, were the only people who actually lived at The Makai.

"I'm sorry I missed it." Sevencea had scared Jim once or twice herself. He seemed to have warmed to her a little, but the poor kid was just terrified of women. Between Maggie, Keisha, and Sevencea, Jim was going to have a heart attack one of these days.

Sevencea relaxed against the counter, listening to the ticking of the clock on the wall. The Makai could be a bustling place sometimes, but it also had moments of glorious peace.

Maggie broke the silence. "Are you going to the last place tomorrow?"

Sevencea looked down, running her thumb over the back of her other hand. "What if he's not there?" The words were barely a whisper.

"Then we form a new plan. We start over, and we keep going." Maggie's reply was prompt and firm. "We'll find your man, *Kama Lei*. In the meantime, you're welcome here as long as you want. Plus, don't forget your blossoming career in photography. The world doesn't end if he's not there."

"Thank you, Maggie." Sevencea laid her hand on Maggie's and met the older woman's eyes. "I don't know what I would have done if I hadn't met Caroline. Leading me straight to you was the best thing she could have done."

Before Maggie, Sevencea hadn't had any human identity beyond her quest to find Jacob. Now, she had friends, a career, and an entire life that didn't have to have Jacob in it. However, if sneaking food from under Frank's nose had taught her anything, it was that brownies were good by themselves, but amazing with caramel. With the help of Maggie and everyone at The Makai, she'd built something great here. It was time to put the cherry on top.

"Every step you take has purpose." Maggie tapped the countertop to punctuate each word. "You're here at The Makai for a reason. Jacob went missing for a reason. You went looking for him for a reason. Even when faced with outcomes we don't like, there's always a design behind the journey. Trust that."

"I always thought of my father as the wisest person in the world, but you're making him work for it." Sevencea squeezed Maggie's hand and released it.

Maggie shook her head and chuckled. "Well, you tell your father he's welcome to join me for a battle of wits any time."

The thought of her father taking to land was amusing, if unlikely. "I'll be sure to extend the invitation," Sevencea promised. She suddenly felt a little wistful for her clan. Hopefully her father wasn't worried about her. She'd told him was she was doing, of course, and he'd given her his blessing. But she was still his youngest, and doing something so unusual had to worry him a little. Hopefully when she found Jacob, she could bring him home with her and finally introduce him to Brineus.

Maggie waved Sevencea away. "Go get some rest. Frank's probably got leftovers in the kitchen if you're hungry."

By this point, offering more gratitude was redundant. Sevencea allowed her parting smile to speak for her.

Chapter Thirty-Seven

It had taken a few pointed glances from Gerald and Meredith, but eventually Jacob did give them some time alone. Reluctantly. He meandered the halls, doing his best to stay busy anywhere except his father's room. When he'd talked to his mother about coming to visit, he hadn't expected her to come so quickly. She was usually busy with work. He also hadn't realized how much he'd missed her until she stood right in front of him.

If the way she'd clung to him was any indication, she'd missed him just as much. He'd never felt more guilty about his graduation meltdown than in that moment. He'd tried to apologize again, but she'd shushed him.

"Already forgiven, dear. We don't dwell, we grow."

With those words of wisdom, she'd released him to go to Gerald. Jacob realized then that, until he'd reacted to his mother, Gerald had no way of knowing she was real. Once Jacob and his mother parted, his parents had fallen into an embrace they took a while to come out of.

Jacob didn't begrudge them time together. If anything, he suspected their relationship needed some resolution just as desperately.

Still, it was agonizing waiting around for an appropriate moment to rejoin them. Nothing he tried to distract himself with worked. A few of the staff members gave him odd looks for wandering the halls, but that wasn't unusual. Dr. Wilcox had kept Jacob's reason for coming to Mana'o in confidence, but rumors had spread anyway. Jacob knew no one thought he should be there.

The smallest part of him was starting to agree. He didn't know how he'd imagined a mermaid. Maybe he never would. Still, his father had a point. Dr. Wilcox had a point. They'd both tried to tell him this entire time that his situation wasn't proof he was sick. He still thought that an imaginary romance with a mermaid should have warranted a little more concern, but maybe he shouldn't have assumed his whole life was over so soon.

Jacob halted in the middle of the hallway. He hadn't made that assumption just because of Sevencea. He'd made that assumption a year ago, when his father first got sick. Jacob let out his breath, his gaze vacant as he stared into the distance. Maybe this whole thing was a self-fulfilling prophecy. Had he imagined Sevencea because he'd been so sure he'd get sick someday?

Down the hall, Gerald's door opened. His father's head popped out and glanced in both directions. When he spotted Jacob, his eyes lit up, and he made a "come here" motion.

It took Jacob a second to realize he was being summoned. He walked to his father's room, then stopped in the doorway. His mother sat in Gerald's normal chair, looking unusually at ease. Gerald had retreated into the room and sat on the edge of his bed, facing Meredith. He gestured for Jacob to take the second chair.

"When was the last time we were all together?" Meredith asked, a little wistful.

They had to think about that for a moment. Jacob finally answered. "Christmas before graduation."

Meredith's expression contorted briefly, then smoothed back out. "I'm sorry I haven't made being here in person a priority. For both of you." She paused and looked to Gerald, then Jacob. "I've talked about this a bit with you both already, but I wanted to say it as a family too. I thought taking care of what we'd built," she reached for Gerald's hand, "was the best way I could care for you, while you were being treated for your illness. I didn't even think that you might need me somewhere other than the command seat of our company." Her lips tilted upward on one side.

Jacob felt a knot in the pit of his stomach. Why had he lashed out at her at graduation? Why hadn't he just talked to her? "I know you said not to keep apologizing, but I am sorry, Mom. I should never have shredded our relationship the way I did."

Meredith reached for him with her other hand. "Your anger, volatile though it may have been, was born from a place of love, dear. I hated it when we weren't speaking, but I always knew you felt you were defending your father. I was merely biding my time until I could explain my side. I didn't realize that we all needed to air out a few things." She looked back to Gerald, a softness in her expression.

Gerald squeezed her hand. "You know I supported your decision. I may not have agreed with it fully, but I understood it. I love that you wanted to help me and protect the work we'd done together. You want to problem solve for everyone. That's not a bad thing, Merry."

Jacob's eyes filled with moisture. He hurried to blink it back. Aside from that awful hallucination, he hadn't heard his father call his mother "Merry" since the last time they'd been together. If anything was proof that his parents were getting back on the same page, it was this.

Meredith spotted the gleam in Jacob's eyes and held up her hands. "Oh no, dear, please don't cry, you'll set me off. I'd much rather we spend some quality time together." She reached for him, squeezing his hand with an encouraging smile.

Jacob laughed and blinked rapidly, dispelling the still-forming tears. "Me too, Mom." He glanced over at his father, who was staring at the ceiling. "You okay, Dad?"

Gerald nodded, tilting his head down to meet Jacob's eyes. "Yeah, sorry, I just figured if we were trying to all start crying I should head this," he gestured to his face, "off early." He reached up to rub at his eyes, then held out both hands in a thumbs up. "I'm good."

Jacob snorted at the same time his mother let out a musical laugh. They made eye contact again, smiled, and promptly continued laughing. Gerald joined in easily, his own laughter boisterous in the small room.

There was a lightness in Jacob's chest, a sensation he'd forgotten the feeling of. His frustrations, anger, and fear from this last year just didn't seem important right now. Some of it he'd already let go of, and the relief was so much stronger than he'd realized. Maybe this whole thing was the reason his mind had invented Sevencea in the first place. To bring him back to the present, where he could acknowledge his flaws and repair his relationships. To make him start living again. Maybe it had worked.

As the laughter died down, Gerald cleared his throat. "We were talking a little, Jake, about you." He released Meredith's hand, clasping his own hands in front of him.

"About me, what?" Jacob prompted. His eyes darted between his parents. Neither of them were giving clues with their expressions.

Meredith, her other hand still clasping Jacob's, gave him a light squeeze. "We think you should go home, dear."

Jacob slowly nodded. "I've been starting to think along those lines," he admitted. The exact thought hadn't yet come, but he'd been headed there. The natural conclusion of believing he'd trapped himself with fear was to face that fear, and leave behind the safety net, the contingency plan, that he'd insisted on. His place at Mana'o was just proof he'd been planning his life in terms of when he would get sick. When had he chosen to stop living?

Gerald's eyebrows rose. "I thought we were going to get more pushback on that." He held up his hands. "Not that I'm complaining."

Jacob chuckled. "I've been thinking about it a lot, today especially. I've kind of figured out what I've been doing to myself." He paused, looking between his parents. "When I found out you were sick, Dad … Well, we all know how I reacted. Between my anger at you, Mom, and the fear that whatever Dad has could be hereditary, I was a mess. Except I didn't want anyone to know that, so I channeled those emotions elsewhere. Like, moving to Hawaii to be near Dad, but cutting myself off from everyone else in the process. I think I convinced myself I had this inevitable fate, and that it wasn't worth living my life if there was going to be this disease waiting for me. And that's not fair to you either, Dad. Your life isn't over because you're sick. You live here, sure, but you're still living. I wasn't even thinking about how what I was doing must have looked to you. I don't think I meant to stop living, but once I had, I didn't know how to fix it."

Meredith stood and moved her chair next to Jacob. She leaned over and pulled him into a hug. Jacob melted into her shoulder.

"I tried telling you," Gerald reminded him. "Sometimes flat out, and sometimes I hinted at it, but you didn't believe me. The lies we tell ourselves are powerful."

"I still don't know what the mermaid thing was about," Jacob admitted. Calling Sevencea by name felt too close to saying she was real. Maybe she was based in some reality, but he wasn't ready to deal with that yet. "But you know that movie *It's a Wonderful Life*?" His parents nodded. "Maybe my brain was acting like my guardian angel, showing me something that would make me start living in forward motion again. Like a kick-start."

"I love that movie." Meredith kept one arm around Jacob's shoulders and smiled at him. "There's some good lessons in there."

Gerald offered a reassuring smile as well. "If it took an imaginary mermaid to make you want to live again, then I don't care if you end up with a wood nymph or a goblin next. So long as you don't close yourself off."

Jacob blinked at his father, then dissolved into laughter.

Chapter Thirty-Eight

Day 27

The taxi idled in the cracked parking lot, waiting for Sevencea. She walked outside, camera bag slung around her neck. The morning sunlight was already beating down, promising a warm day. As she went to get into the car, a spasm rushed through her legs. Sevencea faltered and clutched the door.

"Ma'am, you okay?" The older woman driving the cab twisted around with wide eyes.

"I'm fine, thank you," Sevencea reassured her. She glared at her legs. She was not planning to end her search for Jacob by breaking her neck in a parking lot. Once she found him—because she *had* to find him on this trip—she needed to make a quick trip back to the ocean. A visit to Athys might not be amiss either. She might not have been following the rules he'd given her to the letter, but maybe he could make an improved version that wasn't quite as dangerous.

"All right, if you're sure."

The woman pulled the cab out onto the road, and they set off. Mana'o Treatment Center was Sevencea's last shot, and also the furthest away. The drive would take over an hour, plenty of time for Sevencea to explore all possible scenarios and get worked up over at least a few of them. The longer trip was a lot more expensive, but as it turned out, being a professional photographer was kind of lucrative. At least, in Sevencea's limited understanding of money. Given that she hadn't intended to start a photography business, she was doing a decent job at it.

In a week, there would be a physical magazine in the world with the notation, "Photo by Sevencea," under several of the photographs. The greater population of the island would see her work. More importantly, they'd see how she'd learned to use Jacob's magic. In a way, succeeding at photography almost made her feel guilty. Was she stealing his magic by using it herself? She remembered the look on Jacob's face when he'd given her the underwater camera and the guilt fled. He would love that she was still using a camera. She couldn't wait to tell him about it. Sevencea smiled and leaned back against the seat.

The one thing that had given Sevencea pause in arranging the details for the magazine was that she didn't have a surname. Maggie didn't seem to care, but Sevencea had thought that it might be an issue for Janet. When she'd asked if it mattered, Janet had written back that it didn't bother her in the slightest. According to Janet, if it worked for Beyoncé, it was worth trying.

Sevencea had needed to look up Beyoncé to understand the sentiment, and ended up with a few pulsing melodies stuck in her head for the rest of the day. Still, the comparison seemed complimentary. With everything else looking up, Sevencea could only hope and pray that her success streak would carry through today as well.

After a long and uneventful drive, the taxi finally slowed as the driver turned into a parking lot. She put the taxi in park, turned around, and offered Sevencea a bright grin. "You have arrived, my dear. Want me to wait?"

Sevencea gnawed on her lip. "No," she decided, pronouncing the word with more syllables than normal. "If I end up needing a ride, I'll call for a new cab." She glanced at the meter and dug for the money in her camera bag, handing over the required amount.

The driver looked skeptical, but accepted the money. "All right, if you're sure. Good luck."

Sevencea glanced back over her shoulder as she exited the vehicle and offered a grateful smile. She took a deep breath and stepped forward to the doors. Either Jacob was here or he wasn't. This was it. She pulled the door open and stepped inside.

The woman at the reception desk had dark blonde hair and a pleasant expression. She looked up to greet Sevencea, then seemed a little taken aback, likely by all the pearls the mermaid still wore. She recovered quickly.

"Welcome to Mana'o. Can I help you?"

"I'm looking for Jacob Pearson." Sevencea fought to keep her voice from shaking. "Can you tell me if he's here, or maybe his father?"

Something crossed the woman's face, then vanished too quickly to identify. "I'm afraid I can't give you any information, ma'am. Unless you're family."

Sevencea squeezed her eyes shut and reopened them, focusing on the woman. "It's important," she insisted. Her voice cracked a little. "Please, can you just tell me if either of them is here? I need to know."

"It's against policy," the woman offered. She sounded apologetic, despite her professional tone.

While it had been against policy at the other two facilities, Sevencea had still been able to find out that Jacob wasn't there. Stealing verbiage from those conversations, she tried again. "I don't need any confidential information. I just need to know if they're here. It's not a complicated question!" She took a deep breath, trying to keep her expression calmer than she felt.

"Everything okay in here?" A large man in a nurse's uniform came around the corner. He eyed them both warily.

"I need to know if Jacob Pearson or his father are at this facility," Sevencea explained again. "Please, I've been looking for him for weeks!"

The facility employees shared a loaded glance, then both shook their heads. "We can't release any kind of information, ma'am," the young man told her.

"You have to!" Sevencea exclaimed, beginning to lose her tenuous grip on her self-control. "I didn't come all this way for nothing!" She'd known there was a chance he might not be here, but to be told nothing was worse.

The woman leaned over to a pager system, her brow furrowed. "Security, to the front desk please. Security, to the front desk."

"Ma'am, I'm afraid I'm going to have to ask you to leave," the nurse said. He held out his hands in a placating gesture.

"Quit acting like I'm going to attack you," Sevencea snapped. She rolled her eyes at the man's stance. "I'm not leaving until you tell me if he's here or not." She adjusted her own stance to something hopefully more resolute.

Whether the nurse had a response for that was unclear. Two large men in matching uniforms entered the room. They were looking right at her, and not in a way that suggested she would get what she wanted.

"Ma'am, we need you to leave, or we will help you do so." One of the new arrivals spoke. The other one loomed beside him. "There's nothing here for you."

Sevencea wilted. The words cut through her bravado and pierced the hope she'd allowed to balloon in her chest. She'd failed at the final stop on her quest. Maggie might think there were more options to be pursued, but where else was she supposed to start? Tears pricking her eyes, Sevencea nodded at the guards and escorted herself outside.

To her surprise, the taxi was right where she'd left it. The passenger's side window rolled down, and the driver leaned across the seat. "I had a feeling." Her tone was kind. "No luck in there?"

"No luck," Sevencea echoed. Her voice sounded drained of life, but she couldn't bring herself to care yet.

"Hop in, my dear. Let's get you back home."

Funny, Sevencea mused, how home meant The Makai now. Where else would she go? The ocean was still a home, but she didn't have a purpose there, or anyone to share it with. Her family all had roles that didn't involve her. At The Makai though, she was part of something. They were a team, a different kind of family.

Sevencea met the driver's eyes in the rear view mirror and nodded. "Yes. Home sounds good."

Maggie was waiting when Sevencea returned. Sevencea had managed not to cry during the drive back, but she could tell her eyes were red-rimmed. Maggie took one look at her and pulled her into a hug.

Sevencea burst into tears, tightly returning the embrace. "I know you said we can keep trying, but I don't know what else to do." Sobs punctuated the words. She hated sounding so out of control, but her tears were unmanageable right now. A surge of pain flooded her calves. Sevencea made a choking noise and tightened her grip on Maggie for support. She didn't have the energy to worry about her legs right now.

Maggie stroked Sevencea's long hair and made soothing noises. "We just talked about this, *Kama Lei*," she murmured. "This isn't the end."

"It feels like it," Sevencea countered. She sucked in a deep breath and repressed a hiccup.

Maggie pushed Sevencea away. She held her at arm's length, with a hand on each of her shoulders, and raised an eyebrow at her. "Why are you here?"

"To look for Jacob!" Sevencea blurted. Maybe she hadn't always had her mission at the forefront of her mind, but it had always been the main goal.

Maggie scowled at her. "That may have been why you first set foot on this island, but it is not why you are here. Tell me, why are you here?"

Sevencea hesitated. Thankfully, the distraction allowed her to breath more easily, and her tears were subsiding. Her cheeks itched where moisture was drying, but she wouldn't dislodge Maggie's arms to scratch her face.

"You are here to be a light," Maggie said firmly.

"Oh." Sevencea blinked. She hadn't thought of her purpose in that way, but she liked it.

"Who needs you?" Maggie continued, her eyebrow raising again.

Sevencea sniffed a little. "I'm guessing the answer isn't Jacob?"

Jacob *did* need her, but she was less sure how to help him now that she didn't have a plan to find him.

Maggie chuckled. "He might, and we'll see what we can do about that, but he's not the only one. You have a family, yes? And you have all of us, here. You make my life interesting. You're helping turn Jim into a somewhat coherent young man. You're an extra set of hands and a friendly face for Keisha. And something about you has made you the only person Frank will allow to help in the kitchen. We all need you, in our own ways. You have a place here."

Sevencea's eyes filled with tears again. "Thank you," she whispered, trying to stem the flow. "You're all like family now."

"What is your goal?" Maggie asked, her voice quieter now.

Before, Sevencea would have said, "To find Jacob." Now, she gave it some thought. "To learn. To gain more mastery over my magic." Her hand went to the camera bag. Her magic of bringing humans below the ocean surface was for her mermaid life. On land, Jacob's magic had clearly extended to her. The more she used it, the more she loved it. Now that a career was growing before her, she felt a sense of purpose she'd never achieved underwater.

Maggie didn't bat an eye at the word magic. "You have a passion and a skill, and people willing to help you build a career. You've got this little motley crew here at The Makai behind you. And you bring light into all our lives, whether you mean to or not. So no matter if you ever find that missing boy of yours, he does not define you or your journey." She released Sevencea shoulders. "Understood?"

Sevencea pulled the older woman into another hug. "Thank you. For everything, but especially for not letting me wallow."

Maggie chuckled. She returned the hug, then pulling back with a wry smile. "Anytime, *Kama Lei*. Go wash your face, all right? Take a breather, then we'll find you some work to keep you occupied."

Sevencea nodded. She took a deep breath as Maggie stepped away. She'd ruminated over the blessings of what she'd found on land before, but now, with Maggie's words rattling around her mind, she felt peace washing over her. Jacob was important. He would always be important. But she *could* live a life while she was looking for him.

Chapter Thirty-Nine

That afternoon Jacob began to slowly pack his bag. He'd barely started, when Dr. Wilcox appeared in his doorway.

"Jacob, do you have a second?"

Jacob glanced up with a pair of underwear in each hand. He flushed and hurriedly dropped the clothing into his bag. "Yeah, sure. I'm just, well, I'm actually packing."

Dr. Wilcox's eyebrows flew up. "You're going home?"

"I think so. I've had a few epiphanies since the last time we talked. It's time for me stop living in fear, to stop putting my life on hold." Jacob's commitment to his new life outlook grew firmer with each passing hour. It was a relief. He'd been concerned he might wake up having changed his mind entirely.

"All right then." A beaming smile crossed Dr. Wilcox's face. "Good for you. Can I steal you away though, for a minute? I need to show you something."

"Sure." Jacob side-eyed the doctor as he followed him out of the room, but Dr. Wilcox offered no clues.

They headed down the hall and into the doctor's office. Dr. Wilcox gestured for Jacob to take a seat. The older man opened a laptop and clicked around.

Jacob gave it a minute, then lost the battle with his self-control and blurted, "So, what's going on?" His eyes darted between the computer and Dr. Wilcox.

"We had an odd incident this morning." Dr. Wilcox tapped one finger against his desk in a slow rhythm. He looked uncharacteristically hesitant.

"Okay…? What does that have to do with me?" Jacob glanced at the laptop again. Dr. Wilcox didn't normally use a computer when they met. Its presence was giving him pause.

"All right, let me try and make this easier. If I were to describe a blonde woman with blue eyes, an athletic figure, and a lot of pearls, you would think of…?" Dr. Wilcox trailed off, his eyebrows raised expectantly.

Jacob inhaled sharply. He squinted at the doctor, brow furrowed. Where was this going? "You're obviously describing Sevencea," he snapped. "I mean, blonde's not quite the right word for her hair, but it's close enough. She wears this long strand of pearls that's looped around her neck, and she's got some kind of headdress piece with a pearl right here." He poked himself in the forehead. "Her tail—" He stopped himself. He was supposed to be figuring out why he'd imagined a mermaid in the first place, not dwelling on the imaginary details.

Dr. Wilcox nodded. "That's what I thought. We had a disturbance in the lobby earlier. A young woman made a scene. She bore a remarkable resemblance to your description of your mermaid. With the notable exception that this woman had legs." His lips twitched toward a smile.

Jacob's breath caught. Why was this happening? Why, when he'd finally reached some kind of peace with his fears, was Dr. Wilcox dangling this kind of hope in front of him?

"Sevencea wasn't real," he bit out. His eyebrows drew together, and he glowered at the doctor. "Best case scenario she was just a really detailed dream."

"Jacob. I would not be bringing this up if I didn't think there was a chance it was legitimate. My goal is not to harm you." Dr. Wilcox folded his hands.

Jacob offered a reluctant nod of acknowledgment. The doctor evaluated his expression for a moment, then reached for the laptop and spun it around. A security video filled the screen. Dr. Wilcox clicked the play button, then sat back, watching Jacob's face.

The picture was clear and detailed, not like the black and white, grainy images Jacob expected from movies and television. The video moved in slow motion, giving Jacob time to absorb every detail. He could see the receptionist—whose name he could never remember—and the woman approaching the front desk…

"Holy crap."

Dr. Wilcox grunted, the noise filled with undisguised satisfaction.

Jacob's whole body felt numb. Was his heart still beating? He couldn't tell. "But … she has legs?" Jacob leaned forward to get a better look. He stared at the screen with wide eyes, studying the woman he'd convinced himself was fictional.

She was standing! She had legs! Nice legs, too, as far as he could tell, but more importantly, legs! Her beautiful tail flicked through his memory. He frowned at how vivid it was. Then again, he'd also been certain she wasn't real.

"She was asking for you." Dr. Wilcox folded his hands on the desk, studying Jacob.

Jacob felt his heart stop. "She's real." The words were barely a whisper. Jacob cleared his throat, then looked up from the screen to meet Dr. Wilcox's eyes. "Why would I think she was a mermaid?"

Dr. Wilcox frowned and evaluated Jacob for a moment. "There's plenty of possible explanations. I know you don't like it when I call you a hypochondriac, Jacob, but there are cases of people actually worrying themselves into poor health over fears of illness."

Jacob ran his hand through his hair, releasing his breath. "Yeah. Yeah, maybe." He'd been mulling over possible explanations. That one was sounding more and more likely.

The doctor nodded, his expression sympathetic. "I truly think you convinced yourself that you were going to inherit your father's illness, despite all evidence to the contrary. Then, when a girl you met didn't come around for a few days, you created a scenario that validated your fears and came here. Clearly, this young woman has been missing you. She was quite upset when Daisie wouldn't give her any information."

A cold shock traveled down Jacob's spine. He started in his chair, "She left! She doesn't know I'm here! How am I supposed to find her?"

Dr. Wilcox winced. "Hmm. I don't have an answer for that. According to Daisie she came here in a cab. I'll look into it and see what I can find out, all right?"

Jacob nodded absently. She'd been there, at Mana'o, and now she was out of reach again. If Dr. Wilcox didn't figure out a way to track her down, Jacob might actually lose his mind. Of course he could do his own digging, but where could he even start? Also, the receptionist's name was Daisie? He really should try to remember that. For the first time in weeks, hope pulsed in his chest and he didn't push it aside. "Please, I have to find her. I need to understand."

"Trust me," Dr. Wilcox sighed, "I'd love to understand too."

Jacob skidded into his father's doorway. He grabbed the edge to catch himself and avoid falling into the room.

"Welcome back." Gerald glanced up from his book with an expression caught between concern and amusement. Meredith was on her laptop on the other chair. She looked up, startled.

"She was real," Jacob breathed out. His chest heaved from running down the hallway. "The whole time, she was real."

Gerald fist-pumped the air. "Told you so!"

"You did not!" Jacob protested. He collapsed into his normal chair. "You just asked me yesterday if she could have been an acid trip!"

Meredith snorted loudly. Her hand flew up to cover her mouth.

His father set aside the book and focused on Jacob. "You called me right after you met her and made an offhand comment about imagining her. I told you then she was real."

Jacob did remember that conversation. He nodded. "So why didn't you say anything about that when I checked myself in?"

Gerald snorted. "Jake, you led with, 'she was a mermaid.' At that point I figured I'd leave any determinations on your sanity to the professionals. Just because you don't have what I've got doesn't mean there's nothing wrong with you. We already know you're a paranoid hermit, so—" He shrugged and smirked at his son.

"Gerald!" Meredith's tone was scandalized. She shut her laptop and stood, coming over to rest her hand on Jacob's shoulder. "Ignore him, dear. What do you mean, the mermaid is real? What's going on?"

Jacob shot his mother a grateful look, then rolled his eyes at his father. "Well, she's got legs, for starters. I don't know why I thought she had that gorgeous tail, but she has really nice legs."

Gerald raised an eyebrow at him. He flushed.

Meredith repressed a smile. "How did you find out she was real?"

"She was here!" Jacob flung his hands out. "She was looking for me. I told her about you," he gestured toward Gerald, "so she must have been trying to find me though you. She got chased off by security, but Dr. Wilcox saw the security footage and put two and two together. He showed me, and now I know she's real!" Jacob sighed. His initial high was beginning to wear off, but his heart was still racing. "But there's no way to find her. Dr. Wilcox is going to look into it, but it's not like she left behind a business card."

"You'll find her." Meredith squeezed Jacob's shoulder. "If she was able to track you here, then it's only a matter of time before you two find each other."

"I wish I had your confidence." Jacob reached for his mother's hand. "I seem to default to a pessimistic outlook."

"Scars of a troubled childhood?" Gerald asked wryly.

Meredith glared at him.

Gerald shrugged and mouthed, "What?"

Jacob gave his mother's hand a reassuring squeeze and shot his father a pointed look. "I don't think boarding school made me a pessimist, Dad. It's just my character."

Meredith scoffed. "You're not a pessimist, Jacob; you're overly practical. I should know, you get it from me. You need to take a page from your father's book and realize that just because the worst of two options is likely, that doesn't make it inevitable." She patted his shoulder again, then moved to lean against the bed.

Jacob tilted his head. "Huh. You might have a point."

"Your mother always has a point," Gerald corrected him.

Jacob chuckled and nodded, shooting a smile at his mother. "That's true." Her return smile wrapped him in warmth. He'd had no idea how much he'd missed her until he had her back.

"Now you need to find this girl," Meredith prompted. "Do you know anything that could help us look?"

"Us?" Jacob repeated, his eyes widening. "Wait, you're going to help?"

"As much as we're able," Gerald affirmed. He set his book aside. "This girl is important to you, so she's important to us."

"We just need a plan," Meredith continued. She moved over to the chair where she'd left her laptop, opened it, and set the device on the bed so they could all see it.

Jacob held up his hands. "I mean, I know this is 'The Big Island' and everything, but it's still an island. I could just wander around until I've searched it all. Or I could stay here, in case she comes back." He gnawed on his lip, considering. What if she gave up? What if she left the island and he never found her? He didn't even know her last name!

Meredith was shaking her head, but Gerald spoke first. "You know she's on the island, and there's only around two hundred thousand people here, last I checked. Maybe if you ask enough people, you'll find someone who knows her." He was smirking, but he seemed partially serious.

"You're both being ridiculous," Meredith huffed. She wore her exasperated "business face." "We're going to start looking online."

Jacob blinked. "What, you want me to just Google her?"

"Everyone's on the internet. Especially girls who aren't mermaids." Gerald winked at his son. Jacob rolled his eyes, and he chuckled.

"I guess it doesn't hurt to try." Jacob suspected Dr. Wilcox was already looking online, but doing his own research was probably a good idea.

Gerald patted his arm. "Exactly, Jake. You've got to put some effort into this hunt. After all, if your not-a-mermaid has been looking for you this whole time, the least you can do is return the favor."

"You have a point," Jacob admitted. He moved to his mother's side, then took a seat on the bed and pulled the laptop onto his lap. The niggling fear in the back of his mind whispered that this would all be for nothing. He ignored it. He had to at least try.

"Start with her name," Meredith prompted. She sat beside him, one leg tucked under the other.

Jacob pulled up a browser, typed "Sevencea" into the search bar, and hit enter. He got an initial prompt wondering if he'd mis-spelled his search. Once he'd confirmed he'd typed Sevencea on purpose, he got a few results for microbreweries. Nothing looked related to his mermaid. Or, his human? His mind was still sure she was mythical, despite the new evidence to the contrary.

Meredith made a frustrated noise and shifted the laptop. She leaned over Jacob and added "Hawaii" to the search. "There, see if getting more specific helps."

The new page of results included a recent article about how seasons impact sunsets. "Her name isn't in the search result," Jacob mused. He clicked on the link. "Let's see why this one popped up."

"Hawaiian Shores Today?" Meredith read over his shoulder. She tilted her head.

"It's a local magazine," Jacob explained. "I usually see it at the grocery store." Jacob had never picked up an issue; it was more of a visitor's magazine than a local's magazine. He skimmed through the article, but didn't see Sevencea's name anywhere.

"Try searching the web page." Meredith gestured to the keyboard. "Maybe she's credited as a source?"

Jacob hit the shortcut for the find function, then retyped Sevencea's name. He hit enter. Her name was immediately highlighted. The small font, right underneath one of the stunning sunset photographs, read, "Photograph by Sevencea."

"She's working as a photographer," Jacob breathed, his eyes wide.

Gerald got up from his chair and moved around so he could see the screen. He whistled low under his breath. "Wow, that's a beautiful shot."

Jacob nodded. It really was a gorgeous shot. Memories of teaching Sevencea how to use a camera swirled in his mind. Every moment he'd spent explaining what she'd called his magic must have paid off. The bright colors of her tail swam through his mind again and his brow furrowed. Surely there was a reasonable explanation for that whole mermaid thing. He focused on the website again, looking for any contact information. There wasn't an email address, but there was an email form. The odds of someone actually telling him anything were slim, but he composed a quick message anyway. Then, hoping for actual results, he copied the link to the article, then pulled up his email in a separate tab so he could forward it to Dr. Wilcox. The doctor was just prominent enough in the community to know a lot of people. Maybe he would be able to make some headway with that.

Jacob shut the laptop and handed it back to his mother with a wry smile. "Apparently girls who aren't mermaids really are on the internet."

Chapter Forty

Sevencea had elected to help in the kitchen for the evening. By now everyone knew she'd had a bit of a meltdown over failing to find Jacob, and everyone was giving her sympathetic looks. Maggie was the best at hiding it, but it was still there. Keisha kept trying to give her hugs. Jim gave her sad glances when he thought she wasn't looking. They were all just trying to be nice, but Sevencea didn't want to think about Jacob.

She'd been living with him as the light at the end of the tunnel, and had reacted to the failure of her plan like the light had gone out. Really, she'd never been in a tunnel. She'd been here, on a beautiful island, surrounded by people who cared, and getting better and better at a skill she enjoyed. Maggie was right, it was time to stop wallowing and start living.

Frank was the natural choice for someone to work with who wouldn't give her sympathy eyes or offer platitudes. When Sevencea walked into the kitchen and asked how she could help, he pointed to the ever-present pile of dishes. It was just the kind of busy work she needed.

As she scrubbed, Sevencea allowed herself to think about the upcoming magazine she was being featured in. The news had been exciting, but she hadn't really let herself appreciate it yet. A slow grin spread across her face. People all over the island would see her photography. All her practice to master Jacob's magic had been worth something. It was bittersweet that Jacob couldn't be with her to appreciate this triumph, but using a camera at all was like having a piece of him with her. A piece of him that had given her a purpose and a passion.

Still smiling, Sevencea finished stacking the clean dishes. She sighed. That hadn't taken as long as she'd hoped. Even the pots hadn't had time to get anything crusted to them. A quick rinse and scrub had done the job.

"I'm finished, Frank. Anything else I can do?"

Frank gave the clean dishes a once-over and shrugged. It was the closest thing to approval he ever offered. He waved a hand at some bags on the counter.

Sevencea moved to the bags and peered at them. "Flour, sugar, brown sugar … Do you want me to get these in the right containers, Frank?" Ingredients like this all had their own bins beneath the counters. He must have just had a supply shipment.

Frank nodded, not bothering to turn around again.

Well, that was easy enough. Sevencea hauled up the flour container first. She took care not to open the bag too far so she could control it as she transferred its contents. It was hard to believe that a few weeks ago she wouldn't have had any clue what to do about simple tasks like washing dishes and storing ingredients. It was magical in and of itself to learn the basics of a new world.

With the flour done, Sevencea returned the much heavier container to its place beneath the counter. She began the process over with the sugar. Halfway through pouring the second bag, the strength in her legs evaporated. Sevencea tumbled to the floor with a cry. Her knees crashed against the cool tiles.

Frank whirled around, dashing to her side in an instant. He reached for her shoulders. "Are you all right?"

Sevencea's head snapped up, and she stared at him in unabashed shock. "You talk!"

The older man rolled his eyes and helped pull her up. "Are you all right?" he repeated.

Shaking her head to refocus, Sevencea took stock of her legs. They seemed to be holding her up all right now. Maybe her need to revisit the ocean was more urgent than she'd thought. The realization made her a little sad, though it didn't have to be the end of anything. "I'm okay, I just lost my balance or something."

Frank kept his hands out for a moment, like he thought she might collapse again, then relaxed when Sevencea seemed steady. "Good." He turned back to his work station.

"Wait!" Sevencea thrust a hand out, though Frank wasn't close enough to grab. "I've never heard you say anything before." It wasn't a question. She wasn't sure what her question was. She liked Frank, a lot, but had started to assume he was mute. She'd been too afraid of insulting him to ask outright, so she just followed his lead when it came to communicating. She talked, he pointed.

Frank turned back to face her. He put one hand on the counter, the other on his hip, and nodded. He didn't say anything.

Half a dozen possible questions cycled through Sevencea's head, but ultimately, none of them mattered. Instead, she just smiled at Frank. "Thank you for trusting me." If there was a reason he was usually quiet, his concern for her had overcome it. It was probably the best compliment he could have paid her. She didn't need to press him for his reasons.

Frank's expression softened a little. He reached for her hands, held them lightly, and met her gaze. "Most people bother me. If I don't talk to them, they leave me alone. You don't bother me." He squeezed her hands, then retreated back to his station.

Sevencea stood there for a moment, her mouth hanging slightly open. Then she returned to her work station, grinning a little to herself. "I like you too, Frank."

All she got in response was an annoyed grunt.

Sevencea laughed and returned to the sugar. She'd spilled some when she fell, but a broom would rectify that. She needed to go back to the water, but it was late. As beautiful as the ocean was at night, walking alone to the beach in the dark didn't seem wise, not to mention the potential perils if she fell asleep in unfamiliar waters. She could handle the balance issues until tomorrow. She'd be fine.

Chapter Forty-One

Day 28

Sierra, Echo, Victor, Echo, November, Charlie, Echo, Alpha."
Dr. Wilcox shot a scowl at his phone and waved at the door to motion Jacob in. "Yes, I understand that it's an unusual name." He sighed. "I just want to know if you have an address on file. She's a contract photographer for your magazine. Sure, I'll hold." Rolling his eyes, Dr. Wilcox tilted the phone away from his face to address Jacob. "Sorry, I'm trying to get someone at Hawaiian Shores to talk to me. I know people there, but unfortunately I don't think they're going to give out personal information."

Jacob dropped into his normal seat and shrugged. "Not surprising. You realize that's literally what kept Sevencea from finding me yesterday right?"

Dr. Wilcox rolled his eyes again, this time at Jacob. "Ah, Kevin! Finally. Sorry to be a bother, but I'm trying to help someone locate one of your contractors. Any chance of getting an address?" He nodded once. "I figured that would be the case. Tell you what, if it's not too much trouble, can you get me the advance digital copy of the next issue? Great! Thanks, man, I appreciate it." The doctor hung up, sat down and turned to his laptop.

"Digital copy of what?" Jacob leaned in. It had been hard to sleep last night, knowing Sevencea was out there. All his fears, both during their relationship and after he left for Mana'o, seemed small now. How had he ever let them dominate his life? He was ready to start living again, but he couldn't go home until he knew where Sevencea was. He had to apologize for running out on her.

"The next issue of the magazine," Dr. Wilcox explained. "Sounds like your girl has a few new photos in there. We might be able to figure out where on the island she's based from those. It's not much, but it's a start."

"No, that's a lot." Jacob stood and grasped Dr. Wilcox's hand. The surge of hope he'd been experiencing since yesterday was practically making him giddy. A massive grin covered his face. "Seriously, thank you. You've been a huge help during all of this."

Dr. Wilcox offered a sincere smile and firm handshake in return. "It's been my pleasure, Jacob. I like you, and you deserve to be happy." He glanced at the laptop. "Ah, perfect, here it is. Come over here, and we can look at this thing." He double-clicked on the newly arrived email attachment and pulled up the magazine spread.

"Try searching for her name," Jacob advised. "It's faster." He clenched his fingers against the desk, then forced them to relax. This needed to work.

Dr. Wilcox nodded and typed in the search. "Aha! Looks like three results." Both men leaned in and examined the first photo.

"It's a dock." Jacob squinted at the photo in search of identifying features. Not for the first time, he felt a prickle of guilt for not spending more time exploring the island. He'd hit up some of the

main highlights, like the volcano, but he was woefully understud-
ied for having lived here an entire year.

"It's Kailua-Kona," Dr. Wilcox gestured to the screen with his
finger. "I've been to this dock, on a fishing trip last year. See the sea
glass hanging off that post? I remember that. Kailua-Kona is on the
opposite side of the island from here. Let's look at her other photos. Maybe we can narrow down where in that area she's operating
from."

Jacob watched the doctor check on the other two photos. One
was a close-up of some kind of bird. The other appeared to be a
garden. The text around the garden stated it was a place called The
Makai.

"That's a bed and breakfast, I think," Dr. Wilcox mused. "I've
never been there, but I've driven past it. It's got a thatched roof, if
I remember right. Maybe you could call over there and see if they
know her?"

Jacob's heart picked up its pace. "What if she isn't there?"

"Then you keep looking," the doctor replied promptly.

Jacob huffed a laugh and nodded. "All right, that's fair. Since
you're on the computer, can you find me a phone number for this
place?"

After some typing, Dr. Wilcox grabbed a sticky note and scribbled down an address, phone number, and a name. He held it out
to Jacob. "Looks like the owner is a woman named Maggie Iona. If
anyone knows your girl, it's probably her."

"Thank you," Jacob said fervently. He gripped the sticky note
like it was a lifeline and dashed out of the office. He had a phone
call to make.

Jacob bounced up and down on the balls of his feet, his cell phone in one hand and the sticky note in the other. He didn't have the nerve built up to actually dial yet. The idea that the woman on the other end might not be able to help him warred against his hope that she knew where Sevencea was. Jacob clenched the note. Screw it. Nothing ventured, nothing gained. And if she *did* know where Sevencea was he would gain so much.

"All right, here goes." Jacob dialed the number and held the phone to his ear. Inhale, exhale. Worst case scenario, he didn't learn anything new. He was still in a much better place than he'd been a couple weeks ago. He now had hope, no matter the outcome of this call.

"Makai, how can I help?" A woman's voice answered, deeper than Jacob expected.

"Hi, I'm calling for Maggie Iona?"

"You've found her, with very little effort," was the dry response. "What can I do for you?"

Jacob relaxed a little and leaned against the wall. "I saw a photo of the garden at your establishment, and I'm looking for the photographer. I was hoping you might know her. Her name is Sevencea." He held his breath. This was it. The woman's next words would either guide him to the woman he'd fallen in love with, or leave him scrambling for new leads. Hope ballooned in his chest, and he let it grow. Hope would carry him through.

Maggie paused. "She's helping a guest at the moment, but I can take a message." She said it so plainly, like her words weren't an earth-shattering revelation.

Jacob lurched forward from the wall. He held his cell phone out for a second, staring at it wide-eyed, then brought the phone back to his ear. "She's there?" His heart paused, waiting for confirmation that it could resume beating.

"She's here," Maggie confirmed, "She's just busy right now. Can I get your name and number?"

"Jacob," he blurted. His name sounded raspy from the lack of air in his lungs. Sucking in another breath, he added, "Pearson. My name is Jacob Pearson."

"Ah." Maggie made a noise halfway to a snort, but loaded with sudden comprehension. "You're that man she lost. She's been looking for you. Come on over and find her, all right? You have the address?"

Jacob opened and closed his mouth twice before managing a reply. "Yes, I've got it. Thank you, Ms. Iona. You just made my day."

"Miracle worker is on my business card," Maggie agreed. "See you soon, lover boy." She hung up.

Jacob sagged against the wall, cell phone still in hand. "She's really there," he breathed. Saying it didn't make it easier to believe. But, if Maggie was telling the truth, he could just drive across the island and see for himself.

That thought had him standing straight again, pocketing his phone. It was time to shelf his fear once and for all and go find out why he'd fallen for a beautiful woman he thought was a mermaid. Maybe he was losing his mind a little, but that didn't guarantee impending doom. He grinned. Sevencea was real, and she was just across the island. What was he waiting for?

He took two steps toward the lobby, then came to an abrupt halt. He needed to tell his parents he was leaving, that he'd found her.

The sharp angles of the clinic's hallways made running hazardous, but Jacob was more focused on getting to his parents than the possibility of running into a wall. He skidded to a stop, panting, in front of his father's door.

Gerald didn't look at his son. He stared at the far wall, his eyes narrowed and his teeth gritted. Meredith had her arms around him, running a soothing hand up and down her husband's arm.

Jacob froze. "Dad?" He kept his tone low as he took a few steps toward his father.

"Careful, dear," Meredith murmured. Her gaze shifted to him. "He's having an episode. It's mild, but he hasn't come out quite yet."

"Any moment," Gerald muttered, shaking his head without taking his eyes off the wall. "Any moment, it could attack!"

Jacob pursed his lips and studied his father's expression. Threatening hallucinations weren't the norm. As far as he was aware, it had been a while since his father had been afraid of one of his sensory disturbances. "Dad, what are you seeing?"

Gerald's gaze became unfocused, and his eyebrows drew together. "What do you mean, Jake?"

Jacob exhaled. At least his father knew that he was there. He locked eyes with his mother. Meredith's face was set and determined. She'd sat out so many of his father's episodes, but she clearly wasn't leaving this one. Jacob felt a surge of gratitude.

"There's nothing on the wall, Dad." Jacob kept his tone gentle. "Can you tell me what's freaking you out?"

With a slow, determined motion, Gerald tore his eyes from the wall and focused on Jacob. "It's a giant spider, Jake. It has too many eyes!"

Meredith shuddered. She hated spiders. "It's all right," she murmured in soft tones. "Nothing is there."

Gerald's eyes drooped a little, and his body relaxed.

"Good, Mom, that's helping." Jacob squeezed his father's shoulder. "Dad, I promise you, there's nothing on that wall. You believe me, right?"

"I trust you." Gerald nodded. His eyes darted to the wall, then back to Jacob. "It's too big to be real. You must be right." He shuddered and focused on his son. He lifted one of his hands to cover Meredith's hand and rubbed his thumb across her fingers. "You must be right," he repeated, more quietly.

Jacob's looked at his father's face and his heart seized. How could he leave? Drive an hour away to find a girl? Was that really more important than his family? Jacob gnawed at his bottom lip. The fact that they could talk his father down was a good sign. It meant the medication was doing its job. Still, leaving his father with a non-existent giant spider seemed like a bad idea, even with his mother there.

Gerald blinked, keeping his eyes closed longer than normal before reopening them. "I'll be okay, Jake," he breathed.

Jacob started. His eyes snapped back to his father's. "I know, Dad."

"You have somewhere to be," Meredith stated. Jacob looked up at her with a raised eyebrow, and she smiled. "You know where she is, don't you?"

"I…" Jacob stared at his father, then his mother. "Yeah. I think I found her."

"Then go get her," Gerald ordered. His eyes cleared as he focused on Jacob. "I'm fine, Jake. Merry's here. You have a life to live. Don't you dare let that girl get away because you're sitting here fretting over me."

Meredith reached out to Jacob. She grasped his hand and squeezed it tight. "I'm not going anywhere."

The fear and worry seeped out of Jacob. His father would be all right, and more importantly, he wouldn't be alone. Jacob glanced toward the door, rocking on his feet. Even with his mother there, it still felt wrong to leave when his father wasn't doing well. Gerald reached for Meredith again, as if using her to center himself. His eyes were more focused now, and he wasn't looking at the wall anymore. Maybe Gerald was almost free of the hallucination? He seemed more firmly planted in reality than a moment ago.

Meredith shot Jacob an exasperated look. "He'll be fine, dear. Go, please."

"Go, or we'll ground you 'til you're thirty," Gerald muttered. A slow grin crossed his face.

The rest of the tension in Jacob's shoulders bled away, and he snorted. "You can't ground me. I don't live with you."

"Semantics." Gerald waved him off. "Seriously, Jake, go. I wasn't too deep in before Merry caught it. You both helped. I'll be okay, I swear."

"Okay." Jacob nodded and headed for the door. He glanced back once, just in time to see his parents smile at each other. That was enough reassurance. Despite the illness, his parents had their own version of happily ever after. It was time to find his.

Whether or not Jacob needed to return to Mana'o was debatable, but he didn't bother packing. His first priority was finding Sevencea. He'd figure out the next steps later. He moved through the lobby at a quick pace. He felt jittery, like he was perpetrating a jail break. He'd checked himself in voluntarily, and was allowed to leave whenever he liked, but it still felt odd to just walk out after living here for so many days.

"You headed out, Mr. Pearson?"

Jacob halted abruptly in the middle of the lobby. He turned to the receptionist. What had Dr. Wilcox called her? Daisie?

He opened his mouth, then closed it again. He didn't need permission. "Yeah," he said, trying to project confidence. He felt like the new kid at boarding school, testing the rules. "I'm headed over to Kailua-Kona for a bit."

"Huh." Daisie studied him over her glasses. "Right, well, enjoy the drive."

"Thanks." Jacob nodded and looked back toward the front doors. "If all goes well, I might be back with a guest."

"Mmhmm," was the only reply he got.

Allowing himself a small smile, he headed for the doors. If none of this worked out, he didn't want everyone here to feel even sorrier for him. He shook his head. No more fear. It was time to drive across the island and find his not-a-mermaid.

He chuckled. Because that sounded completely practical.

Chapter Forty-Two

Sevencea swiped her hair out of her face and stuck her head under the stairs. She wielded the feather duster at the cobwebs like an axe. She'd been busy all morning, and hadn't made it to the ocean yet. She hadn't collapsed again, but her legs had felt weak all day. As soon as she was done with this task, she would make a run for the beach. Her heart was racing, but that could be from how many times she'd been up and down the stairs today.

"Sevencea!" Maggie bellowed up the stairs. "Your boy toy is in the lobby!"

Sevencea bolted upright and cracked her head on the stairs. She grabbed a banister and steadied herself. Had she heard that right?

"What are you talking about?" she yelled back. No response. She set the duster down and shook her head, massaging the spot where she'd bumped it. Apparently she'd only get an answer if she went downstairs.

Sevencea moved quickly down the final steps, ready to ask what in the world Maggie was actually trying to say. She came to an abrupt halt at the bottom of the stairs. Jacob stood in the middle of the lobby, gnawing at his lip, hope in his eyes. He was here!

Sevencea barely managed a choked exclamation before she hurtled herself toward him. She threw her arms around Jacob's neck. Her excitement came out as incomprehensible noises, but it didn't matter. Jacob's arms were firm around her, and he was making just as many excited, nonsensical sounds as she.

"I'll leave you two alone," Maggie announced. From the corner of her eye, Sevencea watched the older woman disappear. She'd have to thank Maggie later, yet again.

For now, she focused solely on Jacob. He still smelled the same, just with the absence of the salt spray. That would make sense if he'd been away from home.

Jacob picked her up and spun her around, a broad grin on his face. "I can't believe I found you," he murmured. A pained look crossed his face, then vanished.

Sevencea squeezed him again, then let him go so she could see his face more easily. She grasped his hands. "Where have you been? How did you find me? I've been looking for you!"

Something like guilt flitted through Jacob's eyes. "You came to my father's treatment center," he explained. "It's called Mana'o, and I've been staying there. One of the doctors saw the security footage and showed me. Up until yesterday, I thought I'd imagined you."

He looked her up and down, his eyes pausing for a moment on her legs. "Even now, I can hardly believe it's really you!"

Sevencea glanced down at herself and spared a moment to be grateful she was wearing her tail skirt. It was her favorite piece of clothing, and she was pleased Jacob could see her in it. Her top was a light blue t-shirt with a tie in the front, and she hadn't bothered to put on any shoes while working.

Jacob's words registered, and her eyes narrowed. "Wait, you were at Mana'o and they still kicked me out?" She made a noise that was almost a growl. "I only wanted to know if you were there! They couldn't tell me that much?"

Jacob winced, rubbing his thumbs across the tops of her hands. "I know, but I'm so glad you came. If you hadn't, I never would have known to look for you." His breath caressed Sevencea's cheek.

Sevencea released a heavy sigh and dropped her head. The pearl on her forehead rolled. "I'm sorry I was gone so long. My brother kept me busy while he was making the potion for me. I wanted to surprise you, but by the time I got to your house, you were gone."

There was a pregnant pause. Jacob took a small step back and squinted at her. "What potion?"

Sevencea took a quick look around to make sure no one else was in earshot, then gestured downward.

"It gives me legs. My brother's magic allows him to create potions that do all sorts of things. He had me playing errand girl though to earn mine, so every time I tried to visit you, I got to the beach too late. And like I said, by the time he finished the potion and gave it to me, you were already gone."

Jacob stared at her, his mouth hanging open. His face was the definition of shock. "You really are a mermaid?" He said it so quietly she almost didn't hear him.

Sevencea closed her eyes tight for a brief second. This was exactly what she'd been afraid of. It was her fault Jacob had left. Her fault he thought his mind had betrayed him. She let go of one of his hands and reached for his face. She stroked his cheek with her thumb.

"Oh, Jacob." The words were a wistful sigh. "You have such a gift for seeing the beauty of the world. You always saw me for who I was. I'm so sorry my absence gave you any reason to doubt that."

"You're really a mermaid." Jacob said the words like he was

testing them. His eyes stared past her, unfocused. He blinked and returned his gaze to Sevencea, tilting his head a little. "So, you went to get legs so you could come experience my world? The way you showed me yours?"

Sevencea grinned and nodded. "Exactly. It's only temporary, but as long as I go back to the ocean once a week, I can drink the potion without it causing me any harm. I've been on land for almost two weeks now, working here and looking for you." She felt a twinge of guilt. She should've taken care of the ocean trip first thing this morning.

"I can't believe I've been checked into a care facility when you were here this whole time," Jacob muttered. He rubbed at his forehead.

"Hey." Sevencea squeezed the hand she still held and raised an eyebrow at him. "From what you'd told me, you had reasons for your concern. I'm sorry for my part in it."

"It's not your fault," Jacob assured her. "I've done a lot of soul searching lately. I basically stopped living because I was afraid I'd get sick like my dad. Your disappearance just played into my own paranoia. I'm not going to live like that any longer, I promise."

Sevencea moved in and hugged him again, holding him as tightly as she could. "I'm so proud of you," she murmured against his chest.

It was funny, as a human she was quite a bit shorter than him. If she could stand on her tail, she'd probably be taller. As that thought crossed her mind, her whole body went limp. Jacob was calling to her, but he sounded distant, his words unclear. She couldn't respond. Something hard lay beneath her. Had she hit the floor? How had that happened? Jacob's face hovered above her, creased with worry. She tried to open her mouth, to tell him she was okay. No words came out. Instead, the world around her went dark.

Chapter Forty-Three

Jacob caught Sevencea's head as she slumped to the ground.

"Sevencea?" His voice was desperate as he gave her a light shake. No reaction. "Sevencea!" Still nothing. Had she passed out? What was happening? She was limp in his arms, and Jacob felt his heart rate pick up as panic set in. Was she even still breathing?

"No, no, no," he muttered. He tried to throw his memory back to high school health class. He needed to check for a pulse. Jacob fumbled for the right spot on her neck, pressing close to her jaw and relaxing a little when he actually found her pulse. He still couldn't tell if she was breathing though. Jacob lifted her limp form closer to his chest, listening for any signs of life. Yes—there! She was breathing, but it was a shallow sound.

Jacob's breathing was rapid. He'd only just found her! She couldn't leave him now, not after everything they'd both endured.

What was it she had said? She had to go back to the ocean as part of whatever potion she took? Had she not gone back recently enough? Jacob couldn't think of any other reason for a healthy mermaid-turned-human to collapse.

"Okay," he murmured. Reaching under Sevencea's neck and

knees, he picked her up as carefully as he could manage. "I'll fix this, I promise."

He stood in the middle of the empty lobby, Sevencea's body draped over his arms. Her hair tickled where it brushed him, but he couldn't enjoy any part of having her so close. Where was he going to take her? He didn't know this side of the island very well. The ocean would be to the west, but where was the closest access? He could feel his heart rate continuing to climb, and took a few deep breaths.

"It's going to be okay," he murmured, to himself and the mermaid in his arms. "I'm going to take care of you, I promise."

Whatever he was going to do, he needed to do it now. Jacob headed for the front door, moving as swiftly as he dared without jostling Sevencea too much. Driving would be faster than running, especially carrying someone. He reached his car, opened the door, and set Sevencea down gently in the front seat. Running to the other side, he jumped in and started the engine. With no clear plan yet, he peeled out of the parking lot.

Jacob took two deep breaths, trying to settle himself. He scanned the road, reading every sign for hints that water access was just ahead. "I just promised my life wouldn't be ruled by fear," he muttered. "Imagining worst case scenarios won't help either of us." Jacob's heart still tried to beat out of his chest, but his mind grew clearer. This was a problem he could solve, he just needed to do it quickly.

"All right, don't worry, I'll fix this." Jacob glanced at Sevencea. Was he talking to her or himself? He went back to scanning road signs. He needed somewhere he could throw a woman's body into the ocean without inciting panic. He couldn't help Sevencea if he got arrested for disposing of a body. His lips twisted, and he looked at Sevencea again. She would probably find that funny if she was awake.

Getting her in the water needed to work.

All the signs they'd passed so far were for resorts. Resorts usually meant crowds. He needed something smaller. He couldn't risk being stopped before she got help. This side of the island had a lot of rocky outcroppings that dropped off into water. He only had to find the right spot.

Sevencea's breathing picked up, a pained, labored sound. Jacob looked over, stricken, to see her skin paling by the moment.

"Screw it." They didn't have time. Jacob got off the highway at the next opportunity. He drove past shopping and residential structures, heading straight for the edge of the island. Finally, there it was! The ocean came into view as he crested a hill. Jacob could have wept at the sight. How was he going to get out there though? Jacob gnawed on his bottom lip, debating the wisdom of just jumping off the nearest available ledge into the water. He was speeding down the road, so he almost missed the turn for the public parking. At the last minute he jerked the wheel, sliding into the lot and into a parking place without hitting any other cars.

Jacob exhaled, but the adrenaline was still racing beneath his skin. Sevencea didn't have time for this. He leaped from the car, kicking his sandals off into the foot well and patting his pockets to make sure they were empty. Racing around to the passenger's side, he slowed just enough to extract Sevencea without bumping her against the frame of the car.

She sagged in his arms, paler than death. Jacob bit back a cry and adjusted his grip, tilting her head against his shoulder. If it was less obvious she was unconscious, it would be easier to get to the water.

Now that the water was right in front of him, Jacob could see what hadn't stood out from a distance. Boats! And where there were boats, there was a dock. "C'mon, Sevencea, hold on," he murmured, moving down the slope. When the dock came into view, Jacob uttered a silent prayer of thanks and sped up. The dock was short, and no one was around to interrupt. The hot pavement burned his bare feet. Jacob picked up the pace again, running for the dock.

The pavement gave way to wood, and Jacob threw all his remaining energy into one last push, surging forward to the edge of the dock. Sucking in a breath, he launched off the dock, Sevencea still cradled in his arms. They landed in the water with a massive splash. Jacob felt his feet hit sand as they sank. They weren't deep enough. Sevencea probably needed to stay submerged for the magic to work, right? He renewed his grip on the mermaid and pushed off, kicking as hard as he could to take them deeper.

This was going to work. It *had* to work.

Jacob glanced upward as he swam. Light glistened off the surface of the water.

Sevencea's hair floated around her face. She looked mysterious and ethereal, just like the first time he'd seen her underwater. Only this time, her eyes were closed, and her whole body was lax. Carrying her underwater was far more difficult than carrying her on land, but Jacob didn't relax his grip.

The water blurred his vision. He blinked hard. He had to keep watch on Sevencea. If this didn't work, she would drown. Something brushed his leg, and his gaze moved down to her legs. It took everything in him to not to inhale. Her tail fin had erupted from where her feet had been moments ago. Jacob's eyes widened as her legs snapped together. He released Sevencea, letting her float as her skirt dissolved into individual scales, coating her legs.

Jacob watched eagerly, focusing on her eyes, but Sevencea didn't move. Her scales were all in place, and she looked almost like normal. Except she was still too pale.

"Sevencea?" Her name escaped, Jacob forgetting for a brief moment that in this world, without her, he couldn't breathe.

As the lack of air started to tighten his chest, Sevencea's eyes flew open. She let out a wild gasp, breathing the ocean in deeply. Her color was slowly returning as she heaved. Finally looking up, she met Jacob's gaze and alarm flashed in her eyes.

He'd been so distracted by her transformation—something he could witness endlessly and not tire of—that his oxygen needs had gone ignored. Jacob's mouth opened involuntarily and the ocean rushed in. His eyes bulged, and he spluttered. He tried to swim upward, but inhaling saltwater had disoriented him. He kicked ineffectively, his throat burning and vision cloudy.

Sevencea rushed forward with a powerful flick of her tail. She wrapped her arms around him and stilled his flailing. Holding him tightly, like he'd held her, she pressed her lips to his.

Jacob buried his hands in her hair and kissed her back. All the longing of the last few weeks, all the hope and desire he'd tried to write off as illness, was channeled into that kiss. Sevencea was solid, but soft, beneath his hands—real, not a figment of his imagination. He couldn't truly fathom that he'd ever doubted her. They broke apart, both breathing heavily. Jacob's eyes went wide. Breathing! He'd been so caught up in the kiss that he hadn't even noticed Sevencea's magic at work.

"You saved me," he murmured.

Sevencea pulled him close, their foreheads almost touching. "You saved me first." She kissed him again, lightly on the lips.

"I was afraid I would be too late." Jacob reached up and traced his fingers lightly along the side of her face, gazing into her bright eyes. He never again wanted to see those eyes closed with such terrifying finality. "I'm so sorry I left the beach. I didn't have enough faith in my own sanity to wait for you."

"I'm sorry I was gone so long," Sevencea replied, her tone soft. She offered him a wry smile.

Jacob chuckled and shook his head. "Maybe it needed to happen. I hate that we lost that time, but a lot has happened to me. A lot of good, to be honest."

"Me too," Sevencea admitted. "Some things I would never have expected, but now I can't imagine my life without them." She smiled at him. Her face glowed in the light streaming through the water. "I found my way in the world, and it led me back to you."

Jacob nodded. Yes, that's exactly what had happened. His heartbeat picked up, and he inhaled deeply, relishing the oddly familiar sensation of breathing in ocean water. "I need to tell you something. Something I wish I'd said weeks ago. But now it's truer than ever."

Sevencea just looked at him, but her eyes twinkled like she knew exactly what he was about to say.

Jacob pulled her close and kissed her, a brief, soft moment. "I love you, Sevencea," he whispered. He'd been certain of the words before he said them, but aloud they sounded even truer. An uninhibited smile spread across his face as pure joy filled his heart.

Sevencea returned his grin with a delighted laugh. "And I love you, Jacob. We dove headfirst into new worlds for each other. How could our bond be any less than love?" She took his hand, entangled their fingers and squeezed.

Jacob found himself getting lost in her eyes as they floated together. They were holding each other now, both safe, whole, and most importantly, together. Eventually they relaxed, both laughing a little.

"I need to be down here for a while," Sevencea admitted sheepishly. She glanced down, and Jacob noticed her bodice had returned. Her wet t-shirt clung to it. "My potion is also back at The Makai," she added, "You'll need to grab it for me before I can come back on land."

"I can do that," Jacob assured her. He watched while she fidgeted with the t-shirt, pulling it off and ridding herself of the wet fabric. He envied her that. His own pants and shirt were not going to be fun to swim in—or traipse around in soaking wet.

Sevencea offered him the shirt. "Can you hold onto this for me?"

Jacob chuckled. "Of course." He tucked the fabric into one of his pockets, then added, "So you're planning to come back on land?"

Her expression softened. "I may have come on land for you, but I've found a home there too." She squeezed his hand again. "There's a purpose for me there, and people who need me. It's different from being here." She sighed, her tail flicking. "That reminds me, I have your camera. I brought it with me from your house."

Jacob blinked at her. "You took my camera?"

"It was the closest thing I could have to you." Sevencea shot him a wistful smile, her expression guilty and apologetic all at once.

"I'm glad it helped you," Jacob said. "Your photography is how I found you."

For that reason alone, he was grateful. If photography had also helped Sevencea learn what she wanted to do with her life, he would willingly share that dream with her.

Her expression brightened. "Then we should both be grateful that you taught me."

She fluttered her fingers, still entangled with his, then flicked her tail and dragged him forward. "Like I said, I need to be down here for a while. Do you want to come with me? Swimming might be a little hard without your flipper-things."

"Come with you where?" Jacob asked, intrigued. It didn't matter that the swim might be hard. He would gladly go with her.

The mischievous grin he'd grown to love spread across Sevencea's face. "To meet my family."

Chapter Forty-Four

The swim was long, but Jacob made it without complaining. Sevencea kept finding herself staring at him fondly. Usually when he wasn't looking, but he caught her once or twice. As they approached her clan, she heard him suck in a breath, but not exhale.

"Relax," she murmured. "He's going to love you."

"I'm relaxed," Jacob assured her.

She raised an eyebrow at him. "Not even a little nervous?"

"Excited," Jacob corrected. He reached for her hand and brought it to his lips, interlacing their fingers. "I'm eager to meet anyone who's important to you."

Sevencea flushed and pulled him along. "Flatterer," she teased.

They hadn't yet reached her home when Brineus approached. Sevencea grinned at her father—he must have been keeping an eye out for her return. The older merman swam forward and pressed a kiss to the top of her head.

"Welcome home, my minnow." Brineus offered Sevencea a fond look, then leveled an expectant stare at Jacob, holding up a whirlpool in the palm of his hand.

"It's nice to meet you, sir." Jacob kept his eyes squarely on

Brineus's face instead of the threatening swirl of water.

Brineus grinned. His eyes went from Sevencea's lightly flushed face to Jacob's earnest one. "So, you're the human that so interested my daughter."

Jacob glanced at Sevencea. His expression shifted from apprehension to something soft and warm. "I'm honored to be the subject of her interest."

"You can relax, Jacob." Sevencea nudged his shoulder. "My father is trying to intimidate you, but he's perfectly friendly. Right?" She looked pointedly at the whirlpool.

Chuckling, Brineus dissipated the whirlpool. "It's a simple way to get the measure of someone new." Sevencea shot him a look, and he grinned. He moved forward, extending a hand to Jacob. "It is nice to meet you too, Jacob. I know my daughter would not be so taken by someone unworthy of her affections. I look forward to getting to know you as she does."

Jacob flushed with pleasure. Sevencea enjoyed his pleased look. She moved forward and hugged her father. "Thank you," she murmured.

"Of course, my minnow." Brineus pulled her in for a hug. "Will you be staying, or do you have obligations on land?"

Sevencea reached for Jacob's hand again. "I think I'm of both worlds now," she admitted, looking into Jacob's eyes. The prospect of telling her father she planned to spend a lot more time on land made her stomach flutter, but she could already see acceptance and a hint of pride on his face.

As she began to explain to her father about her time on land, Jacob listened as intently as Brineus. Sevencea realized as she spoke that he too was hearing most of her story for the first time. She kept hold of Jacob's hand the entire time, appreciating his solid presence. Sevencea felt lighter when she came to the end. Having her father know everything was a relief; having Jacob at her side was a dream come true.

"So I have people who need me, a job that I care about, and a place in that world." She offered her father a smile. She loved him dearly, but he'd known as long as she had that her place wasn't with her clan. At least, not full time.

"I'm so proud of you," Brineus replied. His eyes shone brightly, though a twinge of sadness hid in their depths. "You have my full support, so long as you promise to come back and visit as often as possible."

"You know I would, even if it wasn't required by Athys's potion," Sevencea promised. "I may have found a home on land, but this is still my home too."

She glanced to Jacob. His expression was almost more supportive than her father's. He would be the first to encourage her to visit her family when she needed to. That was one of the perks of falling for someone who cared deeply for his own family. He understood her love for her first home.

"Will I be meeting this brother of yours?" Jacob glanced around like he expected Athys to pop up from behind a rock.

Sevencea chuckled. "Eventually. I need more of the potion from him. Though I'm not sure if he's around today."

Which might be a good thing. Sevencea was grateful to Athys, but she wasn't eager to introduce her human love to her brother. Athys's protective instincts could lead to some exceptional teasing and pranks. One day it could be amusing to let Athys have his fun, but today she just wanted to be with Jacob and figure out what the future would look like.

"I'll make sure he mixes the potion for you," Brineus promised. "He's not here right now, but I'll see that it gets to you, one way or another. Maybe he can help me come visit you someday." Her father winked at her.

Sevencea grinned, unable to stop the picture of her father and Maggie staring each other down that popped into her head.

"You're welcome anytime." Jacob squeezed Sevencea's hand.

She took it, intertwining their fingers. The plans being laid spoke to a long future together. It was exactly what she hoped for.

Sevencea suggested they return to Jacob's beach, instead of swimming all the way back to where he'd left his car. That way he could change into dry clothes. Then Jacob could call a cab to take him back to his car, get her potion from The Makai, and drive to Mana'o on the opposite side of the island. Sevencea would spend that time underwater. Jacob would deliver her potion to her on the east side of the island, and she could come with him to Mana'o to meet his parents. It was a convoluted plan, but Jacob agreed it was a good one.

Sevencea spent the rest of the day underwater, stretching her tail. She hadn't pushed herself in a bit, so she used the time to exercise by lapping the island. Of course, she thought of Jacob often, but especially as she passed his beach. Everything she'd dreamed of was coming together. She had two families now, a love that had withstood trials, and a blossoming career. Sevencea couldn't keep the smile off of her face. As the sun dropped toward the horizon, she emerged on the east side of the island, browsing until she found the beach that seemed directly below the path of airplane after airplane. Jacob had given her the airport as a landmark, so she hoped she was in the right spot. The sun was leaving purple hues in its wake as it set. Sevencea wondered if she should be feeling tired.

Between her collapse and her workout, perhaps she should've been, but instead she felt energized. She also felt more than a little foolish for risking her health unnecessarily. Jacob had already made her promise not to do it again. She'd readily agreed.

Sevencea relaxed in the water, floating with just her head above the surface.

"Sevencea!"

She spun to the beach and grinned. Jacob stood on the sand, waving.

"You made it!" She swam closer.

Jacob waded into the water. He wore shorts and a fresh t-shirt. She swam as close as she dared without exposing her tail—to where Jacob stood calf-deep in the ocean—and he handed her the potion.

Sevencea took a quick swig, then tucked the potion into her bodice. She looked to Jacob, enjoying his expression as he watched her transformation for the first time. His eyes were comically wide as he watched her tail split.

"Does that hurt?" he asked, his voice hushed.

Sevencea waved her hand. "Sort of. More than anything it's disconcerting, but it gets easier the more I do it."

Her legs finished forming as she spoke, and she laughed and got to her feet.

She strode to Jacob and planted a kiss on his cheek. "Did you miss me?"

"Every minute," Jacob confirmed. He gave her a proper kiss in reply. "Ready to meet my parents?"

Sevencea nodded. She'd wanted to meet Jacob's father, of course. Discovering his mother was here too was even more intriguing. It warmed her heart to know that Jacob had begun rebuilding his relationship with his mother during the time they'd been apart.

The drive to Mana'o was short, but the sky had darkened by the time they pulled into the parking lot. Jacob strolled to the front door, holding Sevencea's hand and whistling. She couldn't hide her grin. Had he ever been this carefree before?

As they walked inside, the receptionist's mouth dropped. It was the same woman she'd spoken to before. Sevencea waved at her.

"Daisie, this is Sevencea, my girlfriend. Sevencea, this is Daisie." Jacob gestured between them, and winked at Sevencea.

Sevencea offered the woman a pleasant smile and gestured toward the inner door. "I'll be going inside this time," she announced.

Daisie gaped after them as they disappeared through the door.

As the door shut behind them, Jacob snorted. "Sevencea, victorious?" He grinned at her.

She shrugged and her cheeks flushed. "I worked hard to find you!" she protested, trying to suppress a grin of her own. "Let me bask in my success a little!"

"Technically, I found you," Jacob reminded her. She responded with a withering glare, and he smirked. "Team effort?" he offered.

Sevencea rolled her eyes, but smiled and nodded. They continued down a hallway until Jacob stopped and motioned for her to wait where she was. He approached a doorway and knocked.

"Hey, Dad, are you feeling better?" Jacob asked, his voice soft.

"Jake! Hey, how did it go? Did you find her?" An excited voice called from inside. It sounded much like Jacob's, but older and more cheerful.

Jacob glanced back and motioned for her to come forward. Sevencea walked up beside Jacob and took in the room. An older man leaned forward in a chair, a book in his lap. A woman sat beside him, her entire focus centered on Jacob and Sevencea. A little self-consciously, Sevencea gave a half-wave. "Hello."

"Dad, Mom, meet Sevencea." Jacob held out his arms like he was presenting her.

His father's jaw dropped. His eyes jumped from Sevencea's face to her legs, then to Jacob's face, then back to Sevencea. She risked a glance at Jacob's mother. The woman watched her thoughtfully.

"Whoa." Jacob's father nodded to himself. He stood, crossed the room, and grasped Sevencea's hand. He lifted it to his lips and lightly kissed it, just as his son had done earlier. "It's an honor to meet you, my dear."

Sevencea flushed and her apprehension bled away. "The honor is mine, Mr. Pearson. Jacob speaks very highly of you."

"Call me Gerald, please. This is my wife, Meredith." Gerald motioned to the woman. She came to her husband's side and shook Sevencea's hand.

"We've heard a lot about you," Meredith said, her tone vague on whether that was a good thing. She had a sternness to her that Sevencea recognized from some of Jacob's expressions.

Gerald grinned. "The way Jake speaks of you, I feel like I'm meeting royalty." He glanced pointedly at his son. Jacob just shrugged. Gerald moved back to his chair, gesturing for everyone to follow.

"Come in, please, don't just stand there. We don't bite, I promise." Gerald chuckled to himself as he took a seat again.

Once Jacob's parents were seated, Sevencea sat down next to Jacob on the bed.

"So, where have you been? Why did Jake come racing over here, convinced he'd dreamed up a mermaid?" Gerald leaned forward and clasped his hands in his lap.

Sevencea looked to Jacob. It may have been her secret to tell, but these were Jacob's parents. It was up to him whether or not she should share all the details. A hint of a smile crossed his lips, and he nodded. So, he was letting her make the choice.

Sevencea took a deep breath. This was her first time reveling her secret to anyone but Jacob. It was fitting that it was to his parents.

"I *am* a mermaid." She held her breath. They both just blinked at her. "I was gone for over a week because my brother made me work for him while he prepared a potion that would give me legs. By the time I returned to Jacob's beach, he was already gone."

"Huh." Gerald leaned back in his chair and folded his arms across his chest. He glanced at his wife, an eyebrow raised. "What do you think, Merry?"

Meredith made a noise of consideration. Her entire bearing was of someone used to being in charge, but her firmness softened every time she looked at her husband or son. She glanced toward Jacob. "I assume this isn't some sort of elaborate prank?"

"You assume correctly, Mom. She's being one hundred percent honest." Jacob clasped Sevencea's hand, and they squeezed each other's fingers at the same time. Jacob must be nervous too. That helped calm Sevencea's own beating heart.

"Huh." Meredith leaned back in her chair. "A mermaid indeed."

She appeared tense and didn't seem to know how to relax. It had taken Jacob a while to accept that Sevencea was a mermaid. His parents would likely need some time too. What if they objected? Approving of their son's love was one thing, accepting that she wasn't human was quite another. Sevencea held her breath, waiting for one of them to say something.

"Well, as long as Jake's happy, I don't care if you're secretly a dragon." Gerald shrugged. He glanced between Meredith and Jacob and winked at them both.

Laughter burst from Jacob, and he tilted to the side like his laughter might knock him right off the bed. A few tears escaped his eyes. He wiped them away as laughter continued to shake his body.

Meredith smiled, her most carefree expression so far. "I'm with my husband on this."

Sevencea looked between them all, her brow furrowed. "I'm definitely not a dragon."

That started a fresh wave of laughter from Jacob. Gerald joined, and gradually Meredith began to chuckle. Giggles of her own rose to Sevencea's lips and the last of her tension bled away. Maybe she didn't need to overthink things. Both of Jacob's parents seemed pleased she was there, mermaid or not. Maybe that was enough.

The laughter continued until a man appeared in the doorway. He caught sight of Sevencea, and his eyes lit up.

"So, this is our mystery girl!" He reached forward and shook her hand. "I'm Dr. Wilcox. I help treat Mr. Pearson here, and I was attempting to convince Jacob he wasn't sick when you showed up and proved me right. Thank you for that." The doctor wiggled his eyebrows in Jacob's direction.

"It would have been great if I wasn't kicked out of the building the first time I showed up," Sevencea pointed out. "We could have had this reunion two days ago."

Dr. Wilcox coughed. "Yes, well, I am sorry about that. Anyway, I'm glad we were able to find you. Now all we have to do is figure out how Jacob got it into his head that you were a mermaid!" He chuckled and shook his head.

Sevencea grinned and shot Jacob a wink. "I'm secretly a dragon too."

The Pearson family and Sevencea dissolved into hysterics again. Dr. Wilcox looked puzzled, but he joined in the laughter and didn't question it.

Epilogue

Day 300

"Have you seen my lens cap?" Jacob called. He picked up and set down pillows on his living room couch at random and scowled when the black circle he was hunting for didn't appear. The lens in question sat on the table, waiting to be packed.

Sevencea walked in and hung her purse up on the rack. The extra house key jingled as she tossed it back into her bag. "Not unless you left it at my place. But Maggie would have given it to me already."

Jacob shook his head. "No, I've had it here since the last time I was at The Makai. Hang on, I'm going to check the bedroom again."

"You don't actually need it," Sevencea called after him, amusement clear in her voice. She wasn't wrong. He could simply borrow one of her lens caps. Their camera accoutrements were starting to become indistinguishable from each other's.

"I'm not going to risk someone knocking my camera into the sand again," Jacob called back. Sevencea would need to keep her lens protected for the same reason. Shooting photos on a beach filled with people could be a hazard. He gave the messy surfaces in his room a skeptical glance. He'd been meaning to organize in here. Sevencea kept her room at The Makai pristine.

"Okay, that's fair," she admitted. "Don't take too long though. Maggie's expecting us."

A loud poof sounded as she took a seat on the couch. Jacob grinned. It was the kind of thing that would make his father laugh too. Gerald's treatments were going as well as ever. He wasn't much worse, but he wasn't better. According to his doctors, having Jacob and Meredith around more had helped the most. Speaking of which, Jacob's mother should be back in town soon, fresh off some big deal she'd closed. Since her first visit while Jacob was staying at Mana'o, she'd made an effort to visit the island every few weeks.

Maybe Jacob wouldn't have his father forever, but he had his family for now. That was a huge blessing.

Then there was the wonderful blessing that was Sevencea.

He hadn't foreseen the success Magical Ocean Photography would enjoy when he and Sevencea officially went into business together. But between Maggie's contacts and their combined talent, it was easy to get jobs.

"Do we know this couple?" Jacob considered his chest of drawers. He might have an idea where his lens cap had ended up after all.

"Not this one. Keisha's wedding is in three weeks. Remember, I have to be a bridesmaid *and* help you shoot."

"Right, right, I knew that." A sympathetic noise escaped Jacob's lips and he nodded. Sevencea had been thrilled when Keisha asked her to be a bridesmaid, but neither of them were looking forward to an evening of split responsibilities.

Jacob pulled open his sock drawer and glanced over the contents. His lens cap lay on top, where he'd set it in his distraction a few days before. "I found it," he hollered.

"Awesome, let's go!" There was a second poof noise. Sevencea was back on her feet.

Jacob smiled at her enthusiasm. These days, Sevencea was on land the majority of the time. The best part of owning their own business was that she could go back underwater pretty much whenever. Jacob had also picked up a hobby of finding unique ingredients for Athys's potions, something that endeared him to Sevencea's brother more than he'd expected. It had the side benefit of keeping them on Athys's good side, meaning Sevencea had a steady supply of the potion she needed.

Over time, he and Sevencea had developed a unique and wonderful routine.

Jacob snatched up the lens cap and slid it into his pocket. Glancing down at the newly revealed patch of drawer, Jacob spared a smile for the small black velvet jewelry box nestled between a pair of socks. "I'm coming," he called. He slid the drawer closed again. "Let's go make a wedding magical."

Acknowledgements

This story has been in my heart and on the page in many forms for a long time, and there are a great number of people who've played a part in its journey. Whether or not I've remembered to list them here, I am grateful for them!

First and foremost, my family have been great supporters of my love of storytelling for my entire life. I am extremely grateful for their encouragement through this process. My grandmother, in particular, was instrumental in ensuring Jacob and Sevencea's story was told. Without her insistence, this book likely would not exist.

To my friends who are excited whenever I have a new story to share and my friends who put up with me always talking about writing – thank you for being there.

I also need to thank the many people who played a part in the polishing and development of *Head Over Tails*. Lindsay A. Franklin, The Armorers (my first critic group), Amy Brock McNew, and Caroline Puerto all helped edit, beta read, and guide the story in its early drafts.

I can't talk about editing without mentioning my dear friend Jen Lindsay (of The Writer's Wellspring). Her work on *Head Over Tails* was essential in preparing the book for querying, and the story would not be what it is without her help. Even aside from her professional assistance, her encouragement and support throughout this process has been a literal godsend!

Speaking of support, I also need to thank my lovely Ladies of the Realm Table, Bonnie, Emily, Kate, and Abigail. We support each other through the highs and lows of querying our books, and their support, excitement, and encouragement during the high of *Head Over Tails* being released has meant the world.

Of course, I have to thank the incredible team at UUP. Everyone has been amazing to work with, and I'm so grateful they fell in love with Jacob and Sevencea. Every step of the process has shown me just how much they care about me and my story, and I'm so grateful they are my partner in bringing *Head Over Tails* to readers.

I'm also grateful for the Realm Makers community, for bringing all the professionals who worked on this book into my life, and so many of my good friends.

If you're reading this, I am most definitely thankful for you! I've been waiting a long time to share Jacob and Sevencea's story with readers. Thank you so much for taking the time to read about their adventures!

Last, but definitely most important, God's fingerprints are on every single part of my adventure with this story. I am forever grateful to be a creative made in the image of her Creator.

Love and live boldly!

-Brianna Tibbetts

About the Author

Raised on a steady diet of rich fiction, novelist Brianna Tibbetts has been writing exciting, speculative worlds as long as she can remember. Currently based in the Pacific Northwest, she reads voraciously and writes extensively. In everything from short stories to series, Brianna demonstrates her passion for lively stories infused with faith. In addition to writing, her other superpowers include being ginger and yarn crafting. When she isn't spending time in her own creations, she loves indulging in the fictional worlds of others.

We at Uncommon Universes Press hope you enjoyed this book, Uncommon Reader! Please feel free to post your honest feedback in a review on any major platform.

Visit uncommonuniverses.com to sign up for the Uncommon-Reader Newsletter and get the latest in thrilling book news from UUP (and a 10% off discount on an autographed paperback).

Visit briannatibbetts.com to sign up for Brianna Tibbetts's newsletter and get exclusive updates.

Thank you for reading!

CPSIA information can be obtained
at www.ICGtesting.com
Printed in the USA
LVHW031917060322
712467LV00003B/10